BEAUTY

A Novel

SUSAN WILSON

SCRIBNER PAPERBACK FICTION
Published by Simon & Schuster

SCRIBNER PAPERBACK FICTION
Simon & Schuster Inc.
Rockefeller Center
1230 Avenue of the Americas
New York, NY 10020

First Scribner Paperback Fiction edition 1997
Published by arrangement with Crown Publishers, Inc.
SCRIBNER PAPERBACK FICTION *and design are trademarks of Simon & Schuster Inc.*

Designed by Nancy Kenmore
Manufactured in the United States of America

1   3   5   7   9   10   8   6   4   2

Library of Congress Cataloging-in-Publication Data
Wilson, Susan, date.
Beauty : a novel / Susan Wilson.
p.   cm.
I. Title.
[PS3573.I47533B4   1997]
813'.54—dc21   97-16841
CIP

ISBN 0-684-83422-7

Dedicated with love to my family

I know that the legend of

Beauty and the Beast is possible.

Like the fairy tale, this true story has a

lovely heroine and an ugly hero.

Unlike the fairy tale, it isn't Beauty

who needs to discover the man inside

the Beast, but the Beast himself.

Being a true story, there are no physical

transmutations, only intellectual ones;

the only magic mirror that of

the soul in love.

HARRIS BELLEFLEUR

Love looks not with the eyes, but with the mind,
And therefore is winged Cupid painted blind.

WILLIAM SHAKESPEARE,
A MIDSUMMER NIGHT'S DREAM,
ACT I, SCENE i

There is many a monster who wears the form of a man;
it is better of the two to have the heart of a man
and the form of a monster.

MME. LEPRINCE DE BEAUMONT,
BEAUTY AND THE BEAST

Prologue

CROMPTONS HAVE ALWAYS BEEN PATRONS OF MILLERS. For centuries in England, and since 1635 in New England, the aristocratic Crompton family has sat for formal portraits painted by Miller artists. It is said that the only reason we found our way to America was because the Cromptons, though strict Puritans, desired to keep the tradition and imported the Miller family.

I've seen many of the portraits: long-nosed, high-browed, blue-eyed faces looking out over starched ruffs or lacy jabots; fashions of their times revealing more about the era than the sitter. Personal interests hinted at: the first Neville Crompton standing, one hand on the head of a greyhound; his great-grandson sitting, one hand on a globe, as their fortunes began to encompass shipping and worldwide commerce.

My ancestors were good at what they did. Their works are important enough in antique art circles to warrant hanging in small museums in this country and England. One, a portrait of Neville Crompton, even hangs in the Yale Center for British Art in New Haven.

Yes, Cromptons have always been patrons of Millers.

Chapter

1

MY FATHER HELD OUT THE LETTER IN A HAND THAT shook a little with the tremor he'd had since my mother died, the sheaf of paper quivering like a breeze-rattled leaf.

I wiped the paint from my hand on my rainbow-streaked jeans and took the thick vellum. I scanned the typed letter, two paragraphs, brief and to the point.

"What do you think, Alix?"

"I thought the Crompton line had died out."

"No, this must be the son of the man my father painted." My father shrugged. "Too bad he's decided to follow the tradition. He's out of luck."

"Why?"

"Alix, you know I'm no portraitist."

I did know. The bold talent, which flourished over the course of four hundred years, had been diluted and grown weak until it was only by force of family legend that any of us called art our livelihood. A good commercial artist, my father was not gifted, though he made a good living. I was too honest with my father to disagree with him. Although he could do a credible job, there would never be anything remarkable about his painting. "So what are you going to do? Break with tradition?"

My father took back the letter, squeezing it along the fold. "You go. You're the real artist in the family."

"No, I couldn't, Dad. It's your commission, and besides, he wants Alexander Miller."

"He's written to Alexander, but he'd be far more pleased with the work of Alix."

I remembered then the first time my father had seen my work. Not the art projects of an adolescent, but my first real attempt at disciplined art, a portrait of my mother. I'd worked on the charcoal sketch in secret, slipping into the art classroom after school, not letting anyone see it. Drawing my mother's youthful face from memory, trying not to show her recent pain and withdrawal in the picture. It was an optimistic picture, a pretense she'd never left us.

He'd held the small picture out at arm's length. It trembled slightly, making me aware for the first time that his hands would always shake. A curtain fell across his gray eyes and his face became unreadable as he studied the sketch. Picking at the dry skin of my lips, I waited for his verdict. He set it down and slowly shook his head from side to side. Oh God, I thought, he hates it. Then his eyes cleared and he held me close.

•   •   •

"You take the commission," my father repeated.

"You know I dislike portraiture."

" 'Dislike' doesn't count." He stuffed the letter back into the tissue-lined envelope and tossed it into a pile of mail. "He's offering good money."

My father rarely yelled when we were children, but his words often struck their mark, drawing us back in line, and now his words were more than clear. Since my layoff the previous fall from the private girls' school where I'd taught Art Appreciation, my father had financially supported me in my attempt at making a go of being a full-time artist. It was a trade-off: I attended to his household needs and he paid my rent.

"A working artist doesn't always work for his own muse."

I wanted nothing more than to go home. But my paints were open and the canvas stretched and the light in the small studio I shared with my father is best at that time of day. I touched one finger to the envelope. "I'll go for you. But I think you're wrong—surely you can do a portrait."

He hunched over the kitchen table, pressing his hands down. "Go back to work, Alix. Your paints are getting dry."

. . .

"So who is this guy?" Mark slipped his wool sweater over bare skin.

"A rich patron, just like a modern Medici, supporting the arts." I stuffed my hair into a scrunchie and ran some water into the kettle. "Believe me, I'm not crazy about doing this, but my father can't." I didn't want to go over the same ground with Mark. Once over with my father was enough.

"How long will you stay there?"

"I'm hoping he'll let me take a few Polaroids and come back here to work on it. I'll have to spend a little time interviewing him so that I know him well enough to paint a decent portrait. I simply can't paint someone I don't know."

"Is that why you've never painted me?"

"Who says I haven't?" I countered, pulling down mugs from the shelf. "You were the rooster in the piece I just sold. Didn't you recognize your eyes?"

He smirked and I could see his withdrawal into poutiness, which had little to do with my remark and much to do with my not being around and available. A thirty-something photojournalist, Mark was talented enough to earn a living at it in our small New Hampshire town by freelancing for city newspapers. He was passionate only about his work, and it was often when his artistic star was low in the sky that he would come around and make noises about permanency. Sometimes I was almost suckered into thinking that maybe my determination to be successful in my art could peacefully coexist with husband and children. Then I would come to my senses. What woman could flourish as a painter as long as there were the constant demands of other people's needs?

I set his mug in front of him and kissed the top of his head. "I won't be long."

He didn't answer, instead flipped through an old *New York Times Magazine*, squeezing the pages at their corners as he turned them, leaving them creased.

.   .   .

The day I left was one of those crystal days in midwinter, the air so cold it hurts to breathe. The sky was an empty jewel-blue. The car, mercifully, turned over on the first try, and I threw the Sentra into first gear. Iced gravel spun out from under the tires as I backed out of my driveway. I spotted Mark's truck coming toward me and we stopped side by side on the deserted country road.

"Don't be gone long, Alix."

"It's a job, Mark. I'll be gone as long as it takes."

"You are a painfully slow painter."

"Only when I'm creating. This is replication of what is there. A man's face."

"Where will you be staying? Maybe I'll come up." The words came out of white puffs darting from between his lips.

"You can't. I'm staying at his house."

"Do you have to?"

"Mark, let's just leave it alone. I'll be home as soon as I can." I suppressed my impatience enough to throw him a kiss, but he made no move to catch it.

. . .

Leland Crompton lived at the northernmost tip of the state, beyond the reaches of the national park in the White Mountains. From my southern town it was a drive up the highway for a couple of hours and another hour or so on secondary roads.

"They lived in Boston when my father painted Walter Crompton," my father said, studying the map through his half-glasses. "Beacon Hill." I'd stopped by his house on my way out of town.

"Long way from Beacon Hill, this Riseborough." I took the sheet of paper and folded it, tucking it into my purse. "I'll find it."

With typical, less endearing than annoying, parental cautions, my father urged me to fill up the tank twice and check my tires.

For once I held my tongue and bit back the retort "I'm thirty-six years old, Dad!" I didn't even think to say, "Then *you* go." Instead I gave him a hug. "I'll be fine, don't give me a thought." I was more mellow than usual that morning. We walked out to my car together; he leaned on my arm as we came across the snowy lawn as if afraid of slipping. When I hugged him good-bye, he felt warm to me and a tiny alarm bell jangled. "Are you okay, Dad?"

"Fine, Alix. Just tired."

Before I backed out I sat and watched as he made his slow way back to the front porch. When had he grown so feeble? Overnight he'd gone from vigorous middle age to old. I was glad then that I'd held my tongue.

The stinging sunlight sparkled off the latest snowfall, and traffic was heavy before Waterville, my halfway mark. I allowed myself one quick lunch stop and checked the hand-drawn map Leland Crompton had sent with his retainer. What had seemed relatively clear before now seemed threaded with erratic blue pen.

Now, off the highway, down a switchback road etched into the cleavage of a pair of mountains, I pulled the Sentra off the road to study my map in the waning light. Sunset comes earlier in these regions where the mountains obscure the light by late afternoon. Clouds had come in, urging their way over the tops of the mountains, lowering to meet the rising mists filtering between the pines, and I clicked on the overhead light. Then I got out of the car and took a handful of clean white snow to wash the headlights. I stretched and breathed in the cold mountain air. A light breeze stroked back my hair and I pulled my collar closer. It was suddenly fully dark and the deep blue of it touched me. There were no artificial lights here beyond my headlights. Could I ever imitate this exact shade of blue-black without masking the density or losing the depth? Could I paint the portrait of a stranger? I shivered and climbed back into my car. Illuminated by my headlights, the lumps of snow along the edge of the road looked like pearls.

Another half-hour of right turns and left forks and suddenly I caught sight of lampglow in the distance. A massive iron gate stood open, a wrought-iron rose tooled on it. In the light of my high beams, I could make out iron thorns. Compulsively I checked the directions crumpled in my hand. Yes, this was my landmark. I turned the Sentra into the mile-long drive and wound my way up the hillside between even rows of pines.

The drive circled in front of an imposing fieldstone house with hipped roof. I could see a wing striking out away from the main house, its symmetrical match on the other side. A massive central chimney sent a fine mist of wood smoke to the sky. Twelve mullioned windows looked out over the front, but only two downstairs windows showed any light.

Suddenly the front door opened and an older woman darted out, her hands fluttering as she half-galloped over to the car. "Willie will get your things, never mind that, come in, come in." Her barrage after so many hours of silent thought seemed an assault. "You needn't—" She stopped in mid-sentence. "I'm sorry, I thought you were the painter fellow. What do you want?"

"I *am* the painter fellow."

Three distinct lines formed over her nose. She stepped back from the car and let me out. "Willie will bring your car around to the garage." She pronounced "garage" in the English way, a curious affectation in an otherwise ordinary New Hampshire accent.

Like an automaton, I handed my keys to Willie, a stooped middle-aged man who spoke not at all but bobbed his head and would not look at me.

As I slammed the trunk lid down I chanced to look up and thought I saw a curtain move in an unlit upstairs window.

Walking ahead of me, Mrs. Greaves led me into the house. "Well, well, well, you ain't what we expected." She snatched my left hand, darting at it like a pigeon on breadcrumbs. Her hand was soft, the thousand lines in it smooth as lines on paper. "Who are you?"

"I'm Alix Miller. When my father couldn't come I did." A little heat of embarrassment licked at my face. "I'm here to paint Mr. Crompton's portrait." I tugged to release my hand, but her grip was firm.

"Why didn't you tell us you were coming instead?" She strengthened her hold.

"I don't think I thought it really mattered." And I wondered why it should have. "I'm a Miller and an artist."

"You're very pretty." Mrs. Greaves dropped my hand. "Not married?"

Surprised by her non sequitur, I merely shook my head.

I followed Mrs. Greaves up a long flight of stairs to my room. A mahogany banister ran in a slow curve up the stairs to the gallery. I trailed my fingers on it, marveling at the warmth and smoothness of its unbroken length. I could not find a join anywhere along it, as though the whole thing had been coaxed out of one great length of wood.

All along the gallery portraits hung. A little beat of excitement lurched in my heart at the sight of my own ancestors' work. I wanted to stop to examine them, but Mrs. Greaves's quickstep along the gallery and down another corridor allowed no dallying.

"Dinner is at eight," Mrs. Greaves said, opening the door to my room. I stepped in and she closed the door, pulling hard against the swollen jamb.

By some magic, my bags and canvases and paint box were already in the room. The room was large—a pair of long windows filled one wall, a double bed with a blue coverlet stood foursquare on the left, and a double dresser with a narrow rippled mirror stood opposite. Two good engravings were the only decoration. An Aubusson carpet in deep blues and maroons was bordered by a hardwood floor. The walls were the faintest blue. A very masculine room, it had the faint odor of cedar. From somewhere in the house I could hear classical music, then it stopped and I heard nothing more.

. . .

I had more than an hour and spent it unpacking and washing up. Dinner at eight. I had brought only one dress and hoped that if dinner at eight was de rigueur here that my host would not mind seeing it on me for a few nights running.

I brushed on blush and stared into my own hazel eyes, recognizing the nervous tension in my smeary attempt at eyeliner. If he was anything like his house, my host would be imposing. I had tried not to imagine Leland Crompton at all. How old he was, forty or sixty, pleasant or taciturn. I had no idea, and my anger at my father for putting me in this position fermented. Had the house been in Boston, or a modest garrison colonial in Newburyport, it might have been easier, but this English country house surrounded by miles of desolate mountains had an ominous quality about it, unrelieved by the cool Mrs. Greaves and the silent Willie.

I was ready when at seven-thirty there was a tap on my door and Mrs. Greaves came in. "Mr. Crompton begs your pardon, but he is not feeling well and will not be able to join you at dinner."

A surge of relief belied a bass note of disappointment, but perhaps it would be easier to meet my patron in the light of day.

. . .

A wash of moonlight spread across my room, bathing everything in a silvered half-light. It woke me and I rose to draw the curtains closed. For a moment I looked out of the mullioned window, the bulk of the surrounding mountains a dark backdrop against the milky light illuminating the courtyard below me. Something moved. The pallid moonlight was swept with a shadow, then empty again. I could not tell if it had been animal or human or just my imagination.

"MR. CROMPTON WON'T BE DOWN TODAY, BUT ASKS that you make yourself comfortable. The house is yours to use, and there are some fine walks if you've a mind to hike." Mrs. Greaves had finished clearing my breakfast dishes. I had half-expected her to forbid me some portion of the house.

"If he's not well, I can come some other time." I set my coffee cup back into its saucer, a schoolgirl's hope of early release waiting to be tapped.

Mrs. Greaves sighed. "No, he wants you to stay."

Visions of an invalid floated through my imagination, my setting up my canvas in a dimly lit sickroom, some old geezer in a wheelchair scowling back at me, his lower body covered by a dull-colored afghan, just the tips of his leather-soled slippers peeking out. Shaking off the image, I nodded at Mrs. Greaves. "Of course I'll stay."

The landscape in the bright morning light was magnificent and I itched to make some preliminary sketches. I take ideas from nature and convert them to shapes and colors and textures, which sometimes others find attractive. A mountain may be only hinted at in the finished work, but its essence, its soul, is there. So I took a small notebook, bundled up against the cold, and let myself out the back door. A bank of garage doors faced me and I peeked in to see my car sandwiched between a station wagon and a sports car completely shrouded in canvas. I dug my mittens out of the glove compartment of my car and set off.

I noticed tracks in the snow, large footprints and beside them the tracks of a dog, the pairs of prints interweaving as the dog had crossed and recrossed the man's path through the formal garden as it terraced downward toward the woods. They branched away and were lost beneath the pines, where the snow had toppled off the warming branches. I plodded on, watching for blaze marks laid out along the way.

Higher and higher I climbed, my breath moistening the scarf around my face. Despite the cold I grew warm and unzipped my jacket, letting the fresh, cold air cool me. I pulled off my hat and shook out my hair. The cathedral pines whispered above me, bending gently to warn one another of this intruder in their midst. I reached a promontory, which thrust out from between the pines and extended out over a view of the valley that now lay beneath my feet. Wind-dusted rocks offered a decent dry seat and I took out my pad and began to sketch.

I drew until my fingers were numb and my seat frozen. The light had already begun to change and I realized I had been gone for hours. I grew a little nervous when I couldn't see any blazes on the trees nearby and I wondered how long I had traveled without noticing any. Worse still, my footprints in the snow had been covered as the rising wind had blown snow off the pines. "Well, this is a fine mess," I quoted to myself, and headed downhill in the resolute belief that downhill would eventually lead to a road. By now I was cold and hungry and feeling very stupid. How long would I have to be gone before someone sent help?

The annoyance I felt quickly transmuted into genuine fear when I could find no blazes and every trail dead-ended in brush or rocky outcroppings looming above me in malevolent bulk. Dusk was closing in with winter suddenness and I knew that even if I found the marked trail, the light blue blazes would soon be invisible in the color-robbing gray of twilight. I started running, the calf-deep snow pulling on my muscles, holding me down like seawater. All the stories I had ever heard of lost hikers popped into my head like rabid prairie dogs, and I fought against panic.

I tripped over a buried root and pitched headlong down the steep slope, unable to prevent myself from tumbling for yards before coming to a halt against the rough bark of a fir tree. Stunned, I lay panting and didn't hear anyone approach until a gloved hand reached down to me.

"Are you all right?" a deep voice asked me. "Are you hurt?" So resonant was this voice it seemed as if I were being spoken to by an echo.

"No, yes, no, I'm all right I think." I took the proffered hand and was hauled to my feet to look into the most grotesque face I had ever seen. Mere bad looks or horrible accident had not shaped this face. Deformity had done this. A heavy brow rose up over deep-set eyes. The cheeks were of unequal shape, giving the face a twisted, asymmetrical look above a prominent jaw. The hatless head was large, like a paper bag children have stuffed and drawn a face upon. His nose was large and hooked and his ears, beneath a thick mop of graying brown hair, were like saucers. It was almost as if the craggy outcroppings had suddenly transmogrified into a man. My instinctive revulsion showed, and he dropped my hand.

"The house is straight ahead, beyond that spruce, no

more than a hundred yards." He turned and walked away with an ungainly gait. A large mongrel burst out of the woods and came to heel beside the man.

Ashamed at my rudeness, I called after him, "Thank you!"

He waved a hand without turning around, as if he had not expected anything different from me.

. . .

Once in the kitchen, Mrs. Greaves fluttered her hands and chided me for my foolishness, unwilling, evidently, to believe that I was a seasoned hiker. "I just lost track of time." I patted my pockets. "Damn."

"What?"

"I've lost my notebook."

"So you've nothing to show for your foolishness?"

"I suppose not."

"Mr. Lee says he'll be down for dinner. You go have a hot bath and dress now. I'll send up tea."

"Mr. Lee?"

"I've known Mr. Crompton since he was a boy. Since he turned fourteen I've called him Mr. Lee." Mrs. Greaves set a tea tray on the counter.

"What's he like?"

She moved to the sink and began running hot water. Her face was reflected back in the darkened window; I could see the furrowing of her brow as she wrestled with her answer. "What does he look like or what is he like?"

"The latter. I'll see soon enough what he looks like." I thought back to the encounter in the woods, a little hunch forming.

"Mr. Lee is a nice man. I think it's safe to say that. Not given to anger. Quietlike."

"What does he do for a living, or for fun? I like to know

my subjects before I paint them, not from only their lips, but from those around them."

"He writes. You know, novels and such. Stories. Good ones. I think he does that for fun as much as for profit. Between you and me, he need never earn a penny of his own in his lifetime." She shrugged a little, as if to minimize what she had said, and set the kettle on the stove. "Run and get your bath."

    .   .   .

I paused along the gallery to study the portraits, taking childish pleasure in seeing the artists' names on the tiny brass plaques. Alfred Miller, 1723; Ezekial in 1752; a second Ezekial in 1767. The eighteenth-century Cromptons all sat, the colors in their clothes still lovely in shades of blue and cream and brown. I liked Ezekial's work. He gave a little more depth to the painting than most of his contemporaries, the roots of Dutch painting evident in his style. The first portrait was of an eighteenth-century Crompton family—father, mother, and three boys, ages about three through seven. The second, of the same family fifteen years later, wives and grandchildren at the feet of the patriarch. I tried to sort them out from the first portrait, but the numbers were wrong, one of the boys was gone.

    .   .   .

The long refectory table was set at either end, two places separated by the candles, whose yellow flames wavered as I walked by. My host was not yet there and I felt awkward about sitting, but did not know where else to go. Instead I stood by the long window and looked out into the night. Floodlights illuminated the terrace, brushed clean of snow. Ironwork benches flanked the perimeter, and again I saw the rose worked into the filigree. I could hear a chiming clock strike eight. I wandered around the formal room, admiring the antique china displayed in a breakfront and the small landscape hanging beside it. As I turned away from the painting, my eye fell on my notebook, set beside my plate. I touched its cover and opened it. The felt-tip marker had gotten wet and the sketch of the valley had bled, making a flannel patchwork of it.

"I think it's still a nice picture," Leland Crompton said as he came into the room.

"Thank you, but it was only a rough draft for concept." I had guessed that my patron was the man I had encountered in the woods and so managed to cover my shock at seeing him again.

He limped into the room and stood at my seat, pulling it out for me. I sat and he went to his own. "Mrs. Greaves is a very fine cook. I hope you'll enjoy your stay with us."

I lay my napkin across my lap and sipped my water, all the while wondering if I had offended him earlier.

"Thank you for rescuing me this afternoon."

"You were nearly here."

"I feel rather foolish. . . ."

He cut me off, not impolitely. "It happens."

I did not know which he meant, my being lost or my rudeness.

The candles were thick and obscured my view of him. Mrs. Greaves brought in the soup course, dimming the lights with the rheostat as she left the room.

We made the small talk that two strangers are given to when forced together. Nice weather, cold for this time of year, how was the drive up. All the time my mind teased itself with the question, How am I ever going to paint this man? How am I ever going to stare at him long enough to replicate that face? Why does he want me to do this? Soup cleared, the main course was brought in and we struggled through the second course of conversational ploys. How long had I been painting, what school? I realized he was doing the questioning and cast about for a question of my own.

"Mrs. Greaves tells me you are a writer."

"Yes."

"Novels?"

"Yes. And short stories."

I had not opened any conduits with that gambit. "Mr. Crompton, I need to get to know you a little if I'm to paint you."

"Yes, I suppose that's true."

He was silent for a time, busy with the remains of his dinner. Then, finally, he folded his napkin and rose. "Ms. Miller, will you please excuse me." He held up one large hand to keep me in my seat. "Please, stay for dessert and coffee. The television is in the room third door on the right from here. Make yourself entirely at home." He moved awkwardly away from the table and walked out of the dining room with an obvious self-consciousness, utterly aware of my eyes on him.

.   .   .

Alone again at breakfast the next morning, I made up my mind to leave. This was a useless exercise and I had work at home to finish before my show in March. If he wasn't going to sit for me, was only going to leave me to cool my heels in this lovely house with the wonderful meals, well, forget it. I ripped the ruined sketch out of my notebook and threw it in the wastepaper basket. The sky had clouded up overnight. If I got an early start I could be home before it began to snow in earnest.

Just at that moment of decision, Mrs. Greaves came into the dining room. "Mr. Crompton will see you in the solarium." That was it, then, my window of opportunity closed. When I didn't move she snatched at my breakfast dishes. "Go on."

The south-facing solarium extended into the formal garden and I imagined that in summer it was like being out of doors. The surrounding mountains were bluish above the snow, pine trees and bare deciduous branches making a mosaic against the sky. A bird feeder hung in the near foreground, filled now with flickering chickadees. The light, even on this overcast day, was wonderful.

"Will this do as a studio?"

"Absolutely . . . it's perfect." I walked around the space, holding out my hands to see where the shadows might lie. I couldn't have built a better studio.

"I had it added on a couple of years ago. It really doesn't fit the architecture, but I love it."

He was looking out over the garden, his hands on his narrow hips. From the back, except for the slight hunching of his shoulders, he could have been normal.

. . .

My canvases and paint box had been brought down and I fussed with the easel, struggling as usual to get the stripped wing nut positioned just so in order to keep the easel standing. He watched me for a minute, then fished an elastic band out of a ceramic pencil holder and in a moment had jury-rigged the easel into a more or less secure stance. I set a rectangle of stretched canvas on the easel and lowered the brace to hold it. We stood side by side for a moment, both looking at the blank canvas, a snowy lawn as yet undiscovered by dogs and children. I was struck then with sudden doubts that I could do the job. As if aware of my thoughts, Lee moved away from me.

"Where do you want me?" he asked, and then hunched

himself over to the corner I pointed to, sitting in one chair, then another as I directed.

"This will take some time," I cautioned. "From beginning sketch to detail, this could mean some very long hours."

"I'm aware of that."

"I could take some photos and paint from them. Then you needn't spend all day sitting."

"No. This is the way it has always been done. This is the tradition between our families, isn't it?"

"Yes, I suppose it is. I hadn't thought of it that way. Tradition."

"Like Tevye, we have our traditions that make life bearable." He hooked his heels into the rungs of the bar stool he sat on. "Now, how should I sit? As you can see, I have no bad side."

I smiled at his wry remark, feeling a little pang of relief that he had acknowledged my difficulty.

I tried to pose him verbally, barking directions like some demented furniture mover. "Up-to-the-left-no-down-a-little . . ." In Life Art class, models posed for us. Smooth-skinned, wraith-thin, or muscular, completely at ease sitting nearly nude for strangers, the check at the end of the session no doubt making up for these theater majors' vestigial modesty. With casual fingertips, we'd move the various models through poses of our own desire, touching them into shape as if they were clay, not flesh. Faced now with this imperfect and shy man, I could not bear to touch the misshapen face, though my words could not contrive the most genuine pose. When my instructions became ridiculous at last, I set down my pencil and swallowed my hesitation. I saw the squeamishness in his eyes, and like an animal unused to being touched, he flinched reflexively against the feel of my fingers on his chin. Except that it

21

was misshapen, it felt like any chin, vaguely rough, as if his razor were old.

I looked down as I pressed his large, gnarly hands together on his knees. I was surprised at their feel, warm and smooth, the large knuckles belying the softness of the skin on the back of his hands. There is such intimacy in touching someone's hands, shaping them or guiding them. I wanted very much to turn them over, to feel the palms, to get a sense of his labors. But I didn't.

"Now, Mr. Crompton, you must try to look relaxed, like you have your portrait done every week." I stepped back to my easel, pencil poised.

He laughed. The sound boomed from his barrel chest, startling me into laughter. "Lee. Please. If we're to spend hours in each other's company, I prefer you call me Lee, if I may call you Alix."

"Okay. And remember, if you want to stop at any time, just get up. I'm a cruel artist and forget my subjects are alive."

After a few minutes of silent work he cleared his throat in a stagy manner. "Alix, you must overlook my bad manners yesterday. I'm not used to society and it takes me some time to regain the social graces."

"You've nothing to apologize for," I answered, knowing that it was I who should be apologizing. But I couldn't bring myself to speak of our encounter in the woods, was too cowardly to say why I had reacted so abominably. Instead I countered, "I should apologize for not warning you my father couldn't be here."

"No matter. A Miller paints a Crompton in any event."

"Tradition."

As a sip of wine after abstinence warms the heart and sends a message of relaxation to the body, I was suddenly at ease. Lee's friendliness this morning soothed away the strain of new acquaintance. Both of us shy, we had somehow moved past the first barrier.

.   .   .

Over the next few days, our sessions settled into a routine. I'd breakfast alone, then join him in the solarium by eight. He had a marvelous stereo system and the four morning hours of work were accompanied by a wide range of music, from Respighi to Neil Young. He was a patient sitter and had an unlimited ability to remain still. The light was best in the morning and we kept to only those hours before lunch. After lunch he'd retire to his own work and I was left on my own till dinner. Much of the time I spent sketching versions of the slowly developing portrait.

It had been a long time since I'd drawn from life. So much of my work was pure imagination that it took some time to harness the necessary discipline. I was so often taken with painting the beautiful, or representing emotion or thought with visually exciting color or shape, that to render on canvas a true representation of someone whose exterior is so grotesque was a challenge. There have been artists who have made the normal grotesque. I was attempting to make the grotesque normal.

"YOU HAVEN'T SEEN THE WHOLE HOUSE, HAVE YOU?" LEE asked one morning as he handed me a mug of coffee. As we took a ten-minute break I watched him discreetly as he walked around the room stretching this way and that to loosen joints stiffened by two hours of motionless sitting. I had passed from visitor to artist and observed everything about him with an anatomist's eye.

I'd been there for four days and had seen only these few rooms downstairs and my bedroom. "I'd love a tour." I sipped the coffee and added a half-teaspoon of sugar.

"Good, after lunch I'll show you around."

"It won't interfere with your work?"

"My work is just at that stage when the characters are being completely willful and I can't make them work. Exactly the time to take an afternoon off." He climbed back on the stool and fell easily into his pose. He'd never mentioned his writing before and his speaking of it now pleased me in some little way.

· · ·

We toured the house after lunch. Lee was patient, letting me admire the great many works of art he had displayed on the walls and in various niches. "Much of this belonged to my parents and grandparents. I've added only a little in the past few years."

"Do you go to the auctions?"

"No. I have a man who knows my taste and sends me descriptions." He touched a painting into line.

We came to the library, a lovely dark green room with walls of books and an old-fashioned sliding ladder to reach the ceiling-high shelves. The deep green carpet absorbed our footsteps; instantly our voices dropped to hushed library tones. I ran a finger along the spines of the many hardcovers filling the bookshelves, smiling at common interests and authors. John Gardner's *Grendel*, *Freddy's Book*, and *Nickel Mountain* were prominent among the fiction.

"Are your books here? The ones you've written, I mean."

"I write under a pseudonym," he said, and handed me a hardcover copy of a mystery novel. *Another Fine Mess*, A Tyler Bent Mystery by Harris Bellefleur.

"You! You're my favorite, I've read all of this series!" I was laughing and hugging the book to me. "Why ever did you kill off Molly Tripp?"

"She was becoming a nag," he retorted and that bell-like laugh sounded up from his chest. I handed him back the book, but he shook his head, resembling in the muted light of the library the head of some great beast. "I killed off Molly, not because she was a nag—that was a flip remark —but because all of Tyler Bent's partners end up dead. If I had spared her, why who knows, maybe they would have had to sleep together. Tyler is a man doomed to be alone."

Again, I handed the book back to him, but he pressed it back into my hands. "Please, keep the book. I'd like you to have it, unless you already do?"

"No, I don't have my own copy." I opened it. "May I ask for an autograph?"

He seemed oddly pleased. "I never get to do this."

Slowly it dawned on me how isolated Lee Crompton was.

"Let me think of something suitable and give it back to you before you leave."

We wandered up the stairs to the gallery, where I was able to tell him a little about the painters of his ancestors. "Ezekial was better than Alfred, he had a clearer touch with expressions. Alfred was a little heavy-handed." I pointed to the second Ezekial painting. "Who's missing in this one? One of the three boys isn't there, but I can't tell which one."

"Roger, the middle son. He died shortly before his twenty-third birthday."

"How sad," I murmured. "How?"

"Disease." He paused. "It has been suggested that he had the same disease I have. Acromegaly."

I looked at him, his profile massive in the late afternoon sun. "Have there been many cases in your family?"

"One per century documented. I'm the twentieth-century man. There won't be any others."

"Yes, genetic counseling is really a modern miracle," I said without thought.

He looked at me with something of a rueful smile playing about his mouth. "That doesn't enter into it for me."

The tour seemed to end at that moment and Lee excused himself to write some letters. I stood for a long time before the eighteenth-century Cromptons and wondered at a disease that would leave its mark upon a family in such an insidious way. In the centuries before ours such anomalies were sometimes called punishment, or the work of the devil. I knew a little about the disorder, a pituitary tumor that caused abnormal growth in the head, hands, feet, and thorax. But how a man of twenty-three might die of it I couldn't figure.

. . .

When the phone rang that afternoon I realized that I had not heard any phones ringing during the week I'd been at Riseborough, which had made the house seem all the more peaceful. That the phone was for me was a jolt, and I was immediately concerned. I hadn't called my father since coming to Riseborough, and now the flicker of concern I had felt when I left him sparked again, mingled this time with general guilt.

But it was Mark. "When do you plan to come home, Alix?" He was on the cordless phone and his voice was tinny, a vague hum surrounding his words. "You remember I've got a dinner on Saturday and you promised to come with me."

"Mark, I'm not finished, not nearly," I protested, and immediately began to get angry. As usual, his needs and desires were immediate and pressing.

"Alix, you've been there since last Saturday. Surely you get the weekend off. You can go back."

It would do no good to remind him that his creative life had kept him away from several important occasions in my life.

"Look, it's not like you're up there because you want to be," he said. "Weren't you just going to take a couple of Polaroids and come home?"

"It's working out just fine doing it from life," I admitted to him and, I realized, to myself. "I'm enjoying it."

But in the end I promised to come home on Saturday and attend the newspaper awards dinner. Though complaining all the while about having to wear black tie, he pressed me enough that I was certain he expected to receive an award. It would be a big moment for him, and of course I should be there. I tried not to think of my March opening. I knew he wouldn't attend. Despite knowing the

27

date for months, he'd planned a backpacking trek with some buddies that same weekend.

I hung up the phone and leaned against the kitchen doorjamb. "Damn him," I muttered, and smiled at Mrs. Greaves.

"Boyfriend?"

The term seemed dated. "Sort of. I don't know what he is." I helped myself to a cup of coffee from the Mr. Coffee. Sliding onto a stool, I leaned both elbows on the counter. "Tell me about Lee. What was he like as a boy?"

"Why?"

"I don't know, just curious about him."

Mrs. Greaves poured herself a cup and looked at the clock. Sighing, she nodded. "He was a little hellion."

This was so far from what I expected her to say that I choked.

"I mean he was a determined, sometimes not very nice boy. Oh, he was good enough as a child, but adolescence burned in him like fire. One scrape after another. Very full of himself and with a God's-gift-to-women attitude, which I sometimes think was his downfall." Once again she looked at the clock, then at me. Something in her attitude had softened, and she motioned for me to follow. "He hasn't always been like he is now. I'll show you."

She had a suite of rooms off the kitchen. On every surface were photos: family groups, individuals, pets. I realized then that there were no photos anywhere else in the house, only the paintings. She took a small photo in a cheap metal frame from her nightstand. "This is Lee at fifteen."

An adolescent boy looked out from the picture. Too unformed yet to be called handsome, it was a nice face, just on the edge of solidifying into manhood, the fair down on the upper lip still safe from the razor. I was caught by the dark blue eyes, much like those of an idealized cherub in a Renaissance painting, but it was the charming smile that lit the boy's face that held my attention, and I could see that despite the horrific changes the disease had made in Lee's face, it hadn't touched his smile.

"That would be his second year at Groton. Here"—she handed me a second picture—"this is fifteen years later. You can see the beginnings of the disease."

A candid shot, taken at some unexpected moment, with Lee not looking at the camera but away. The boy in the first picture had changed, changed beyond growing from a boy to a man. His hand, resting against one cheek, was outsized, the swollen knuckles obvious in the close shot. Though his features had not enlarged grotesquely yet, his face was softer, less defined, and his ears and nose were already large. His eyes were no longer willful but locked in private thought and I knew before she said it that this was the last photo taken of Lee Crompton.

"We came to live here a year or so after that picture. It was the family's summer home, and Lee has made it his home since then. We've been here nearly ten years."

"Where are his parents?"

"Divorced years ago, when Lee was at Groton. His father died some years after your grandfather painted him; she's still alive, living in Boston. She doesn't come." Mrs. Greaves took the picture out of my hands, looking at it before placing it beside another. "He grew into a nice man, didn't he?"

Her words surprised me, then I understood what she meant. "Yes, he is a very nice man."

She wiped her hands down the length of her white twill apron and left me standing there. A sudden chill wafted from a slightly open window.

• • •

At dinner I told Lee that I would have to spend the weekend in Boston. I explained about Mark's dinner and the possibility of his receiving an award.

"You must be very proud of him," he said, not looking up at me.

I stared a long while into my soup dish. "I am."

"You don't sound convincing."

I looked through the candelabra at him. "Don't I?"

"No. Why?"

"Sometimes I think it would be easier to be unconnected."

"How can you say that?"

"This relationship sometimes takes its toll on my art. He resents the time I spend on my work."

"He's said that?"

"Not exactly, but sometimes Mark gives me the impression that he believes that his work is more important than mine because mine is, I don't know, somehow less tangible than his. I've never reported on street people in Nashua and my abstracts don't often sell." I caught myself. Why was I telling Lee this?

"He was probably raised to believe that a man's work is always more important than a woman's. So many men have been lost to their own self-importance that way."

"Lee, are you a feminist?" I teased.

"Alone here, with only the company of a strong-willed housekeeper and a weak-minded gardener, yes. I am an advocate for women's rights, for social reform, for many causes I can touch only through my own wealth."

I set down my spoon and Lee rang for the second course. "I'm thinking I should probably leave Friday." I knew Mark wanted me home Friday, but I hesitated. "Though maybe I should head back earlier. I hate to sound trite, but I haven't a thing to wear to this dinner."

"I have hundreds of catalogs. Why not look through them, and if you find something it can be delivered almost in no time."

After dinner we settled into the television room and against the background of some shlocky Sunday night movie, we thumbed through stacks of catalogs.

"How about this?"

"Too young."

"Or this?"

"Too old."

"You'd look great in this."

"Too risqué! What about this?"

"Not risqué enough. You want to be dynamite, don't you?"

And so it went until he found exactly the right dress. "Perfect."

"Perfect."

. . .

"Bad-dog, come back here!" Lee bellowed after the ugly mongrel who accompanied him on his walks. "Damn it, Bad-dog, leave it!"

The rangy mutt pulled his nose out of the carrion lying in the snow-covered road and loped back to Lee. "Good Bad-dog." Lee bent to whack the beast on his springy ribs.

"Good bad dog? Isn't that a trifle oxymoronic?"

"He was mostly bad dog when he arrived here. His real name is Ralph, but Bad-dog has always suited him better."

The dusty afternoon sky threatened more snow, a pinky

aureole surrounded the sun as it lowered. We'd been walking since lunch, a long, wandering walk while Lee pointed out favorite places and birdlife. The snow-laden air was warmer than it had been and didn't send us back to the house for a long time. Our progress was slow, convenient logs offered us frequent resting places. Although he was solicitous of me, I knew that the effort to carry around his own weighty limbs tired Lee, and I was happy to pace myself to him. The fresh air brought color to his cheeks, tinging his ears pink.

"Oh, look"—I pointed down the slope beyond the guardrail—"a pond. It looks like someone's shoveled it."

"Wiggy's Pond, best skating around." He stepped forward. "Do you skate?"

"Not very well." I moved ahead of him, sliding a little down the tree-crowded slope. "Look, there are kids skating, let's watch." But when I turned, he was gone.

I scrambled back up the hill and caught up to him. "Hey, wait up!"

He slowed, but did not stop. When I finally drew beside him, he was apologetic. "I'm sorry, it's just that I don't like to be seen by children. They often get frightened."

"Those weren't small children, Lee, they were teenagers."

"They're worse, they don't run away."

. . .

By the time we got back to the house it was much colder and Mrs. Greaves had hot chocolate ready for us. Leaving wet boots and gloves in the kitchen, we dropped jackets in the hallway and settled in front of the fire in the library, stretching out our stockinged feet to soak in the warmth.

"I didn't mean to be curt back there." Lee eased his bulky frame against the couch. "When I first began to show signs

32

of the disease it wasn't so obvious. I moved about in the world without much difficulty. But as I grew . . . and grew and grew . . . it became more and more difficult. People were curious, but mostly kind. I wasn't treated as my ancestors in acromegaly were once treated, as freak show displays.

"One day I was walking down Boylston Street. My eye was caught by the display in a toy store window and I wasn't looking where I was going. I ran right into a mother and her little girl. The child looked up and took one look at me and began crying. Despite my apologies, the mother raised her hackles and said, 'How dare you be out on the streets to frighten little children!'

"And I couldn't answer. She was right, I had no right to do that. So I retreated."

"You never leave here, do you?"

"No. I can't. I invented handsome, debonair Tyler Bent to live my life for me. Alix, if you had ever seen the fear in that child's eyes, you could do no less." He smiled at me, a lopsided smile that yet had a charm to it. "But, thankfully, you can only imagine it, you will never experience it."

"How could anyone have been that ignorant or cruel?"

"Every time someone sees me for the first time, I see that same look. It is instinctive and unavoidable."

I remembered again my own reaction and I was ashamed.

Chapter

4

A BRILLIANT JANUARY SUN TOUCHED THE PANES OF GLASS in the solarium windows and the warmth filtered into the room. I stood in a tee shirt mixing paints with a palette knife. Lee came in and set down the coffee pot.

"Come give me your opinion," I said.

"Of what?"

"Background color. I would almost paint in the windows and the garden beyond, but I think that the overall effect would be too cluttered."

"Do whatever you think will work. I can't offer an opinion." He edged away from the canvas without looking at it, stopping to pour two mugs of coffee. He carefully measured a half-teaspoon of sugar into mine.

"Lee, you haven't looked at this. Not once."

He climbed on the stool and hung his head a little. "Alix, I'm confident that your work is wonderful, but I will not look at it. That's not meant as an insult to your abilities, but a problem of mine."

"Then why am I doing this?"

"Because it has always been done. Because it will go into storage and some descendant from a different branch of the family will discover it someday and know that Millers still painted Cromptons in the last decade of the twentieth century."

"That's not quite good enough."

"You're right. The truth is, I thought that it was a pity to break the tradition just because I refuse to have it hung. Very simple. But I don't want to see it."

I stood for a long time, unable, it seemed, to touch the brush to the canvas.

"Have I upset you?"

"No. Well, yes. You've sort of skewed my focus. I have been doing this with your approval in mind, and now, if you aren't going to hang it, it becomes unimportant and I could draw a stick figure with blue eyes and call it *Portrait of Lee Crompton.*"

"That would do. Maybe I would hang that."

"Lee, don't be self-denigrating, it's not attractive." I had lost my concentration utterly and began closing up paint tubes with angry, jerky motions. "Let's not work today. Like your characters, if the paint won't go on in the right places, I can't make it."

"I'm sorry, Alix." He slipped off the stool and stepped toward me.

With a hasty jerk, I pulled the sheeting over the untouched portrait. "No need to apologize. It's your portrait to do with as you want. I'm just the hired artist, you're the patron."

I had squeezed paint all over my hands and I went into the tiny lavatory in the hallway to wash. I noticed that there was no mirror in it, and I realized then that except in my own rooms and Mrs. Greaves's there were no mirrors anywhere in the house.

. . .

Half an hour later a light knock at my bedroom door startled me. "Alix? May I come in?"

35

Having spent the last half-hour going over my angry words and trying to gird up my courage to go apologize, I felt my heart begin to pound. "Lee?"

The door opened and Lee came in, pushing it wide as he did. "Do you want to go skating?"

"What about the children?"

"It's a schoolday. There won't be anybody around till after two."

"I don't have any skates." But I was reaching for my sweater.

"I've got a garage full of cast-off skates from dozens of Cromptons. I'm sure we've a pair to fit you." Thirty minutes later we were in the station wagon heading for Wiggy's Pond.

The pond was cleanly shoveled, the white contrails of skaters' blades etched into its surface. Looking straight down I could see the grass frozen in perfect arrangement. Closer to shore the grass burst through the ice in frozen bouquets. Bubbles appeared like evil eyes. Farther out the ice darkened and I could no longer see through it.

Lee knelt in the snow to pull the lacings tight on my skates. My foot in his huge hands seemed as tiny as Cinderella's. His own skates were immense black things with wicked-looking blades. I wobbled onto the ice, taking an exploratory stride before pushing away from shore. Tongue firmly balanced at the corner of my mouth, I completed eight or ten pokey little strides before crashing. A whoosh of skate blades circled around me and Lee hoisted me to my feet. "Like this," he said, and pushed off, gliding around the pond in a graceful arc, great long strides, a quick reverse and a slow glide. I stood frankly open-mouthed. This great clumsy giant could skate like a dancer. The ice freed him from the constraints of gravity. Awkwardness melted away and grace was revealed. My fingertips throbbed to take pencil in hand and record this. He danced around me, pleased with my reaction, executing figures, racing off and back. He came to a sudden stop in front of me, the scrim of ice shooting away from the blade of his skate.

He'd shrugged off his jacket and stood now in a dark blue Norwegian sweater and a cranberry-colored down vest. Warm from his exertions, he'd thrown off his hat and gloves. Thick hair curled about his ears, he pushed it back from his massive brow and cocked his head, looking strangely impish for such an ugly man. After a heartbeat of a pause he held out one hand. "Will you skate with me?"

I put my hand in his. "Like this," he said, and pushed off. Together we sailed out over the pond as the January sunlight struck sparks off the ice. He turned me and slid an arm behind my back; side by side, like contra-danseurs, we glided back and across the ice. We dashed in and out of the shadows of trees that surrounded the pond. Now like waltzers, we faced one another and my strides were mirror images of his. His right arm lightly touched my back, with his left he held my hand. Every few strides, my face brushed up against the slick cloth of his vest. He kept his strokes short to accommodate the difference in our heights. One two three, one two three, we danced over the silver-gray surface. Gracefully toeing the ice, Lee let me slide by him and turned me into a twirl. For one brief instant I forgot he was not an ordinary man. In the next, I was newly startled by his visage, and in the third moment, I knew that more and more I would forget how he looked and think of him only as Lee. He let go of my hand and bowed, his long arms sweeping the ice. "Thank you, Miss Miller."

"My pleasure, Mr. Crompton," I answered, attempting a curtsy.

. . .

Mrs. Greaves had left us a cold lunch, which we warmed with nips of sherry in our coffee. It was Thursday, her half-day off. "She'll have left us something to heat in the microwave," Lee assured me.

"I can cook, she needn't have done that," I protested.

"It's our routine, Thursdays and Saturdays she's off, and every other weekend. She drove a hard bargain coming up to live in this backwater. My mother has never quite forgiven me for stealing her."

"She's very fond of you."

"It would be trite to say that I think of her as a mother, but the truth is, she's been a good friend in some difficult circumstances."

I remembered then what Mrs. Greaves had said about Lee's mother, that she never came up. "If I ask a personal question, please feel free to tell me I'm out of line."

He nodded. "Ask away."

"Do you have friends who come and visit? Tell me you aren't alone here all the time."

"I have two or three friends who come who were at school with me. But, like everyone, they have busy lives and it has become harder and harder for them to get up here. We stay in touch over the phone now mostly. Why do you ask?"

I shrugged. "I don't know. Really." I poured another touch of sherry into my glass. "I suppose that I'm rebelling against the idea of someone so nice being a recluse."

He didn't say anything, simply rubbed a massive hand over his face as if to erase what was there. "Alix, a true recluse wouldn't be in touch with the world as I am. I'm connected through the phone, fax, computer. I can see it, even if I won't let it see me. Accept that"—he held my eye with his—"please."

"I'm sorry, I've absolutely no right to say anything." I looked away from him, releasing us from the topic.

"I have to get to work. I've played hooky long enough."

. . .

The sunlight in the solarium was still bright and I cozied up on the floral couch to sketch. What Lee didn't know was that I was making sketch after sketch of him. Late at night as I sat up in bed, listening to the wind rattle the windows, I took my pencil and pad and drew him from memory. He would never let me photograph him, so I took the day's memories and committed them to paper. Lee pitching snowballs to Bad-dog; sitting on a log gesturing toward some bird in flight; dozing in front of the TV. His hand, long and gnarled, resting on Bad-dog's silky head.

Bad-dog came in and sat beside me, one eye cocked hopefully on the leash hanging on the doorknob. I sketched our morning on the ice, thinking how like a diary my sketchbook had become. Vignettes of a very surprising week. Bad-dog suddenly got to his feet and muttered a little in the instant before I heard the back doorbell.

It was the UPS man with my dress. I raced upstairs and opened the bag. Lee was right, it was dynamite. Short, black, velvet, it had a deep square neckline and a fitted bodice gently flaring as it reached my hips, a dancing dress.

. . .

"Is there a pizza place anywhere nearby?" I asked, joining Lee in the kitchen.

"Tony's, in Riseborough proper. It used to be very good when I was a kid. Why?"

"I just thought instead of mucking about heating things, we could get a pizza and some beer." I took the phone book from the shelf. "I'll buy. What kind do you want?"

"They don't deliver."

"I'll go get it."

"Alix, Riseborough is ten convoluted miles away. I can't hope to give you directions."

"So come with me." I saw the reflexive beetling of his brow. "You stay in the car and I'll go in."

"All right." Suddenly he grinned. "It's been a very long time since I've had pizza. Lived on the stuff for years as a kid, but Mrs. Greaves won't let anything remotely take-out into the house."

"Then we'd better burn the box!"

That incredible deep laugh sounded again, driving Baddog to his feet. "Bundle up, we'll take my car."

. . .

Underneath the canvas cover lay a 1968 MG. Bright red and pristine, the two-seater sat like a toy beside the Chevy wagon. Lee rubbed a gloved hand along the door. "My high school graduation gift. Can you believe it, such a waste on a boy. I never worked for it, barely appreciated it. Only through the grace of God did I never rack it up, though I had enough opportunities."

"It's beautiful. What's the word . . . mint. Mint condition."

"Willie is the curator for this museum piece. He spends half his time with it. His greatest pleasure is when I let him drive it to the gates." Lee pressed a button and the garage door raised itself. "Hop in."

I eased myself into the cockpit of the passenger seat and fished around for the seatbelt. The top was down, and I was grateful for the blanket Lee pressed around me.

Willie's care was evident in the immediate turnover of the engine, no hesitation, no sputtering. Lee slid the car out of the garage, and in a smooth arcing motion we were out on the long drive and flying between the trees. I felt as if I were skating again, so smooth was the feeling beneath me, so cold the wind whistling over my head.

Riseborough is one of those quintessential New England towns, a lovely big common bordered by white-fronted stores and brick banks. Oak trees planted a century or more ago give the grassy common character, as do the trees arcing over the wires along Main Street. Here and there stumps of the victims of blizzards and disease poke up, put to use now as kiosks and found-mitten holders.

A blue neon beer sign announced Tony's Pizza. Lee pulled over on the green side of the street. "I'll just spin around the block while you go in."

He dug into his back pocket, but I stopped him. "I said I'd treat!" I got out of the car and darted across the empty street. Tony's was a slice of every American pizza place. The odor was exactly the same as the place in my town. Strong cheese, tomato sauce, and beer. The wood floor was gritty with tracked-in snow and there were rings on the counter from wet bottles of beer and cans of Coke. "Miller," I said, and laughed when the guy behind the counter lifted a Miller beer from the cooler. "No, no, pizza for Miller!" The men around the bar hooted. "I'll buy you a Miller." "Wouldn't mind getting my hands around that Miller." "Need some help with that?"

I shook my head, aware of the flirting and not offended. "Thanks anyway, but I've got a date."

One of the men got a little more aggressive and stood up. "Yeah, but I bet I'm more of a man. Ditch him and come with me."

I held the pizza out in front of me and glared at him. He was shortish, middle forties, a little paunchy, with the look of a man who was probably considered a prize in his youth but had gone downhill and didn't realize it. "Sir, my date's easily twice the man you are." I shoved my way past and escaped through the door.

The MG was nowhere in sight, so I ducked into the pharmacy next door. I picked up some pantyhose and shampoo and poked my head out again. There he was, once again across the street in the darkness of the unlit green. One last stop at the package store to buy the beer and we were quickly out of town. "I like Riseborough. It's a real small town and hasn't been discovered by the chi-chi set yet."

"I suspect because there's nothing up here to attract them. Too far to commute to Boston or even Nashua comfortably. No college, no ski resort. There is a small artists' collective, but nothing really active. People are born here, and either live here and die here or leave and never return."

"You weren't born here." I felt the warmth of the pizza against my jeans.

"No, but it has proven ideal for me. Being limited in my social life, the scenery has its compensations." He came to a stop sign.

"Don't you get restless?"

"Of course. Sometimes I take drives at night and go for miles, all night sometimes. I go to Vermont, or down to Boston and just absorb all the sights. I sit in dark parking lots in malls and watch families and couples. It's fodder for my pen. That helps the restlessness. Especially if I accidentally encounter someone. My resolve becomes renewed."

"Resolve to stay out of sight?"

"Yes."

"Then it must have taken a great deal of courage to invite me to come and paint you."

"You may recall, it was your father I invited." He chuckled and I blushed a little.

"When was the last time you met someone new?"

He shifted, his big hand bumping my knee. "A couple of years ago."

"Tell me about it." The shadows from the overhanging trees darkened the tiny open cockpit even as the lights from farmhouses flashed across our faces.

"As you can imagine, anyone with a big house on a remote road in the mountains becomes an object of curiosity. Most of the town elite, if I may use the term, know who I am and"—he gestured with a hand—"what I am. The local Episcopal priest comes and is comfortable with me. The town clerk sends me absentee ballots and we talk on the phone. My dentist, obviously, and my physician are friends. But, on occasion, I am forced to go out. I'd been having trouble with my eyes. One of the manifestations of acromegaly is rapid onset of blindness, so I rushed to the ophthalmologist. Even as scared as I was, I was very careful to make a late appointment and to explain that I have certain anomalies that might be disturbing. No problem, Dr. Lewis knew all about me. Well, he neglected to tell his office secretary. Alix, you should have seen her face. You'd think I was Frankenstein's monster." His laugh began to rumble.

"Lee, that's awful. What kind of adult would act like that? Weren't you hurt?"

"I've long since gotten over being hurt by ignorant reac-

43

tions. But it isn't fun and not worth the freedom of being at large in the world. No, my freedom is cerebral, my night drives satisfactory after a fashion."

He turned into the driveway.

"But would you rather it were otherwise?"

"Would I rather be normal?" The question hung there, and I felt very small.

· · ·

We zapped the pizza back into life in the microwave and settled in front of the fire Lee made. I found a Sade disc and put it in the CD player. Lee raised his bottle. "To half-finished paintings and pizza."

"To half-finished novels and little MGs."

Sade's music lent a sense of poignancy to our little meal. I couldn't put my finger on it for a while, then knew. If this were any other man, we'd be dancing the will-he-or-won't-he-try-to-sleep-with-me-tonight minuet. If he were any other man, I might want him to. I hid behind the beer bottle as I wrestled with my inner shame. I was no better than that mother in Boston or the ophthalmologist's secretary. I could be his friend but I did not want him to touch me as a man.

"When will you go?" His deep voice startled me.

"I was thinking that I should go tomorrow. I need to do some things at home."

"Ah."

"But, if I may, I'd like to stay till Saturday morning." I rushed my words, feeling in some private place that I owed him something. "We can work Saturday for an hour or so and then I won't have lost too much time." I fought back the sense that I was betraying Mark by choosing another work morning over his request to come home Friday.

Lee smiled, and again the charm beat into submission the deformity. "I'd like that. When will you be back?"

"Monday. I'll leave first thing and be up here by lunch." I reached for another slice of pizza. "Is there anything I can bring back? Books or CDs or Chinese food?"

Lee shook his great head. "This may be an outpost, but I lack very little. Just bring yourself back, okay?"

"I promise." And again I felt the poignancy edge into my heart.

THE NEW DRESS HUNG ON A PADDED HANGER, LURK-
ing behind the closet door like some taunting luxury. I
touched the soft fabric of the sleeve and stroked it between
my fingers. I caught sight of myself in the rippled mirror,
hair roughly poked into a scrunchie, baggy blue jeans, and
paint-streaked tee shirt. I thought, Why not? and began to
strip.

After a long shower and half an hour's fussing with my
hair to twist it into a vaguely sophisticated style, I slipped
on the dress. The image that looked back at me in the
mirror now was of another woman. I nodded to myself,
pleased with the results. The short dress revealed flattering
lines, emphasizing the curve of my hips. The square neckline showed off my shoulders, hinting at décolletage. I
slipped on the black pantyhose I'd bought at the pharmacy
the other night and felt that quantum transformation from
ordinary to sexy.

Then I looked myself in the eye. "What *are* you doing,
Alix?" What if he thought I was coming on to him? Would
he assume something I never meant? Or worse, what if he
thought I was teasing him? Could I be unwittingly cruel to
a man I certainly liked but never in the way for which I
was dressing? I beat the panic back. I was a woman who
enjoyed dressing up. Who could fault me for that? Surely
he would know better.

I heard the hall clock chime the hour and knew he'd be in the living room with wine poured. Our habits, only a week old, were formed. A little unsteady on my heels, a great deal of long leg showing, I came down the stairs, one hand gliding along the seamless banister.

Lee held out my glass of wine and raised his glass. "You look stunning. Your friend Mark will certainly approve."

"Thank you. I'm sure Mark will like it, but I wore it because I thought you should have a chance to see what you picked out." I took a quick sip of the chardonnay and cursed myself for behaving like a flirt.

"You need a piece of jewelry. A pendant of some sort. No, silver. Silver beads." He looked into his glass, his massive brow knit in some private thought, then raised his head. "Shall we?" He stood aside as I preceded him into the dining room. I noticed immediately that my place had been set to his left instead of at the opposite end of the long table where I had sat all the other evenings, looking at him through the obscuring prisms of the candelabra.

·   ·   ·

After a few minutes, I stopped worrying that he'd misunderstand my innocent intention in wearing the dress. He got me to speak of my work, my recent goals for myself and my art. I confessed I was not a portrait painter, but an experimenter, using combinations of materials and shapes and forms to express concept and emotion. "I use broken shards and fabric, or varying thicknesses of paper. Color, lots of color. I try to capture the real colors in the world. The night I came here, I kept thinking I needed to capture the color of the night."

He was a good listener, prompting me, asking leading questions to keep me going. "What if, when you finish something, you don't like it? What do you do?"

"Sometimes I cut it up and cannibalize it. Sometimes I just scrape at the canvas and then gesso it over and use it for practice."

"What themes are you working with now?" He poured another bit of wine for me, his hand so large it covered the label. I liked his question, it was the question of an artist.

"Animals. I'm using the features of barnyard animals to represent human characteristics."

"How?"

I thought back to Mark's complaint that I'd never painted him. "Well, cockiness as a rooster's coxcomb. Or small-mindedness in the eye of a chicken." I laughed behind my wine glass. "Of course, an awful lot of what I do is my own private joke."

"You pick interesting human attributes, nothing trite like hate or love." He studied his wine glass, withdrawing for a moment into private thought.

. . .

As he guided me into my car the next morning Lee leaned forward and for a split second I thought he was going to kiss me. Instead he handed me the copy of his book. I opened it up to the flyleaf to read the inscription, "To Alix, with best wishes, Harris Bellefleur." I smiled but was oddly disappointed.

Then he said, "Bring back slides. I'd like to see your work."

A flush of pleasure mingled with the alarm prickling my neck. "I will. I'd love to show you my work."

He stood back and raised one massive hand in farewell. I tooted the horn and arced down the drive. As I passed through the rose-adorned gate I smiled; the coming weekend was just an interruption in a period of very good work.

. . .

My apartment smelled a little funky as I opened the door. Despite the cold, I threw open the windows. The fresh January air barreled in and fluttered the various notes and cartoons magnet-stuck to the fridge. A new note caught my eye: "Welcome home! I'll be by early for a reunion." Almost as soon as I had finished reading the note Mark burst into the room. "Hey, it's cold in here," he said, and began shutting up the windows.

"It smells, leave them open for a minute." I raised the kitchen window again.

Mark reached from behind me and pinned me against the counter, sliding his hands over my breasts. "Hey, I missed you. Did you miss me?" Turning me around, he kissed me, edging his tongue into my mouth. Within seconds we were in the bedroom, his anxious fingers tugging at my clothes. The sheets were chilled, but we soon warmed them. Afterward I lay spooned behind him, one hand on his firm hip. As he dozed, I rose up a little to study his face. Mark's shaggy good looks had always attracted me, long before we'd become lovers. Fair, usually unkempt, his hair was now clubbed back into a ponytail; frilly ends had pulled out from the elastic and framed his face. His hand lay on the pillow, a hand I had drawn many times, long and narrow. I knew the feel of it on my skin and between my hands, I knew that at the base of each finger were hard calluses from woodcutting all winter.

I eased myself back on my pillow, pulling the blanket up to my chin, struggling a little to get it from Mark. I sighed, touching on a melancholy whose source eluded me.

The phone rang. When Mark failed to react, I leapt out of bed and dashed into the kitchen, wrapping a flannel shirt over my nakedness.

"Alix?"

"Lee?"

"I just wanted to make sure you got home all right."

I held the phone close. "Yes, just fine. Got here about an hour ago."

"Good. Well then, see you Monday."

"I'll be there."

"Listen, Alix?"

"Yeah?"

"Knock 'em dead tonight."

I laughed.

"Good-bye."

"Lee? Thanks for calling."

"Who was that?" Mark stood in his shorts, arms crossed over his chest against the cold air still blowing in.

"Lee. Lee Crompton." I buttoned my shirt and pushed past him to get my jeans.

.   .   .

Cautioning me not to be late picking him up, Mark galloped down the stairs and out, his pickup truck leaving a new rut in the sun-softened mud. Pressing my forehead against the cold pane, I stared out at the departing truck and tried to touch the unhappiness within me, tried to give it a name. As if I were some gallery visitor without a guidebook, I wandered about my place, the second story of an old farmhouse, the land around it long since given over to subdivision. I looked at the sum of my exposed life hanging on the walls and stacked behind the couch. Every available space on the walls was covered by my work or by the works of others, including my father's and his father's. Studio photos of generations of Millers loitered in the narrow hallway to my bedroom. Their silver-tinged faces peered back at me as I lingered there. I stepped closer, hunting for resemblances. Were those dead-ahead eyes brown or green beneath the ram's horn eyebrows? Edward Miller, my father's grandfather, sat with an insouciant slouch, surrounded on either side by his coterie. For a short time around 1880 he was famous and followed. His hand, drooping elegantly as his elbow rested on the chairback, was ringless. I held up my own and examined it. Like Edward's mine was ringless, too, and I smiled to think in my veins passed the blood of such a man, whose own hand painted Lee's great-great-grandfather. I'd seen the portrait, a dour old man, his clipper ship fleet represented by a tiny painting in the portrait.

Tradition, Millers paint Cromptons, keeping food on Miller tables and paint in Miller paint boxes. Our two families were inextricably linked, yet knew each other not at all. We wandered through different circles, coming together only once a generation, like some kind of rite.

I looked at my great-grandfather again, trying to read the thought behind the steely eyes. Had you already painted Neville Crompton, or was that in your future?

It came to me then, the reason for my melancholy. I was the last. The last Miller to paint a Crompton. And the portrait I labored over would never be seen.

6

A PERSISTENT BANGING ON THE FRONT DOOR PENETRATED my blow-dryer deafness and I ran to open it, wondering why Mark didn't just let himself in, then remembered that I was to pick him up. A uniformed courier stood there, clipboard in one hand. "Alix Miller?"

"Yes?" My heart beat oddly, a little frightened.

He held out the clipboard. "Sign here."

I scraped a nearly inkless pen over the multipart form, which he pulled apart with a professional snap and handed me the canary copy. He then swung a manila-colored envelope out from under his other arm and handed it to me. Closing the door, I studied the form, the carbon-weak signature of the sender indecipherable. Like a child, I squeezed the padded envelope, feeling the object within. I tugged at the pull tab and shook out a rectangular box. A piece of paper fluttered out behind it, little bits of packing material clinging to it like lint.

Dear Alix,

 I want you to have the enclosed for your dinner tonight. I found them in a dresser in the attic some years ago and was told they were my grandmother's. As I mean no presumption, I hope that you will keep them.

I opened the green velvet jeweler's box. Silver beads lay against satin, their polished surfaces warming in the light. I held them up, admiring the perfectly formed drops as they graduated to a large central bead, beautifully filigreed. Looking closer I could see tiny roses etched into the pattern. I unclasped the old-fashioned box clasp and held the necklace to my throat.

Reflected in the hall mirror, I could see that Lee had been right, the silver beads were perfect with the black dress. I touched the filigreed bead. He meant no presumption, but what should I assume? I couldn't accept a gift like this, I shouldn't—a family heirloom, an expensive piece of jewelry. In the same mental breath I loved how they looked. Okay, I thought, just for tonight. No permanent gift. No matter what he said, a gift like this comes with strings. Long, sticky emotional ones I wasn't prepared to be entangled in.

The morning seemed so long ago. We'd only worked for a couple of hours. Lee had been unable to sit still, complaining of tingling in his hands, something the disease manifests now and again, he'd explained. With Mrs. Greaves out, I'd made us lunch of grilled cheese while Lee shared *New Yorker* cartoons with me. We'd laughed over them and I burned the sandwiches.

I touched the beads at my throat, a talisman. "Don't do this to me," I said.

. . .

The dinner in Boston was predictably boring, speeches laden with inside jokes among the photojournalist coterie. I smiled, laughed, and sipped white wine behind a mask of good humor. My mind crept back to Riseborough, even as my fingers touched the silver beads. My left-hand neighbor commented on them.

"Thank you, yes, a friend gave them to me."

At that moment, Mark chose to swing his attention away from the journalist on his right. "Who?"

A pernicious wave of flush rose up my neck to my face, as if I had something to hide. "Lee Crompton."

Mark's fingers closed over mine as they lay on the white tablecloth. "He's the guy who called you this afternoon. Who is he?" Mark was fighting to keep his voice mildly curious.

"Mark, he's the man I've been painting all week. Remember?" I shot off the answer in a tone designed to imply impatience with his not knowing this.

At that moment the awards program began and Mark let go of my hand. But as the master of ceremonies began to announce the first category, Mark leaned over. "We need to talk about this. Later."

"There's nothing to talk over," I hissed.

"Not now, don't talk to me now."

I began to pray that he'd win an award in the vain hope he'd forget about arguing. I was tired and had no strength to defend something that needed no defending. We'd planned to spend the night at the Copley Plaza, and a night in a hotel room with a man angry at me was not a pleasant thought.

. . .

God heard my prayers, or perhaps Mark's, because he was brought onstage for a prize in a best photo category. It was for his photo of the owners of a local barn holding each other after a horrible fire had destroyed their stock and their dreams. Taken from a distance, the two embracing forms against the backdrop of the burned-down barn was a touching picture and one of my favorites. I had even stolen the emotional theme for one of the unfinished projects slated for my March show.

At any rate, Mark and several of the other prizewinners grouped together and declared open season on Boston.

We roved from club to club, reggae, blues, rap, finally coming to rest at the hotel in the early hours. I lugged Mark's inebriated form into the elevator and then out, fishing through his pockets for the key.

"Easy, old pal." I bent under his weight. "Let's make it to the bed!" I extricated the plaque from his hand and set it on the writing desk.

"Hey, Alix," he called out from the blankets.

"What?"

"Do I need to be jealous? Of Crompton, I mean."

"No. Now go to sleep."

"Good." In seconds he was out, one foot on the floor to prevent the room from spinning around.

I sat on the end of the other bed and stared at myself in the mirror. Slowly I unclasped the beads and took them off, holding them in my hands for a long time before I put them away.

"I REALLY WANTED TO GO TO THE MUSEUM OF FINE Arts." I knew my voice was edging on petulance.

"Okay." Mark's capitulation would have a hook: "Then you've got to treat me real nice." He held open the covers.

"Don't I always?" Shucking off my leggings and baggy sweater, I climbed in to lie next to him. "Didn't I already bring you coffee?"

He rubbed his face against my bare shoulder. "You forgot the rolls."

"Bastard," I cried, and pummeled him until we wrestled ourselves into laughter. Last night's drinking had no effect on him this morning and he was quick and rough. In fifteen minutes I was in the shower. "Make me another cup of coffee," I called as I toweled my hair.

He thwacked my bare bottom as I walked by, jolting my good humor with a little annoyance at this old and irritating trick. I sipped the new coffee and cringed; as usual he'd put in too much sugar.

· · ·

We separated at the museum; I headed off to the newest exhibit in the Gund wing, he off to his own interests. I wasn't taken with the exhibit and in a sudden flash decided to seek out portraits, hoping to find some inspiration among the old order. Finding a bench, I sat down and communed with the several portraits before me. What made them art as opposed to private record? Not every portraitist became famous or hung in a museum, so few of my ancestors had. My painting of Lee had progressed to the point where I could begin detailing it, adding the spark of life to the sketch. Any portrait can be a representation of the outside of a person; a good one speaks of the inner man. I wanted very much to reveal the soul that I had begun to know that lay beneath Lee's horrible exterior.

I examined cheeks and hands and postures and colors in the portraits before me. Finally I decided that my father was right, it was the life in the eyes that made the difference. A really good painter told something about the sitter in the expression. Cunning, mischievous, brilliant, sweet-tempered, or dour.

It shouldn't be so difficult, then, I thought, to paint Lee. With his massive features, deep facial lines, and mobile expressions, I should be able to capture the man behind the distortion with ease. If he would let me—but as soon as he sat, it was as if he became a lifeless statue. A gargoyle. I had not even begun to attempt his face. For the entire time we'd been at it, I'd only created the outline of his form, stroking in cautious hints of the shape of his face. It was only in the little pencil sketches that I had captured him. Those showed life and interest and a human being. From those I could do a creditable portrait. And again I felt that jolt of sadness that my efforts were for nothing. I reasoned with myself, as I sat there in front of a Sargent, that it was his money, his choice what to do with the finished painting. It was never going to be my personal masterpiece, no portrait would be. So what did I care if he stored it for all eternity under a burlap cover in the attic of the Riseborough house? No, that wasn't my problem. That he wouldn't even look at it was.

I shook off my reverie and looked at my watch; within our agreed-upon time frame I had fifteen minutes left for the gift shop. I wandered around the museum store almost as if it were another room in the exhibit. Tiny reproductions of masterpieces adorned book covers and coasters. Instructional toys and silly objects, jewelry and posters crowded the space, filling the visual sense with overstimulation and the spendthrift sense with excitation. I could withstand most of it, until my eye fell on a copper wind chime fashioned with a rose as the central clapper, the five chiming pipes like thorny stems. I could see it hanging in the solarium, could imagine its melodious sound airborne even as my hand touched the display. Delicate tones sprang out, not tinkling but bell-like in their quality.

"Fifty percent off," the saleswoman said as if talking to someone else, then turning to face me. "It really is pretty."

Mark joined me at the cash register. "What'd you buy?"

I showed him and he screwed up his face. "Why? You don't have any place to hang that."

"It's not for me."

Most of the time Mark is amazingly uncurious. At other times he displays a ferreting quality most annoying. "Who?"

"Lee."

"Why?"

"I don't know. It just seems perfect for his house."

Mark was silent all the way to the car. I unlocked it and climbed in, he stood outside. The biting city cold ruffled his fair hair and he shoved his hands into his pockets.

"Come on, it's unlocked," I said, shoving the key into the ignition. "Mark?"

"You go. I'm going to stay in town for another day."

"Don't be ridiculous."

"Ridiculous?" He leaned into the car. "No more ridiculous than buying an expensive gimcrack for a rich patron." With that he slammed the Sentra's passenger door and stalked off.

I felt sick. Leaning my forehead against the steering wheel, I fought tears, not the first I'd felt in recent months. I knew he expected me to leap out of the car and follow him down the street, I knew that he'd close down on me until I declared my error, until I manipulated his forgiveness. I raised my head, tears hardened into stone. I watched his back in the mirror as he strode away, hands shoved in his pockets and head down in his characteristic walk.

"I don't need this bullshit," I said aloud, and turned the ignition key. How dare he make assumptions about me. How dare he sully an impulsive and innocent act with implications. I passed the street I might have turned down to go around the block and head him off. I kept going. I negotiated the light Sunday traffic up Route 9, merging onto 95, all the time driving on automatic pilot while my active attention chewed on Mark's sulk.

It wasn't as if he'd ever said let's get married, or let's live together, or suggested any other permanent arrangement. Then I could understand his periodic bouts of demanding my complete attention. Mark said he was a man on the move, the future could mean Los Angeles or New York or even Europe. That had suited me. Equally, my own declaration, early in our acquaintance, that I could never roam far as long as my father was alive had effectively set the framework of our relationship.

In many ways we were poles apart, yet, like magnets, we could not resist each other. I was rooted, he ready to sever ties; I cared deeply for my father, he could not understand filial attachment and the flashes of jealousy in his petty remarks drove splinters into my heart. He was not above forcing me to choose, and his silence was so much deeper than my father's.

Our art was the thing that had brought us together, and often the thing that set us apart. As a photographer, his stimulus was from the outside, what he saw he reacted to. As a painter, my muse was internal, what I thought and felt brought out to the canvas. I respected his work, he criticized mine in the name of being helpful.

This late in the day on a Sunday in January, the traffic north was minimal and I cruised along, WGBH blaring a Beethoven quartet, the counterplay between the violins, viola, and cello voicing the drama in my heart until the last twisting rise to the tonic chord, which seemed written expressly for my state of mind.

Mark and I had met at a group show in which we both had pieces. I had an abstract in acrylic called *Old Man with Rake* and I watched him examining it, watching for the expression that would encourage me to approach and introduce myself, or, depending, keep my back to him and never speak. I was at the stage in my career when even slight disapproval touched me personally. Attending my own shows bordered on neurotic. For days I would deny I was even going to attend, then worry about what to wear. I practiced witty conversation and defenses for my work. I watched Mark, then walked off.

Driven away from my own work, I set about studying others', coming to rest in front of a dramatic black and white photo of a Peruvian mother and child. Mark was suddenly at my side, studying the same picture, one hand rubbing his short beard, up and down, using just his fingertips under his chin in a manner which would become so familiar to me. "So, what do you think of this one?"

"I like it. It's a marvelous study." I stepped back a little, putting an inch more distance between us. "Who is he? The photographer, I mean?"

"Mark Kramer."

"I don't know his work."

"I'm somewhat familiar with it," he whispered in a gallery voice.

At that moment a woman breezed through, an older man in tow. "Mark, sweetie, I want you to meet Donald Stone." She darted for Mark's hand and pulled him away from me with an icy glance over her shoulder, garnished by a red-lipped smile. Mark threw me a grin even as he was hauled off to do the ingratiating gallery jive.

He found me later, holed up in the gallery cafe.

"Why did you do that?" I asked.

"Do what?"

"Pretend you weren't the photographer."

"For the same reason you pretended you weren't the artist who painted *Old Man with Rake.*"

Flushed, I stammered, "But you didn't like it, and I told you I liked the mother and child."

"I do so like your work."

That was the first great lie he told me. Now he no longer took the trouble to lie, he no longer seemed to care about my feelings, and his truthfulness was hard-edged. "Grow up, Alix," he told me the last time I got angry at his criticism of my work. "Get used to it if you want to make it in the art world."

I signaled for my exit.

ALTHOUGH IT SEEMED AN ETERNITY HAD PASSED SINCE I'd last slept in my own home, I was agitated and afraid that my phone would ring and that I would have to deal with Mark, deal with the reality of him rather than the creature of my imaginary arguments. So deep was my anger that I wanted no possibility of contact with him and thus decided to spend the night with my father. I'd stop home only long enough to throw more clothing in a bag and water my plants. I won only imaginary fights, when every word was orchestrated and my points were heard and scored. When it came to reality, Mark seemed never to stick to the script. My best shots were deflected and used against me. Tired, upset, I had no strength to engage the battle tonight.

My answering machine was flashing like mad. Choosing to ignore it, I emptied my underwear drawer into a tote bag and hunted for the watering can. That done, I shrugged on my coat and flung the bag over my shoulder. The insistent red light caught my eye and I relented. I was being pessimistic, maybe Mark had left a conciliatory message and I was being stubborn.

It was my father: "Alix, call me as soon as you get in," the message ran and his voice seemed tentative, a thread of anxiety woven into the nine short words.

With conflicting disappointment and relief that Mark

hadn't called, I shut the machine off and dashed down the stairs.

. . .

"Dad, what's up?" I called from the kitchen as I let myself in the back door. A slight smell of yesterday's soup lingered and dishes were piled in the sink. My booted foot crunched on broken glass as I walked through the room. I called again, "I'm home, Dad." I bent to pick up the glass, then heard him call me.

I found him in the living room, sitting bolt upright in his favorite chair, his breathing labored and a film of sweat glazing his forehead. "Alix." He smiled, pain erasing the smile instantly. "I think I'm in a little fix here." His fingers clutched at the arms of the chair.

I called 911, and the next few hours were a complete blur. It seemed to me, after the fact, that the ambulance was there instantly. Time lost its power for me, hours seemed seconds. I was suddenly in the small emergency room of the local hospital and a cup of coffee was thrust into my hand. I couldn't tell the nursing staff from the doctors, no one wore whites like on TV, everyone wore stethoscopes around their necks and Nikes on their feet. I focused on giving information. I racked my brain for details of Dad's history. Why didn't I know his medications? Did he take anything? Had he been having problems before this? Allergies? I shivered, an icy breeze slipping in as the pneumatic doors swung open again.

Then I waited. Year-old *Smithsonian*s entertained me while the staff monitored my father, waited for blood-gas tests, made him comfortable. While my eyes read the words, my mind made decisions: I'll monitor his eating better; I'll spend more time with him; I'll maybe even move back home. I sighed involuntarily with that thought.

"Alice Miller?"

I didn't correct her. "Yes?"

Birkenstocks on her feet and baggy sweater over leggings, the doctor led me into a tiny room, the sole furnishing two plastic chairs. "It's not his heart," she began.

A heat wave of relief stung me, quickly doused by her next words: "I want to keep him here and run some tests. I think that we may be dealing with"—she caught herself, aware suddenly of the need to be gentle—"something else."

"What?" I was in no frame of mind for prevarication.

"I think your father may have cancer."

"How can you say that? Why?" I was on my feet, denial spilling from my mouth. "That's not possible. Not again."

"Please, Alice . . ."

"Alix, it's Alix. Please tell me why you think that."

It was too much, too much to take in at once, but over the next few days I learned a great deal about how this evil lies in wait until it can rear its ugly head and steal our loved ones without a by-your-leave.

My mother had died of it when I was fifteen, and the question that spun through my mind now was, why had he lived so long without her only to die of it, too?

Pancreatic cancer. A tumor lying dormant and painless suddenly comes alive and all living becomes dying.

Into subordination go all other concerns when faced with death. When Mark finally called me on Tuesday, I had no strength to care that we'd fought, and he had the grace not to mention it.

"I'm sorry about your dad," he said, but quickly turned the brief conversation toward his own news. Once again his star was on the rise, the *Boston Globe* had offered a good assignment.

"Great, call me when you get back," was all I could manage to say. Mark Kramer was at the wrong end of the telescope and getting farther away from my reality.

. . .

I'd called Lee on Monday, speaking only with Mrs. Greaves, explaining my problem with a sense that someone else was speaking. She murmured, "Poor lass," which sent the first tears rolling. "If there's anything I can do," she said, as had so many others whom I had called with the news.

"No. Thank you, though. If there is, I'll call," I promised her, as I had promised ten others, determined not to call anyone for help, but to shoulder this burden myself and be the brave little trouper I had been when my mother died.

Once the pain had come under control and all the tests had been administered, only one decision needed to be made.

"We'll start an aggressive campaign of chemo and radiation, in Boston, of course. We can maybe eke out another six months that way." Dr. Mulcahey reached for his Rolodex. "I'll put you in touch with a top oncologist at Dana Farber."

"Wait, no." I sat on the edge of the Naugahyde visitor's chair. "We don't want to do it that way. That's not living, Dr. Mulcahey."

Dr. Mulcahey threw himself back in his chair, which protested with a squeak. "Alix, it's your father's decision, but I don't think he should give up."

"I don't call it giving up. But you know he saw my mother struggle to fight it, only to finally lose the battle. Every day a skirmish in hell with chemo or radiation or pain. No, Dr. Mulcahey, he knows exactly what he wants and I support him in it."

Dr. Mulcahey shot forward, his chair squealing louder. "Treatments have improved since your mother's illness. Twenty years ago much of what she endured was still experimental."

"Have they eliminated the side effects from chemo?"

"Of course not all." His impatience was beginning to show.

"Is the cure no longer worse than the disease? Have they been able to make the quality of a life in cure as sweet as a clean death?"

"There will be times of remission, when the drugs begin to conquer the cancer, and aren't those few weeks or months infinitely better than letting it run its course uncontrolled?"

"It cannot be controlled, only held back like the Dutch dike. With pain control, and surrounded by people he loves, we can make his last months sweet and uncomplicated." I paced the room now, walking in and out of the patches of sunlight barring the floor through the venetian blinds.

"You are talking about your father's death, Alix."

I stopped, the sunlight and shadows laying bars across my body. "Haven't you been?"

"It may take a year. Are you committed to waiting a year for death, or working for a year to give him life?"

"You bastard, it's what he wants!" I cried out. "It's what he wants. My mother was a young woman, it made sense to fight. But Dad's seventy-three. He doesn't want to do it. I won't make him do it."

"All right, all right"—Dr. Mulcahey threw up his hands in a stage gesture—"then please contact Hospice. Do that much for him anyway."

"We already have." I was outraged, as if giving my father

death with dignity was some sort of filial selfishness. It occurred to me then that in these litigious times Mulcahey was worried that someday I would come back to him and accuse him of not trying to save my father. "I will, Doctor, in no way hold you accountable for our decision."

He looked up at me with rheumy blue eyes peering over the horn-rimmed frames of his half-glasses. To save him denial, I left.

HOSPICE HELPED ME SET DAD UP AT HOME. THEY taught me how to administer the morphine; how much would ease the pain and how much would make him sleep. The living room had been made over into a bed-sitting room, the paraphernalia of illness neatly laid out on the antique breakfront. When he felt better we played games, chess, checkers, and the like. Some days he preferred just to watch television and we spent hours letting Sally Jessy Raphaël and her ilk entertain us with the pathetic of the world. The sunlight played upon the screen, fading it to gray, and he dozed as the guests told their tales like bards of old, entertaining the bored princes. He lay in his recliner, fingers clutching intermittently at the arms. He was withering. The flesh of his forearms raddled now, a million silky lines cascading downward when he raised his hands. I watched his life's juices being sucked away by this invisible tyrant, while all around us were results of his life's work, vital images pulsing with energy. I took to changing the paintings and line drawings so that he could see them all before he went. "Before I go, I want to see . . . before I go." It was as if he were waiting for a flight.

One afternoon he woke with a start. "Alix, go work. You musn't waste light like this."

"No, there will be plenty of light another day."

"Alix, go. You can hear me if I call. Go paint a nice picture for your show."

He'd forgotten that I'd withdrawn my participation from the March show. It was the middle of February and I hadn't touched brush to canvas since that last Saturday at Riseborough. But I had been sketching—sketching my father as he lay there, asleep or awake, comfortable and in discomfort. I was recording it on thick white paper in my notebook. Someday, I knew, it would be translated into a piece of work dedicated to him. I recorded the wasting away, the deepening lines as his face hollowed out. I penciled in the expression of resignation and the grim-lipped fight against despair.

"Alix, go paint. I would really like to know you're working. I hate unfinished projects and the studio is cluttered with yours."

When I began another sally of protest he held up one hand. "For God's sake, child, give me some time alone!"

"Oh, Dad"—I leaned over and kissed him—"of course I'll leave you alone."

. . .

I took him at his word and went home to my apartment, which had grown cold and dusty without me. All the plants were dead. My answering machine light was bleating. I'd left the message where to call on the tape, but evidently someone had left a message here anyway.

"Alix, I didn't want to disturb you, but I thought I'd call and see how you were. It's Tuesday, February second, about six-thirty. Give me a call if you want to talk." Lee's voice was soft and resonant over the speaker, full of concern, and suddenly I wanted nothing more than to talk with him. I felt a jolt of something I could only call home-sickness. Mantra-like, I kept thinking I want to go home, I want to go home. I wanted to be out of this nightmare and in a safe harbor. Lee's voice brought me back to a brief time when his home had been a haven of quiet and work for me. I hadn't needed it then, now I longed for it.

My calendar was still on January. I lifted the page and looked at February. Valentine's Day had passed unnoticed and it was now the 17th. He'd called almost three weeks ago and probably thought I didn't want to talk to him.

I twisted the thermostat to 70° and set the kettle on the stove. Coffee made, I punched Lee's number and listened to the ring.

"Hello?"

"Lee?"

"Alix, how are you?" His voice was so sweet that I was unnerved and tears began to flow as they had not in weeks. He kept repeating my name, but I couldn't speak. All of it waited to burst forth, but all I could do was cry. As I sobbed Lee kept up a soothing litany. "Alix, it's okay, let it out. Let it out, let it out. You've been holding on but it's okay to let go."

Finally I reached that plateau where tears and weeping are silly. "Oh, Lee, I'm so embarrassed. You must think I'm a jerk. Calling you just to bawl."

There was a slight pause, a little throat-clearing second. "Alix, I'm touched that you did. I just wish"—he paused again, and I sensed instantly his next brave words—"I wish that I was there."

"Come!" I lurched to my feet. "Please come tonight!"

He didn't say anything, and I could feel his indecision. "Are you sure?"

"Please. I'm at my father's all the time with no one else. Take one of your night drives and come visit me."

"It wasn't my imagination then, was it?"

"What?"

"That we're friends?"

"Yes." I pressed my back against the doorjamb and slid to the floor. "Yes, we are, and on the basis of that friendship, will you come help me sit with my dying father?"

.   .   .

"Dad"—I touched his shoulder—"someone is coming to visit tonight."

"Who?" More and more he disliked having people come to see him.

"Lee Crompton." I took the blanket from him and helped him to his feet. "My patron. My friend."

We shuffled down the hall together. "I can't see anybody," he said before he went into the bathroom. "I can't have anybody see me like this."

I smiled a little. "Lee is different, Dad. He'll understand that."

He shook his head before shutting the bathroom door.

The house had begun to take on the odor of illness and I was painfully aware of it. I set about baking apple pies to mask the punky smell emanating from the living room. Lee would arrive around seven-thirty, and I had stopped at the grocery store for dinner. Dad was still eating at the table, so I'd planned a roast beef dinner for us. That Dad scarcely managed soup most of the time was irrelevant.

I had just pulled the pies out of the oven when the phone rang. It was Mark, and in the instant that I recognized his voice I realized that the ringing phone had made me fear that it was Lee canceling. My relief that it was Mark instead came through in my voice and he commented on it.

"You sound chipper tonight."

"Well enough. Are you coming by?" Mark had come

two or three times in the beginning, but his excuses not to stop by and visit my father had been at the ready recently.

"Actually, no. I'm going to New York tomorrow and I thought maybe you could break away for a little while and we could, well, have a little time together."

"Mark, I can't." I knew that he meant a little time together in bed.

"Alix, you can't lock yourself in that house forever."

"It won't be nearly that long."

"Right, well, okay. But, you know, I'm going to be gone for at least a week." After a beat he added, "Alix, this could be the one. The career booster."

I know he wanted me to ask him all about it, to turn the key that would start him on his career monologue. Ordinarily I would have, but I had a roast to put in and a sick father. I cut him off. "Mark, listen, have a great time and good luck with the assignment. You can tell me all about it when you get back."

"Maybe, maybe I will, Alix. Or maybe I just won't come back. You never know."

"Mark, is that a threat?" A side effect of my father's illness was my own directness, a loss of finesse. There was silence and I filled it. "I don't need your ego, Mark Kramer. I have enough to deal with, so either be my friend or leave me alone."

"Who was that?" Dad asked.

"Mark."

"Will he be coming by?" My father liked Mark, liked his work. He was circumspect about the peculiar relationship we maintained; only occasionally did he hint that it should be more permanent.

"No. He's on his way to New York."

"Still pursuing the big one, eh?"

I smiled. "Something like that."

. . .

The doorbell rang at six-thirty. Despite his being an hour early, I knew it was Lee, no one ever came to the front door who wasn't a stranger. I was acutely aware of the messy pile of wood on the porch and the tatty little rug in the entrance hall. Wishing I'd had time to change, I stroked my hair back and jerked open the heavy oak door.

Time had softened my memory of him and the reality was a little unnerving. He was larger than I remembered him, and I saw the monster before I saw the man. Then suddenly he was Lee, my skating companion and model, and I pushed into submission the involuntary reaction to his looks and concentrated on the kindness of his being there.

I brought him into the living room, where Dad was in his recliner, the IV drip slowly easing the evening's pain. "Dad, this is Lee Crompton."

The drug slurred his speech and fogged his mind, but old social skills carried the day and he extended the hand not engaged to the drip. "Mr. Crompton, my daughter tells me a great deal about you. She's enjoying her stay with you. No, I mean . . ."

"Yes, I enjoyed her stay with me very much." He glanced at me and smiled. "She's also told me quite a bit about you."

The opening gambit made, I slipped away to make us drinks. When I came back laughter greeted me, rolling chuckles from my father's throat, Lee's vibrant roar surrounding it. Somehow I knew I was the butt of their joke.

"What gives, guys?"

With one voice they protested, "Nothing!"

Dad sipped his orange juice and Lee and I had a glass of wine; conversation rolled along gently until Dad fell asleep as he often did after his medication.

"This is a great house, Alix. When was it built, about 1800?"

"Actually, 1783. It's been in the family since the Civil War, when Edward Miller purchased it. He had designs on being a gentleman farmer, so he bought this farmhouse way out in the country surrounded by woods and pastures and set about raising horses and children."

"Isn't he the one who painted my father's great-grandfather, the whiskery old fellow in the blue tunic?"

"That would be about the time, anyway." I sliced off another fragment of cheese and munched it. "Of course, subsequent Millers added and reduced the house to their personal likings and the fashions of the times. Our own improvements have been new PVC pipes and a rather expensive septic system. And, as you can see, we are no longer way out in the country. Not like you."

He finished his wine and set the glass down on a napkin.

"Would you like a tour?"

"I'd love one."

We wandered through the house, lingering here and there as Lee's eye fell upon some antique or piece of art. He seemed so much bigger in the low-ceilinged house; I kept warning him to duck as we passed through two-hundred-year-old doorways with their unforgiving lintels. So much of what Millers put into this house remained. Now that most of the rooms were unlived in, it had the feeling of a museum exhibit. When I lived here the rooms were often winter cold, but my early memories were only of the warmth of the sun coming through the tiny multi-paned window. I was sleeping in my old room now, near the back and overlooking the lower meadow. A childhood room, it bore remnants of teenage fascinations, which my father had never cleaned out. My high school pennant still clung bravely to the wall beside my streaky mirror, where I had spent so much time experimenting with preteen styles.

A photo of my mother in a cheap dime-store frame sat on the nightstand. I'd found it in a drawer and taken it out, propping it against the lamp when the cardboard foot wouldn't hold it. She looked so young, maybe only eighteen or twenty. She wore pedal pushers and a white Peter Pan blouse. In the black and white photo, her long hair might have been auburn or plain brown. She straddled her bike and her eyes were alight with some joke forever a mystery. I had studied that picture, over and over again, trying to hunt down the clue that her life would be over before she was forty-five.

"You look like her." Lee stood at the foot of my narrow bed, his back to the mirror.

I looked at the picture again, picking it up. "I've never seen the resemblance."

"She was lovely."

"She wasn't when she died."

I set the picture down carelessly and it slipped, rattling the glass.

The kitchen ell had been modernized in my grandfather's day, and restored to its oldest form in my father's. This had always been my favorite room, and its soapstone sink and real butcher block offset the dishwasher and microwave. A farm table instead of countertops served as the work area, and an enamel-topped sideboard provided a perfect piecrust-making surface. I stopped to check the roast and light the fire under the potatoes and carrots.

"So where's your studio?"

I'd forgotten I'd told Lee I worked at my father's house. "The studio is through the back door. Would you like to see it?"

In the tradition of New England farmhouses, ours was "Big House–Little House–Back House–Barn." Our studio was in the back house segment, the barn long gone. A short breezeway connected it, open on one side and heaped now with wood. The studio was freezing. The only source of heat, the woodstove, was now dormant. My several abandoned works stood out as the overhead lights came on. Sheets covered the easels and stack of canvases. Dad's work on his drawing table lay under a sheet of thick polypropylene.

"May I?" Lee touched the corner of the sheeting covering my work.

I got that little chill I always do when someone wants to look at my unfinished pieces, but nodded.

He lifted the cover from a small painting, a landscape with bits of real grass and stone worked into the thick oil paint. The predominant colors were blue, red, and yellow. Off to one side was a face, a little like the angels carved on eighteenth-century headstones; round, slightly cherubic, it hovered out of context with the rest of the painting. I hadn't decided whether to leave it in or paint it out.

I puttered around while Lee looked at all my work. Something like staring at the ceiling while the gynecologist roots around, I can't watch anybody examine my unfinished work. The cold in the room began to numb my feet in their thin Keds, and I motioned that I was leaving. "Stay longer if you want to." I went back to the kitchen and poked the carrots with a wicked-looking fork.

"Alix." Lee came back into the kitchen and held his hands near the oven. "Alix, they're great."

"What?"

"What do you think I mean? Your paintings, of course," he chided. "I want to buy the cherub painting."

"I like that, the cherub. I hadn't thought of it that way, but you don't have to buy anything. Please don't feel obliged."

"Alix, I'll feel deprived if I can't have that painting." His shaggy eyebrows rose and fell. "You do sell your work, don't you?"

"I'd be lying if I said I only paint for private expression. Of course you may have it"—I raised the wicked-looking fork—"but as a gift. Don't you even think of buying it. Just tell all your friends what a marvelous painter you've discovered and recommend me."

"I can't . . ."

"I accepted your beads. Quid pro quo, Mr. Crompton." And we laughed.

. . .

Dad sat at his accustomed place at the head of the table in the dining room. Outside the wind had picked up and it sang through the overhead wires, haunting in its almost melodious whistle. Except for my forgetting the rolls in the oven, the meal turned out well. I hadn't really cooked for a long time and was pleased with the result. My often elusive appetite surfaced, the red meat tasting so good after weeks of soups and quick meals. Lee, used to professional cooking in his house, was kindly complimentary. I looked at my father and saw that he'd touched nothing on his plate. "Dad, come on, eat something," I chided. "No dessert if you don't."

He didn't answer and I could see the fog of morphine like an aura around him. His fuzzy gray hair stuck up at all angles from lying on it all the time. His sweater was buttoned wrong, and when he looked at me he looked puzzled.

"Dad, eat something."

"I don't want to," he retorted.

"Just a little," I cajoled, frightened a little at his outburst.

"No."

"Dad." I was angry now, embarrassed that he would be such a child in front of company. I opened my mouth again, but Lee stopped me.

"Alix, leave him alone."

"Lee, he has to eat."

"No, not right now. Let him be."

The tip of my fork rattled against my plate. Abruptly I stood and began gathering dirty dishes. "Why don't you go into the living room and I'll put on the coffee."

I stood in the kitchen, leaning against the soapstone sink and staring at my own reflection in the night-darkened window. I shook my head to clear it of the scene and went back to the dining room to finish cleaning up. Dishes clattered together as I carelessly piled them one on top of the other. I filled the sink and dropped them in; cauliflowers of soap foam splashed over the edge, dripping down and under my feet. I forgot to plug in the coffee maker and made jagged cuts in the pie.

"Alix, are you all right?" Lee leaned against the doorjamb, his head grazing the lintel.

"No. I'm tired and cranky," I answered, and felt a lump in my throat that would easily become self-pity if I let it. "I'm so tired, Lee. He doesn't sleep at night and wants company. It's got to be like being a new mother. Every morning at four o'clock he wakes me up and we sit up rehashing old problems and reliving old pain until he falls asleep again around six and I'm left awake."

"Go to bed, Alix. I'll take care of him tonight. I don't think it matters who sits with him, as long as he has somebody here."

"But there are medications and . . ."

"I will take care of it."

"I can't ask you to do that, Lee. I'm just grateful you came to visit."

"I came to help. Let me."

I was too tired to debate the issue. The tantalizing idea of a night's uninterrupted sleep was too appealing. "Okay, but don't do the dishes. I have all day tomorrow to do them."

"No, I'll stay with him." Lee plugged in the coffee maker. "Go to bed, sweetie."

I yawned, nodding. As I moved out of the room I turned back. "Lee?"

He turned around, his great head canted to one side.

"I'm really glad you're here." From across the room we faced each other and when I looked into his eyes I saw for the first time, in their perfect china blue, the eyes of the boy in the picture. Two things had not been lost to the disease.

BUNDLED UP IN THERMALS AND A FLANNEL SHIRT, I crawled into my bed in the heat-deprived back bedroom and fell into an instant and deep sleep. Sometime during the night I was wakened. I started to climb out of bed, then lay back—Lee's deep voice pierced the night and I knew he was with my father. I closed my eyes again and knew nothing more.

There is a kind of miracle in waking naturally. Eyes open, the miasma of weariness is gone. There is no soul crying out for more sleep. Thus I awoke, the sunlight beaming in through the paned window to lie upon my bed in oblong patterns, illuminating the patchwork like some stained-glass window across my lap. With amused horror I saw that it was after ten o'clock. I bolted out of bed and slipped down the backstairs to the kitchen. A pot of coffee lingered on the burner, my mug waiting for me on the clean table. A note rested against the sugar bowl.

Alix,

Your father passed a fairly comfortable night, I think. I have given him his medication this morning (8 a.m.) and he's eaten a little. I have to go now, but please call me and call on me.

Lee

P.S. I took the painting. I hope that's all right.

L

I bucked a wave of disappointment. I heard the television go on in the living room and went to bid my father good morning.

"Hey, sleepyhead," he greeted me, holding open his arms in a way he hadn't for a long time. I knelt into his embrace and tried not to notice the scent of illness about him. "I like that friend of yours, he's a pretty good card player."

"Does that mean you beat him?"

"Yeah, but he gave me a run for my money."

. . .

That evening I called Lee. As usual Mrs. Greaves answered, but wouldn't put him on the line. "He's upstairs with a migraine. He's prone to them, you know."

"Part of his disease?" I was compelled to ask.

"I guess so. Anyway, he'll be sorry he missed your call."

"Tell him thank you, Mrs. Greaves. Tell him I'm sorry I slept so long that I missed him. Tell him"—I was scrambling now—"tell him I really loved having him here and that soon we'll get back to working on his portrait."

There was a heartbeat of pause before Mrs. Greaves spoke. "Alix, don't encourage him. Don't set him up for disappointment."

I felt myself go scarlet. "Mrs. Greaves, that is the farthest thing from my mind. Please just relay my message." I hung up, trembling from the unprovoked assault on my intentions.

I wondered then how much of her influence had kept Lee a virtual prisoner in that house.

. . .

That afternoon Robin Gates came into our lives. As naturally as a long-time habit, she banged on the back door and let herself in. She plunged in, taking charge without offending, offering encouragement when we would give up, occasionally spending the night when she saw the raw exhaustion creep up on me again. We were lucky enough to receive a morphine pump so that Dad could administer his own dose as he needed it. She played interminable hands of three-handed cribbage and never once lost her temper when Dad became aggressive or whiny. Or even when I became aggressive or whiny.

About my age, she was a widow, had been for two years. Her husband, Daniel, had died of the same cancer my father had. Hospice had saved her life, she liked to say, and so she donated her time as a volunteer, helping others crawl through the same tunnel she'd gone through.

"It's not supposed to be easy. Every emotion you have will come into play. The best I can offer you is that at the end you will go on with your life. Your mourning is now. You have a gift in that you know what's going to happen and you can say all those things you think you need to now, before it's too late. And hold back those things you should." Robin added coffee to her perpetual cup. "And you need to work. Your dad talks all the time about how great an artist you are. Paint something for him."

"It's cold in the studio."

"Build a fire, Alix. Warm yourself."

The stove was full of ash, so first I cleaned it out, then I performed the ritualistic fire-lighting task that had so often been prelude to my work. Bunch up newspaper, crumpling up current events with ads for white sales across the land. With my red hatchet I struck splinters of kindling from old shingles, mingling them with angled ends of two-by-fours gathered from work sites. The flame caught. I fed the incipient fire choice bits of wood, and satisfied at last that it would survive, I loaded the Tempwood stove with two oak logs and set the lid down.

.   .   .

I stood in front of the empty easel, the absence of my landscape with angel conspicuous. Lee had taken the choice from me, whether to keep the angel or paint her away. A stretched canvas sat on the workbench and I took it up, setting it in place of the missing painting. Studying my tubes of color, I waited to warm up. The afternoon sun suffused the room with lemony light and the impression of heat. The studio has three sides of windows and four great skylights, which can open in the summer. The light is unfettered by shadow anywhere and now I stood in the midst of its power and my hand went to the canvas, nearly blinding in its whiteness. I pressed my fingers to it, closing my eyes and imagining what might go there, entering willingly the dream that allowed me to create. Then I reached for my brush.

.   .   .

"Alix, phone call!" Robin called from the kitchen door, shattering my concentration and bringing me out of the dream.

Clearing my head with a physical shake, I set the brush down and grabbed a rag to wipe my hands. Mark's first question was, "Who was that?"

"Robin. She's here from Hospice."

"Nice voice."

"She's wonderful."

"So how are things?" Mark never mentioned my father by name anymore.

"Why don't you come for dinner and we'll tell you."

"I can't, Alix. I'm actually still in New York. I just

thought we could talk a little." His voice is Mark's barometer, revealing emotion when his words do not.

"Sure." I wished I'd closed up my paints, but settled down on the wide-board floor to listen to him. My preoccupations had so removed him from my circle of concern that a flash of guilt jolted me. Beyond our recent troubles, I knew that we cared for each other. He needed to have me listen. "How is the assignment going?"

"Good." Again his voice revealed his inner concern.

"Tell me about it."

For half an hour he filled me in on his assignment, a photo essay on AIDS babies in a hospital in Manhattan. He'd spent the week shooting photos of these children, their parents, foster parents, the staff who care for them. "They wanted my perspective as a small-town writer seeing this firsthand for the first time. It's so horrible, Alix. You have no idea."

"Your pictures will show it to me."

"I don't think I can do it."

"Why?" I sat up.

"Because I can't put what I've seen on paper."

"You've just told me about it. Write it just that way, and the rest will come."

"Alix, they put in my arms a tiny infant. That baby, weak and sick, looked up at me and made eye contact. I held out my finger, and it took it."

"That's sweet, Mark," I murmured, trying to picture him actually holding a child.

"Then, today, they told me he'd died." I heard his voice break and I felt my own tears rise.

"Mark, come home."

"No. I can't. I have to finish it. I just wanted to talk to you about it. I'll do it." His voice had cleared and I could sense his control was back. "If you have help now, why don't you come to New York for the weekend?"

"I can't, Mark. Robin is only here for a little while each day. Besides, I can't leave him now. He's failing fast."

"Okay."

"Mark, it's a little like being with the AIDS babies—there is only a short time to make him happy and comfortable. And that is the only thing I can do right now. Don't ask me to forfeit even a day of it. It would ultimately be a day I would regret."

"You'd regret being with me?"

"Not being with you, but being away from him. Certainly you can understand that?" I was standing now, and the always dormant anger that Mark seemed so capable of provoking in me lately began to awaken.

"Of course I do," he answered, with only a fraction of hesitation. "I'll be home in another week. I'll come by."

"I need you, Mark. I could use your support."

"And I could use yours."

. . .

It was no good, the dream state I had worked in was shattered, so I covered up my canvas and banked the fire. Robin had left and Dad was quiet in a morphine daze. I thumped around the kitchen for a while, sorting out misplaced dishes from Robin's efforts. My mind traveled over the past week, rambling between the effect Robin's presence had had on us already and my conversation with Mark. I wondered, too, why Lee hadn't returned my call and a sudden rise of concern made me drop the dish towel and head for the phone.

Once again Mrs. Greaves answered, but this time Lee was there.

"Lee, are you okay?"

"Yes, why?"

"Your migraine. I hadn't heard back from you, so I got worried."

"How did you know . . ." He paused. "Ah, I think I understand."

"You never got my message, did you?"

"Nope."

"She's very protective of you."

"I know." I could tell by his voice that Mrs. Greaves had not left the room. I assumed Lee was using the phone in the kitchen. "Is your dad all right?"

I told him about Robin and the morphine pump and how quickly, even in a week's time, he had begun to fail. "He can't get out of bed now and Visiting Nurses come in twice a day. Otherwise I tend to him, and I've begun to wish that I'd taken up nursing as my Aunt Mildred always advocated when I mentioned art school. It would have served me well now."

"You're doing just fine. I watched you with him, and I know it isn't easy, being parent to a parent, but you're doing it. Do you want me to come down?"

"Lee, I can't keep asking you to break your schedule. Of course I want you here, but it isn't fair of me to ask it of you."

"Ask me."

"Come."

As winter fought its way toward spring, Lee came three more times. Each time was a godsend, a tiny respite from the routine. Robin had offered to do night duty, but until the very end I didn't want her to put so much of her own time into what really was my duty. Duty is such an intolerant word; I didn't want to shirk my responsibilities, and especially didn't want Robin to disrupt her own life. She had two young daughters to think of. Although, in the end, she did begin spending nights when her mother could take the girls.

When Lee came my father always rallied. Drawing on some strength he kept in reserve, Dad would keep talking for hours with Lee; no subject was excluded except illness. The two of them would wander over current events and sports. So fixed in the extremes of my daily concerns I had let the world slip away, promising to chase after it someday. Then, when Dad would doze off, Lee would make me tell him what I really needed to say. He offered me the comfort of an ear and gentle consolation.

No longer allowing him to slip away while I slept, I rose early on his departure mornings and we breakfasted together, most times discussing the night my father had passed, sometimes seeking neutral topics. Each morning he was a little ahead of me. I would waken to the light buzzing of his razor and then the scent of coffee brewing. I'd come down and often he would be in my studio, enticing embers into a blaze and lifting the sheet on my unfinished piece.

"You didn't do much on it since Tuesday—was it a bad week?"

"No, actually I stood in front of it for hours, playing with it. Sometimes that's almost as much work as using paint."

"Hmm." He nodded over his mug. "Like sitting in front of the screen and playing with one sentence."

"Precisely."

The gray of dawn was just brightening when I walked him out to the station wagon. Our feet made disparate prints in the new snowfall. "See you Tuesday," he promised, ducking quickly into the car.

"Thank you." I rested my hand on his shoulder through the car window.

"For what?"

"Being here." I patted his shoulder. "Drive carefully; they don't always sand right away."

"I will." He started the car with an almost imperceptible shaking off of my hand. "Alix, don't hesitate to call me if anything happens. I can be here in two hours."

A lurch in my belly reminded me of why he was here, the need for his presence was my father's dying. There were, unbelievably, moments when I forgot, when his being here was unfettered by a reason for it. I walked back to the house in Lee's footsteps, marveling that my own fit inside of his.

"DO YOU WANT TO ADMIT HIM?" ROBIN HELD MY HAND as she asked the question.

"No. No, we said we'd stick it out and we will."

Dad lay on the hospital bed, his clouded eyes lighting on me now and again, then drifting away to gaze blankly at the ceiling or the wall. I wiped a bit of saliva from the corner of his mouth.

Robin took the Kleenex from me and threw it away, then turned back to me to fold me in her arms. "Good. I'll stick it out with you. We just need to get Dr. Mulcahey to do house calls."

We laughed, Mulcahey being our least favorite physician on the short list of doctors who had been involved in Dad's case.

In the last three weeks the cancer had moved like an enemy army, stealing away strength and appetite and interest. The television sat silent, its blank gray eye sentinel over the quiet room. Instead I filled the room with music, George Winston's *December* being Dad's favorite, calming him when he became agitated. Never again could I listen to that tape without feeling the emotions that daily trickled through me.

The Visiting Nurses came more frequently. In my more whimsical moments, I thought of them as Crimean War nurses, Florence Nightingales ministering to the terminally wounded. Though neither wore uniforms, their aura was so professionally powerful that the image was undeniable. Strong, efficient, caring without condescension. Tag-team nurses, they swapped shifts and soon Dad and I were never alone.

. . .

"Come on, Alix, you've got to do this for me," Robin chided when I declined her invitation to go out for dinner.

"Robin, you know . . ."

"Alix, it's my thirty-fifth birthday and I'm depressed as hell. You've got to help me get through it."

"Hey, I lived through that one, it's not so bad."

"The heck it isn't. Now I'm no longer in my early thirties! Now I'm Old Widow Gates."

"You're as young as you feel."

"Bunk!"

While all around me the friends of my youth met and married their husbands, had their children, and drew a jagged chasm between our lives, I had continued to live the life of the independent woman, searching always for artistic success and looking down my nose at the trifles of domestic life. Diapers and temperatures and teething became the topics of the conversations my friends had, and if two of them came together, I might as well have dropped in from a foreign country for all the comprehension I had of their concerns. The snappy, irreverent, political, and aesthetic conversations of old were gone and in their place loomed domestic concerns. Flashes of old interests sometimes showed, little blazes of heat lightning, telling me that all this was temporary for them, that someday they would return and engage the outside world again.

Robin was a nice contrast to my other domesticated friends. Her two daughters were past the stages of infancy and early childhood and Robin was independent enough not to need to speak of them in terms of defining her own life.

· · ·

"To age and all its privileges." I raised my glass of Chianti.

"Like what?"

"Like not being carded." I struggled to find another privilege.

"I bet you're still carded some places."

"That's not exactly true." But I was pleased with the compliment. "And you certainly don't look a day over twenty-eight."

We continued on in that vein for a long time, our association being so one-dimensional we had a hard time seeking out other topics. We only knew each other through this episode in my life. "Episode," that's what Robin called it. It was like television. Tune in next week and see if Alix Miller's dad has died and she's gotten on with her life.

But after a glass and a half of Chianti we began to mellow into that freestyle familiarity between women.

"So what's with you and Mark? Your dad seems to think your not marrying Mark has something to do with him."

"Oh God, no. First of all, even if he asked me, I'm not sure I would do it, and I certainly haven't remained an old maid because of Dad." Yet when I spoke those words I wondered at the tinny sound my lack of conviction gave them. Is that what I really wanted, for Mark to ask me to marry him?

"Why call yourself an old maid? Aren't we past that yet? It's the nineties, after all."

"Right. Well, you know how it is. If you haven't been married or divorced by thirty-five, you're either gay or ugly."

"And?"

"Neither. Just not ready to do the domestic bit."

"Artistic temperament?"

"Maybe. Artists are sublimely selfish people. We need privacy and space. I can't imagine myself putting away my paints to go fix dinner or run to a PTA meeting."

"Maybe you just haven't met the right man."

"You have pizza on your chin."

I took a bite of my own, less because I wanted it than I needed to think about what she said.

"So tell me about Lee."

The moment she said his name I realized I'd been thinking about him.

Robin lifted a gooey piece of pizza, catching the string of mozzarella on her tongue and reeling it in.

"You know about him," I hedged.

"Not really. You're very quiet about him. I know more about Mr. Mark than I do this mysterious night visitor."

I pushed the melted cheese back onto my slice of pizza, remembering then that night in Riseborough and our impromptu pizza party in front of the fire. I looked up to meet Robin's brown eyes. "I think he may be my best friend."

"Funny thing to say about a guy."

"He's very special. He's, well, different."

"Nice different?"

I smiled. "Physically different."

Robin's dark eyebrows shot up under her bangs. "How? Is he gay?"

"He has acromegaly. Do you know what that is?"

"Gigantism? Abnormal growth, right?" She bit into a second slice.

"Right."

"So he's not handsome."

I choked on my wine, sending myself into a coughing fit. Control regained, I answered, "No. Rather like a drunk Thomas Hart Benton had drawn him. But he's not horrible," I found myself going on. "He's so wonderful that it's easy to forget he's not easy to look at. I mean, it would be logical that his soul would be as ugly as his face, but it's not. It's like he's trapped in this monstrous body."

"Like the Beast in the story."

I set down my slice of pizza and wiped my hands, surprised at a moistness in my eyes, which was not forced there by my choking. "Yes. Exactly. And like the Beast, he lives reclusively, afraid of other people."

"But not you."

"No. Not me."

"You must be Beauty."

I CAME TO DREAD FOUR O'CLOCK IN THE MORNING. THE Nightingales said it was the hour of death. I don't think they, or whichever one of them it was, meant to upset me, rather that I should begin to expect the end soon. I'd wake, listen, and wait. Straining, I would listen for Dad's stertorous breathing and relax again to fall asleep. If I didn't hear anything, I would creep down the stairs like a child and come to stand beside his bed. I'd watch his labored breaths, my own breaths urging his on.

It was late March and the date of my show had long gone by. I noted its passing with regret, and a little bout of self-pity. Robin caught me arranging what would have been my five exhibition pieces. "Nice stuff."

"Thanks." I flushed a little, taken aback by her praise. "Someday I'll bore you with my portfolio."

"I wish I could do something like this, something meaningful."

"Oh Robin, how can you say something like that? What you do takes more nerve and talent than my meager work here. What you do is so sublimely meaningful. And so lacking in the self-absorption that drives my kind of work."

"Giving the world a great painting can never be selfish," she protested, but I don't think she understood what I meant.

I wanted to explain to her, but at that moment Mark walked into the studio.

I hadn't seen him in a few weeks, not since before he'd gone to New York to do the article on the AIDS babies. As usual, he looked good and I could see a slight rise in Robin's eyebrows. I hastily made introductions and Robin left us alone in the cold studio.

.   .   .

"Will you go in to see Dad?" I asked Mark after a little while.

He looked up from cleaning his camera lens and didn't answer. I could see the reluctance in his hooded eyes. Finally he capped the lens and sighed. "Yeah, I will. Maybe later."

"He'll be happy to see you."

"He barely knows me."

"Mark, I don't believe you!" I heard shrillness in my voice and I stopped. "Look, it's no big deal. Do it or don't. Don't agonize."

"I said later. I mean it." He stood up and came over to where I was leaning against the chopping block. He put his arms around me and slowly rocked me in time with the soft music filtering into the kitchen from the living room. Slowly he lowered his face to mine and kissed me. Meeting the resistance of my hard mouth, he said, "Don't set up walls, Alix."

"I'm not. This is my reality right now, and you need to be involved in it if you care about me."

"I care." Again his mouth covered mine and this time I gave in. "Let's take a little break, you need some diversion and Robin's here. No excuses, get your keys and let's go for a ride."

I would have declined, I would have fought to stay put, but I knew that he was right, a break would do me good. "All right, but just for an hour."

My apartment is less than a mile from Dad's house, so we decided to walk. The fresh March air was still chill from winter's relentless possession; our breath came out in filmy puffs, and I remembered as a child pretending to smoke, my parallel fingers mimicking my mother's cigarette fingers. By the time we got to my place we were chilled by the cold and hot for each other. It had been a long time since the hotel in Boston and my desire had long been beaten back by the siege engines of grief and exhaustion. Heedless of the stagnant cold air of the closed-up apartment, we flung ourselves together like yin and yang.

For a moment all the tension and stress melted out of me and I floated above it all, empty of all emotion, hovering in that touch-made illusion of peace.

. . .

We cuddled together under the body-warmed blankets and soaked in the last rays of afterglow. Finally Mark shifted and sat up, pulling me against his chest. "Alix, I was right."

"About what?"

"They offered me a job, staff photographer."

"The *Times*?" I pulled away from him, but he held me back against him.

"None other. The thing is, Alix, it means living there." His hand stroked my bare arm. "I'll be traveling all over the world, but I'll be based in New York."

This was the point where he was supposed to say, "And I want you to come with me," and the point where I was supposed to say yes. Forget that I hate New York and forget that I wasn't at all sure I loved Mark enough to make that sacrifice. I was at that stage of womanhood where settling down was seriously overdue.

I wanted to scream, "But what about us?" Except that a small, undefined as yet, part of me was wild with the relief that the spectre of permanency in our relationship had now withdrawn. Equally I wondered at his callousness. Had he really seen our relationship as so casual, so insignificant, that I was very nearly the last to know about his move, or had I moved so far away from him in my own recent troubles that I hadn't heard him? As always, nothing was simple where Mark was concerned.

I hugged him and managed to rise above the thousand conflicting emotions fighting for eminence. "I'm happy for you, Mark. It's what you've been working so hard to do."

"I start right away." He shifted a little. "The thing is, Alix, I'm leaving today."

"You've already got a place to live?" I was drowning in a mixture of relief and abandonment.

"I'm sharing with a couple of guys until I find my own place. We're all on the road, so it should work out. No one will be around enough to get on each other's nerves."

"So this is really a good-bye," I said finally, unable to look him in the face for fear he'd be constrained to say something he didn't feel.

"No, no, of course not. I know that once"—he caught himself a little—"once you can, you'll come to see me, and I'll be back as often as I can."

"I'm going to take a shower." I slipped away from his touch and into the icy bathroom.

Running the water as hot as I could stand it, I stood under the stream and shook. The water began to cool as the tank ran out and I slammed the faucet off. Steam filled the tiny bathroom and I cleared a porthole of mirror with the end of my towel. There was my face, pale, darkened only by the circles under my eyes. My hair tumbled down from the towel, and in the harsh fluorescent light I saw a possible streak of silver in the light brown. Not much longer, I promised myself, and realized for the first time the relief I would have when it was all over. I wanted it to be over. I wanted to get on with my life.

Bundling on my flannel robe, I rewrapped my hair and came out into the living room, where Mark lounged, my sketchbook in his lap.

"I'll go make coffee."

I had just put the fire under the kettle when I heard laughter and Mark sidled into the kitchen, my sketchbook in his hands. "Alix, I can't believe you let me be jealous of this!" Hooting with laughter, he handed me the book, its thick pages turned to a sketch of Lee. Underneath I had written, "Lee and Bad-dog in the Library." It was one of the better sketches of Lee, in the sense that it looked like him, a study intended to develop what would go into the portrait. Of course, it was a picture of an ugly man.

"God, to think I was worried."

It was only simple ignorance, but his attitude appalled me. "You bastard," I said, shutting off the burner.

"Hey, Alix, don't get mad. You weren't playing fair with me making me think this guy was a rival." He was still laughing but the raw anger on my face penetrated. "Alix, I'm sorry. I know I was just stupid."

"At one time you might have been stupid to think Lee Crompton was a rival, but certainly not because of what he looks like."

"Alix, take it easy, I was kidding. I'm sure he's a great guy. You just should have told me."

I was beyond anger now. This man was about to leave me behind, and yet had the ego to speak to me of rivals for his attention.

We walked back to my father's in silence. The air had gotten drier and our breath no longer preceded us.

I WOKE ABRUPTLY, FULLY AWAKE AND ALERT. HAD I heard my name or had I dreamt it? Four o'clock. Already the spring dawn was weakening the absolute dark of the night. The cold in the unheated room was winter-deep, and I pulled on a heavy sweater as I went downstairs. As I reached the fifth step, warmth touched me and I could hear the faithful old furnace roaring in the basement. I tugged my hair out from under the sweater and stole toward the lamplight of the living room.

In the past few days he had begun the descent into death. Most of my time had been spent simply sitting next to him; he was rarely awake, as the expenditure of energy he needed to live exhausted him. An IV against the inevitable dehydration, and a catheter discreetly leading out from under the bedsheet to a bottle on the floor were the lines that held him to this world. The Nightingales came twice a day to bathe him and rub soft lotion into his papery skin against the threat of bedsores. He'd become so delicate that even a wrinkle in the sheet could destroy his skin. Even if we were helpless against what was destroying him internally, we could keep his external body comfortable.

Robin sat forward in her chair, leaning over my father but not touching him. She heard my steps and turned with a smile. "Come to him, Alix. It's time." She stood up and embraced me, then left the room. I heard the front door close gently and the start of her engine.

I knelt beside my father's bed. I could hear Dad's breath, raspy in the stillness. The death rattle. In the mild lamplight, his face was gray and whiskery, no longer the face I knew, but the face of a stranger lingering on a foreign shore. The oxygen tubes glistened in the light, yet he labored for breath in the body's own instinctive struggle.

"Don't fight it, Dad. It's okay to go. I love you." I stroked his forehead with one hand, the other clutched his hand. "I love you, Dad."

My father struggled against letting go. The raspy moist breathing increased, irregular, painful to hear. He made sounds, but no words.

I remembered then Robin's talk of helping her dying husband over the bridge to death. I let go of Dad's hands and held my own up to be taken. "Take my hand, Dad. Let me take you there, let me take you halfway. We'll go to the bridge together. When we get there, when we get to the middle, I'll turn around and come back. But you must go on ahead. Mom's there. She'll be on the other side. Come with me, Dad, it's time to go."

Beneath the closed eyelids I could see movement, as if he were watching something.

"It's not a long walk, Dad. There's no pain on the other side. Let me take you."

A flower blooming against all odds, Dad's hand rose from the blanket. The tremor suddenly gone, he placed it in my hand and his fingers closed over mine.

My face wet with unvoiced tears, I laid my cheek against his chest and waited.

EARLY ON DAD AND I HAD PLANNED HIS FUNERAL. "NO use denying it needs to be done"—he'd been a little sharp with me—"and I'd like to have some say. Now, no primitive rituals. No calling hours, no open casket, none of that stuff."

"How about a New Orleans jazz band?" I scruffed a charcoal shading onto the sketch I was making of him.

"That's good. I kind of like that idea. They really know how to send a person off!"

.   .   .

We'd gone with a simple Service of Commitment at graveside. So many of his friends and scattered relatives had responded to our request to come visit him while he was able that we did not feel the need to go further with the ceremonial aspect of his death. They had seen him to say good-bye while it counted. Thus only a handful of us stood out on that mud-rich March afternoon, the air full of imagined spring. The Hospice people, our faithful VNA nurses, one or two friends who were closer than most, and dear Robin made up the majority of the group. Mark had called with his condolences, but had not offered to come.

"Do you want me to come?" Lee had asked, and I knew it was something he would do if I said yes.

"Lee, you don't need to come, I have plenty of support

here now. But I would like to come up and finish the portrait as soon as possible. I need to get away from here."

I smiled at the sudden relief in his voice. "By all means, come as soon as you can. Everything is waiting for you. Just come."

"Okay. I have one or two things to take care of here and I'll be there."

"Alix?"

"I'm here," I said.

"Are you really okay?"

His sweet concern sent a trilling of emotion through me. "Lee, what would I have ever done without you?"

· · ·

It was harder than I had thought it would be. The brief service seemed so abrupt after the prolonged waiting for death. The brown casket perched on the metal bars seemed so sad, impossible that it contained the shell of the man who had been my father. For a moment I regretted not having the archaic open-casket ritual, the primitive need to see the deceased one last time. I shook off the regret, the man who had died with my hand holding his bore no resemblance to the man who had shown me how to put life in the eyes of a painting with a simple stroke. No, eventually I would remember him as he had been, not as he died. Not too tall, a little portly in his middle years. I would remember his laughter, not the emaciated wraith he'd been at the end.

As I lay my bouquet of roses on top of the casket at the end of the service I saw Robin. I smiled at her and was suddenly struck by the fact that she too was soon to be out of my life. I couldn't bear that, and the first tears of the day stung my eyes.

"Stop that right now." Robin handed me a wad of Kleenex. "I'm fixed tight in your life, my friend. You know that the friends of adversity are friends forever. Besides, I want you to be my witness when John and I get married next year." And in that fashion, Robin announced her engagement to the man she'd mentioned with increasing frequency over cups of coffee. A moment later John Betters joined us and offered his condolences in a soft and sincere voice.

Afterward a few people came back to the house. By the time the sandwiches were all gone, the false spring afternoon had given way to snow clouds. The last to go, Robin and John stopped me in the hallway. "We're going out for Chinese. . . ."

"No, you two go on ahead, I think I'll just open a can of soup. I really don't feel like going out," I said, convincing them easily. I hated the idea of being alone, but their apparent need for time together was obvious to me and I smiled as they dashed down the porch steps, promises of an eggroll called back at me. As they drove off, the first flakes of the late season snow began.

The heavy front door closed me in, and I was alone. I puttered about, lining up the many cards that had arrived, sticking my fingers into the arrangements that people had sent in lieu of making a donation to the American Cancer Society. I stood for a moment in the doorway of the living room but did not go in.

I ran a broom down the gritty front hall and shook out the tatty little rug. I stood there on the front porch with the brown and green rug in my hand and snapped it again and again, the bits of sand flinging back and stinging my face. Suddenly the old fabric tore in my hands and I viciously wrenched it in two, flinging the halves out into the yard. Heedless of the cold, I watched in fascination as the falling snow covered the two pieces of rug, burying them.

. . .

In fifteen minutes I was in my car and on the highway.

It had stopped snowing by the time I reached Waterville and the road was clear, so I sped up. My mind was utterly numb, the past three months had succeeded in preventing me from feeling anything right now. I fiddled with the radio and finally shut it off, jamming in a tape and forgetting to switch the mode button. Thus I drove on in silence, occasional tears running into the corners of my mouth, which I wiped away as if they were someone else's.

It was past ten o'clock when I took the exit to Riseborough. It had begun to snow again, the storm following me north. Depending on vague memory to find Lee's turnoff, I ended up in Riseborough proper and struggled to remember how to get there from the green. The convoluted country roads and the total absence of street signs confused me utterly and I had to backtrack to the green. The only lights still on that Wednesday night were those in the pizza place. I parked in front and dashed in, slipping a little on the snowy pavement.

"Do you have a pay phone?"

"There's one at the corner." The man behind the counter was the same as that other night, but this time the place was deserted and he was alone. "Don't go out, use mine." He lifted a black rotary dial phone onto the counter. "Local call, right?"

"Thank you, yes." I struggled to get my trembling fingers into the holes of the dial.

Mrs. Greaves answered with a slightly alarmed tone and I realized that she had probably been asleep. "Mrs. Greaves, it's Alix Miller. I'm so sorry to wake you, but I'm in Riseborough and I'm lost!" I saw the guy behind the counter smirk a little.

Before she could say anything, Lee's voice came on the extension. "Alix, are you all right? Where are you?"

"Tony's Pizza." I smiled at the guy. "I'm sorry, Lee. I took you at your word and just ran off."

"I'll be right there," Lee said, brooking no suggestion that he simply give me directions. I laid the receiver back in its cradle and Tony, as I thought of him, put it back under the counter and then placed a slice of pizza in front of me.

"You can't loiter here." He went back to reading his magazine and I studied the melted cheese atop the slice.

Twenty minutes later I saw the headlights of a car and I went to the glass-front door to see Lee's station wagon pull up beside my Sentra. I burst from the restaurant to the car with more apologies, quickly stifled.

"Leave your car here. We'll come get it tomorrow."

I unlocked the trunk of my car so that Lee could lift my hastily packed bag. The bag from the museum store, long forgotten in the trunk of the car, poked out from under the spare tire where it had lodged. I reached in and hauled it out.

"Hop in." He shut the door for me, and got in.

"I'm sorry to do this to you," I began again. "I probably dragged you out of bed. . . ."

"I did say 'just come.'" Lee laughed, and the sound shattered the embarrassment that had enclosed me.

The snow burst around the wagon in sudden obscuring squalls. Lee drove on, concentrating now on the road. As we eased out onto the winding road that led to Lee's gate, a deer leapt out in front of the car. Momentarily dazzled by the car's high beams, it froze. Lee touched the brake and we slid a little, fishtailing on the empty road. Lee's arm was flung across my chest in an instinctive protective thrust. The deer broke and ran.

A few minutes later we were home, shaking the snow off our boots and creeping through the darkened kitchen. In the library Lee poured us both a little sherry. We sat facing each other in front of the cold fireplace. I sipped the sweet liquor and felt its loosening attributes relax me.

"Was it so very awful, Alix?"

"The service?"

"Yes, the service, that and it all being over. You've been absolutely focused for three months, and suddenly it was finished. Like a competition when you prepare for months for a minute's shot at glory. I suspect that's what made you run away."

"There I was, all alone. All the visitors gone, the flowers already beginning to wilt, and that goddamn hospital bed still in the middle of the living room. What was it doing there? Why were the oxygen tanks and piles of johnnies still there?" My voice began to pitch higher and I was almost sick to my stomach. "I didn't understand. Dad was dead, and everything was still there. Robin is introducing her fiancé and everyone was pretending it was all back to normal. Even me. We all were acting as if he'd just gone out for a walk."

Lee hitched to the front of his chair and leaned his elbows on his knees.

"It was so fucking quiet. Then I tore the rug by accident. I hated that rug, the little one by the front door. The one Dad bought Mom and she hated it too but never told him."

All the built-up tension and anger and grief overtook me then and I shook as if with palsy, but the tears would not come to relieve the pain.

Lee stretched out his hands. "What can I do? What can I do to make it better?"

"Just hold me."

We faced each other. I met his kind blue eyes and read the reluctance in them. I knew what I was asking. I knew it was so very difficult for him. Except on that day when he'd held me in his arms as we skated over the ice, Lee had never touched me, had shied away from being touched.

"I need to be held, I need you to hold me."

"Alix, I . . ." His mobile and ugly face contorted with a private anguish.

"Please."

He stood and opened his arms. I went into their safe harbor and welcomed the weight of his arms around me, tenderly holding me close in acknowledgment of my fragility. His wool sweater scratched my cheek, then absorbed the flood of tears, which, at his touch, were released like poison from a wound. His cheek rubbed against my hair and he murmured to me as if to a child. Slowly his arms strengthened, closer and closer he held me, and my own arms went around him until we held each other.

As naturally as weeping, I raised my lips to his, and for one instant they were gently met. At once he let go of me.

EARLY MORNING SUN WARMED THE SOLARIUM. MY EASEL
and paints were exactly as I had left them back in January,
thinking then that I was only going away for the weekend.
A sheet covered the portrait, and now, alone in the room,
I flipped it back and scowled. It was all wrong. I had
painted the still faceless form of a man, yet even the posture was not Lee at all but some contrived image. Anyone
who knew him would never think a good thing of this
painting. I stirred up a jar of gesso and began painting the
whole thing out. Big fat strokes of white obliterated the
stranger I had painted.

Lee came in, coffee tray in hand. I had the eerie feeling
that no time had elapsed, that I had never gone away. I
had expected some tension between us, the awkwardness
of last night's scene playing itself out in my head overnight, but if he felt awkward, Lee gave no hint of it. When
I looked at him, pouring out the mugs of coffee and measuring out my half-teaspoon of sugar, a curious feeling of
relief flooded me, as if I'd come home from a long unhappy
journey. Whatever else, we were still friends.

"I'm starting all over." I took the mug from him and
pointed to the white canvas. "It wasn't any good."

"Really?"

"I once told you that I needed to know my subjects

before I could paint them. Well, I know you now. What I paint this time will really be you."

"Frightening thought," he jibed, as he went to the stool and sat down.

I shook my head. "No, no more posed pictures."

"How else can you paint a portrait?"

"Just get comfortable and talk with me. I'll handle the details."

"I know what I've missed about you."

"What?"

"Your reticence."

I heaved a wadded paper towel at his head.

·   ·   ·

The morning sessions went too quickly. I knew what I wanted to do, and the paint went on easily, my hand moving instinctively to stroke the colors into place. I deliberately began to slow down, afraid that once done, the planned-for future, the "after it's over" time of new life would have to be invented. My life could not stay the same, yet I did not see the road I wanted on my life map.

"You're looking pensive." Lee came in, lighting the lamp next to me, as it had grown dark.

"Do I?"

"What's the matter?"

I shrugged. "I don't know. Maybe I've just had too much to think about, too many upheavals. I'm feeling a little at a crossroads, and I don't know what to do next. I should decide what to do about my father's house and whether or not to stay where I am. I need to find a job. But I haven't got the strength to face any of these problems."

"So give it time. Maybe in a month you'll know what you want to do." He stood up and rested his hand on the back of my neck. I leaned a little against it. "There's no hurry, Alix. No need to make any choices right now." He dropped his hand and moved to the stereo.

"The other thing is that I know I haven't come to terms with Mark's going to New York. I'm still feeling like a decision was made for me that I had no voice in. On the other hand, I wouldn't have wanted to make that choice out of some misguided fear of being alone." I thought of our last time together. "Truthfully, Mark wasn't always all that wonderful to be around, he can be very ugly."

"Like me?"

I wouldn't let him get away with it. "No, Lee. Not like you." I took the CD from his hand. "You are the most beautiful person I know. Beautiful where it counts"—I pressed one hand over his heart—"right here."

He turned away as always, but not before I felt a crack in the wall around my heart. Just out of sight, I knew my path was near.

.   .   .

I hung up Bad-dog's leash in the mudroom and kicked off my boots.

"Alix?"

"Right here!" I called to Lee.

"Look what I found." He met me in the hallway and we went into the solarium. He handed me two photos.

"Are these your parents?" The photos were of portraits, one of a middle-aged man and the other of an exquisite woman, shown full-length, her sable coat draped dramatically around her.

"Yes, these are the paintings your grandfather did. I was a little boy then, but I remember him. Don't look for any family resemblance, it's long gone."

"Your mother is beautiful." The portrait showed a fine-boned woman, a woman whose beauty had deepened with the passage of time. Probably forty in the painting, she held her head with a tilt to her chin that implied a certain satisfaction with life. A slight smile teased on her lips and I was pleased with my grandfather's work. "Is it like her?"

"Very."

"Mrs. Greaves tells me you don't see her much."

"Ever." He noted my silent curiosity. "We speak on the phone once a week. She just has never been able to come to terms with me."

"Your own mother?"

"Not very maternal, is it?"

"I can't imagine it. She's lost something very valuable."

He shrugged. "My Boston Brahmin mother had one child, probably against her wishes, one who turned out somewhat rebellious, and, in the end, quite unpresentable."

"Surely she loves you?"

He stood contemplating the photo, then said, "In her own selfish way, perhaps."

I touched his shoulder, a comradely touch, and for once he didn't shrug me off.

"So how's our portrait coming?" His abrupt change of conversation startled me out of my thoughts.

"Take a look and see for yourself."

"Someday."

"Someday it will be green with mold in some damp cellar."

"No, I intend to send it to my mother as a gift."

"I thought you were going to store it for some future discovery."

"I'll let my mother do that."

I was shaken a little by his words. I didn't know what to say, so said the obvious. "It's nearly done."

He set the two photos down on the work table near my paint box. Slowly he raised his face and smiled at me. "Go slow, okay?"

"I am."

THE ALMOST SPRINGLIKE AIR OF THE DAY BEFORE CHILLED
dramatically and we were plunged back into winter as a
second March snowstorm blew in from Canada. It seemed
to me as though Riseborough was always in the grips of
winter, and I couldn't begin to imagine the stark oaks on
the town green in full leaf.

Bad-dog whined and paced and finally we shrugged ourselves into our coats and took him out. The big mutt
cavorted around the fresh snow, burying his brown nose
in it and tossing it into the air. Lee tossed snowballs for
him, and we laughed as the puzzled dog looked all around
for the disappearing balls. The storm had subsided by late
afternoon, reduced to fat moist flakes that would not survive the next intimation of spring. A palette of grays
moved swiftly overhead; charcoal gray and seal gray
clouds blew along, the arctic wind freezing them into
shape and sending them to the sea. Above them the pale
gray sky and below a few white wisps clung to the moun-
taintops. I pulled a pencil and small notebook out of my
parka pocket. We paused for a little while at Wiggy's Pond
so that I could sketch.

Announced by the crunch of their footsteps breaking
through the snow-covered grass, two young boys burst
through the tree line, a toboggan skimming along be-

hind them. Reflexively, Lee turned his face away, pulling his hood close. They quickly passed us and disappeared into the woods. Bad-dog trotted off behind them.

"Hey, Bad-dog, come back!" I called.

Lee shook his head, the hood slipping off. "Forget it, he's an incorrigible boy-follower. He'll come home when they do."

My fingers were frozen and I stuffed the pencil and notebook back into my kangaroo pocket. Lee's hand suddenly dipped into my pocket, pulling out the book. He held it up in the fading sunlight, and nodding, said, "Nice, very nice. You've got a light touch with landscape. Will you paint me another one someday?"

My mittenless fingers touched his as I took back the book. I could feel a warmth in my cheeks; the sweet sense of pleasure in his approbation was almost overshadowed by that of his easy familiarity in taking the book from my pocket.

There was a filmy barrier between us. Every day that passed and I painted his portrait and spent hours with him I felt this film bulge with pressure. Someday, I knew, this film, this barrier, would be penetrated and there would be a perfect understanding between us.

· · ·

"That damn dog," Lee muttered as he shut the mudroom door against the frigid air. "I've never known him to not come home."

"Maybe the boys thought he was a stray and took him home."

Lee shook his head. "He's got a license and a name tag, no excuse."

115

"Lee, maybe they took off his collar. You know little boys. 'Hey Mom, look what followed me home.'"

Lee smiled his crooked grin and tugged at my loose braid. "Right." I loved the feel of his hand on my hair.

It was a Thursday, and we helped ourselves to leftover stew as we balanced on the bar stools against the island counter. The tall kitchen windows looked out over the back garden, and as we ate it began to snow again, the hard little flakes sparkling in the floodlights. Just as we finished loading the dishwasher Mrs. Greaves came in.

"Town's all a flutter tonight, Mr. Lee," she said as she shook the snow from her kerchief. "Two young boys've gone missing."

I dropped a fork and it hit the floor with a bounce.

Lee bent to pick it up. "For how long?"

Mrs. Greaves shrugged. "They aren't sure. The kids had a half-day of school today, teacher workshop days or something. You ask me, they're out all too often."

"Mrs. Greaves, how long do they think the boys have been gone?"

"Could be from noon onward. They've got the search teams all forming down on the green right now."

"Mrs. Greaves, we saw two boys this afternoon, near Wiggy's." I shut the dishwasher and looked at Lee. "Who are the boys?"

"Tommy Lewis and Travis something. About twelve years old."

"Travis Michalik. His father is my attorney." Lee turned to me. "Alix, what about the boys you saw today?"

"About twelve would be my guess."

"What were they wearing?"

I thought back—one had waved at me, the one who'd worn blue. "A dark blue jacket and the other one, a brownish down vest and an oatmeal-colored sweater underneath. I could see snow pants on both of them, not jeans."

"Hats?"

"I suppose. Don't all little boys wear hats?" I was a little puzzled at this intense questioning.

"Boots?"

"Yes, and gloves."

"Good, if they're lost, maybe they're fairly well protected."

"They were pulling a toboggan."

"Ah"—Lee rubbed his chin—"dressed for sledding. Probably headed for one of the clearings."

Then I recognized it—it was Harris Bellefleur working. Lee reached for the phone.

"The police pretty much figured out the same thing we have," Lee said, hanging up. "But knowing they were near Wiggy's might help narrow the field down. They've got about fifty searchers."

"Will they let us know if they find them?"

"I hope so." Lee stared out into the floodlit backyard. "I should have looked at them, Alix. Maybe then they would have run home instead of going on. After all, the woods are full of monsters."

"Lee, that's absurd."

"It's happened before."

"And I should have called out to the boys, asked where they were going."

"At least you looked at them, and you've got an artist's eye. The detail on the boys' clothing identified them immediately to the police."

"I'm glad of that."

He stood for a long time leaning against the kitchen window; only the periodic tapping of his fingers against

the molding revealed his inner agitation. The snow dazzled like silver confetti in the floodlights, hard and cold.
The wind swirled it into eddies that skipped along the
brick walkway. Beyond, out of reach of the floodlights, yet
luminous in its bulk, lay the mountainside.

"Every year or so someone dies on that hill." He shifted
his weight, the crookedness of his shoulders becoming
more pronounced.

"Lee, I'm sure they'll be all right. It hasn't been all that
long." Even as I said them, the words seemed ludicrous,
platitudes from bad television.

"Eight hours is a long time, Alix. Exposure is a hell of
way to die."

"What can we do?"

Lee turned away from the window. "I can search through
the trails above here. There are a lot of connecting routes
between here and Wiggy's, and if they were looking for
new toboggan runs, they might have ventured too far and
ended up over this way. If Bad-dog's with them, he'll hear
me a long ways off. I just have to whistle and listen."

"My very first day here I got lost in those woods. By the
grace of God I tumbled out of them and landed, as I recall,
at your feet."

"I remember." He placed one great hand on my shoulder.

I touched his hand and gripped his wrist. "I'm going
with you. No one should go out alone on that mountain."

He didn't argue, only increased the pressure on my
shoulder slightly before pulling away.

· · ·

The needle-like snow beat on us, clinging to eyelashes and
scarves, burning the skin with cold. We carried heavy

flashlights and in his backpack Lee carried a thermos of hot coffee, dry mittens, socks, and a wool blanket. I carried a second wool blanket in my backpack with sandwiches. Mrs. Greaves had packed this winter picnic with disapproval evident in her tight lips. "You'll catch your death and to what end? Let the officials do their job."

"Mrs. Greaves, that's not very neighborly of you," Lee chided gently.

"Police will find them." She jammed the sandwiches into my backpack, nearly taking me off my feet in doing so. "Miss Miller needn't go with you, she should stay here with me."

"Mrs. Greaves, I couldn't sit still. Really, this is what I want to do."

"Uh huh." There was something so skeptical in her eyes that I turned away. It was as if she doubted my intentions.

After we were out for about an hour, I knew that Lee was right, exposure would be a hell of a way to die. I tried not to think of the two boys, huddled together, the snow settling over their cold bodies. And where was Bad-dog? We whistled until our lips grew chapped.

The new snow wasn't deep, but pockets of old snow, preserved beneath the canopy of pines, caught us at the knees, sucking us down and filling our boots. Despite the high-tech L.L. Bean clothing I wore, I was soon cold to the bone. The wind spun the treetops, its cold exhalations stinging our faces, blowing the needle-hard snow into our eyes and mouths. We both wore woolen scarves looped across our lower faces, but the driven snow eagerly worked its way into the folds and against our skin, where it instantly melted into a cold wash.

We worked our way east to west, then back, dog-legging

up the southern face of the mountain. Lee directed our progress with a compass and fluorescent paint. It would not do to lose us, too.

I stumbled, catching my foot against a hidden root. I hit the snow hard with an audible *whoof*. Lee was by me in an instant, lifting me from the snow and brushing it from the front of me. Only his eyes were visible between his hat and the scarf.

"I'm okay, Lee." I let him help me to my feet.

"I think we should stop here."

"What?"

"I mean to rest for a few minutes. It's nearly midnight."

He pulled the scarf down and I remembered then my reaction to him the last time he had pulled me from the snow. But now it was not revulsion that shuddered through me.

"Lee . . ." I wanted to say what I felt, but there was something in his form, hunched over the thermos as he poured out the coffee, that twisted my sentence into something banal. "Thanks for picking me up once again."

"Never too often." He chuckled.

The little warmth I had enjoyed while moving dissipated, and I began shivering.

"Here, take one of the blankets." Lee reached for my discarded backpack.

"No, we'll need it dry when we find the boys."

I could tell by his silence that he had begun to doubt.

"We will find them, won't we?" I sounded like a child struggling to maintain a belief in the tooth fairy.

"I don't know, Alix. But I have to keep trying." The steam from the coffee he held in his hands rose, giving his monstrous face an ethereal and primitive look in the yellow torchlight.

"Do you know these boys well?"

"No. I know Jerry Michalik, the one boy's father. Decent chap. Always speaks of his son when he comes to the house. A hockey player, good student. His best pal is the other boy, Tommy. His parents run the bed-and-breakfast on the main road into Riseborough. They're both in sixth grade. Both honor roll students." Lee sighed then, and downed the last of his coffee.

"How do you know all this?"

"I read. The *Riseborough Sentinel* is a weekly paper devoted to telling neighbors about one another. I know more through that and my three or four loose connections in this town than I bet most people know about their neighbors in any city. And let us never forget the incredible information highway that is Mrs. Greaves."

I laughed, but felt sad. It wasn't the same. Not the same as potluck suppers and attendance at church, not the same kind of intimacy that bonds a person to their town or their neighborhood or even their family. He knew of them, yet he had not let those boys look at him as he'd sat there that afternoon enjoying the same last effort of winter as they were.

"Do you want me to take you home?"

"No!" I recapped the thermos. "I'm in this as long as it takes."

"Okay."

Suddenly I needed a simple hug. Just that kind of human contact that would confirm our resolve. I hesitated, though, a fraction too long and he shrugged on his backpack and consulted the compass. "This way," he directed, and I followed.

· · ·

Mercifully the wind died down just after midnight. The still air was bitter cold, but suddenly we could hear the echo of our calls, and in the stillness our footsteps crunched in the hard old snow, underscoring the silence between our shouts. We climbed higher and higher into the wooded mountainside, the undergrowth thickening and the rocks beginning to jut out. The moon edged its way from behind the broken clouds and silvered our path.

"Lee, I can't believe that they could have come this far. It would have been dark two hours after we saw them, and they would have been lost long before they got this high."

"Maybe. But there's a clearing near the summit; if they made straight for that they might have actually gotten there in time to do some tobogganing. I think they might have gotten lost coming back down." Lee put his hands around his mouth and called, "Travis! Tommy!"

Our ears strained to hear the sound of young voices calling, or a dog barking. Nothing.

"After this pass we'll head west only. If I'm correct in assuming they did get to the summit, they'll have come back down initially on that side." He sounded breathless, his voice, raw from shouting, was gravelly.

"Lee, don't you think you'd better stop for a few minutes?" He was pushing himself, I knew it. Our sedate walks had often tired him, his awkward shape forcing him to work harder than another man might.

"No," he answered a little sharply, then stopped. "I'm sorry, I don't mean to be short with you. You've been great all night. I am a little tired, but, Alix, I don't dare stop. It's getting so late that any lost time could mean the difference."

"Lee, maybe they've been found. I don't think you should kill yourself."

"It doesn't matter. We keep at it, I keep at it, at least till dawn."

"Why, Lee?"

"Because . . ." He stopped, some truth captured before it slipped out.

"Lee? Why is it so important you find them?"

He came to a full stop then, the moonlight throwing his long shadow over me, his face reduced to only his eyes looking back at me with a sorrowful fullness. "Alix, once I was a man who had the same desires as any other to have children. Yet I never will, so the children of this little town . . ." He stopped, then went on. "Because I live life vicariously, I feel these boys are mine."

"But you won't even let them see you."

"No, I won't. But I read about their schoolboy victories and their Halloween parties and their acceptances to Harvard or their marriages to out-of-towners. I watch their growing up from my house on the hill and I know them. They don't need to know anything about me. That isn't important."

He turned back to the path and called, his hoarse voice barely carrying. I came up behind him and laid one hand on his arm, then shouted the boys' names as loud as I could. My echo reverberated back into my ears, mocking the timbre of boys' voices.

.   .   .

"Listen!" Lee hissed, bending a little to catch the sound. A crashing sound, undergrowth being buffeted, and suddenly Bad-dog burst through a stand of brush, tail wagging, long ears flapping with some doggy joy at finding his master standing there. Lee pulled off his mitten and thwacked the big dog on his side, then ran his hand down the silky reddish fur. "He's warm, his topcoat. He's been lying down on something—or someone—warm." Lee pulled his mitten back on and began retracing Bad-dog's footprints. The dog had scuffed through the snow, and in the light of the flashlights the parallel lines of his track were easy to follow.

Within minutes we found the toboggan, upended but not broken. We called more frantically. Now our greatest fear was that they had been injured, yet there was no sign of them near the sled.

"Most likely they deserted it when they realized they were lost," I conjectured.

"I don't think so. That's an expensive toboggan. Knowing young boys, they probably wouldn't dare leave it, more afraid of being yelled at than of being lost. I don't think they're far. We need to head downhill, bearing west."

I was slightly mystified. Then I remembered, this was Harris Bellefleur. Smiling to myself, I stepped into his footprints.

.   .   .

"Tommy! Travis!" Our voices wreathed the night with puffs of frozen exhalation. Then, like a miracle—no, more like a wish unexpectedly granted—voices answering ours.

"Here! Over here!" Just above and to the west, their sweet boy voices chimed through the dense undergrowth and we crashed through it, no longer mincing around the difficult thickets. The ancient tangle of puckerbrush and thorny whips of vines seemed to fight back, but Lee plowed on ahead.

There, huddled together beneath barricaded evergreen branches, were the two boys. Bad-dog immediately burrowed back in with them, turning back to face his master, his silly dog eyes delighted with his find.

"Are you okay?" Lee knelt in the snow in front of them, and I saw that he'd pulled his hat low and his woolen scarf tight around his face. Only his eyes showed and then only when the light from my flashlight touched him.

"We're so cold." One boy's voice shook more from emotion, I think, than shivering. They were beyond shivering. In the harsh beam of the flashlight they were blue with cold.

Lee quickly removed his gloves and touched their faces. I did the same and was alarmed by the depth of the cold. It was almost like touching the dead.

"I can't feel anything," the boy with the blue coat said.

Lee unzipped his coat and then began removing the boy's boots. He looked at me and I bent to do the same with the second boy.

"Travis, put your feet here," Lee said, and pulled the boy's feet under his sweater and against his bare skin. He winced with the cold, then laughed. "It's like shoving an icicle down my shirt!"

The boy laughed a little, but the tears of pain still glinted in the flashlight's glare.

In the meantime I had done the same with the second boy, who had to be Tommy. Feet secure against my body, I began rubbing his hands. They were so cold that my own seemed to burn with the touch of them.

"Get the blankets, Alix."

I wrapped the boys in the two woolen blankets and fished out the dry socks.

"Better?"

The boys nodded simultaneously.

"Okay, everyone onto the sled." After hefting first Tommy and then Travis onto the toboggan, Lee carefully tucked the blankets back around them, a shadow play of tucking little children into bed.

He picked up the rope and tugged. We were on a fairly

level piece of ground and the toboggan stuck a little. He shifted it, then pulled again. I knew then that his strength was going. He'd exerted himself far beyond his reserves. I stood beside him and grasped the rope in my own frozen fingers. Together we pulled and the sled broke free.

"How did you know he was Travis?" I whispered as we hauled the toboggan.

"He's wearing a Blue Devils' jacket. Hockey player. Tommy didn't make the team." He leaned closer and whispered, "Not a very good skater."

"You really do know them, don't you?"

"Yes."

I laughed and tried not to think of the pain in my feet.

．　．　．

The first light of dawn grayed the sky as we descended the mountain. Rather than moving westward in the hopes of meeting more of the search party, we simply descended, following our own fluorescent blaze marks. It took forever, as we struggled to follow paths clear enough to pass the toboggan through. The boys fell asleep on the sled, Tommy's head pressed against Travis's back, Travis asleep bolt upright. Their sleeping bodies seemed so much heavier than their awake ones.

I moved like a sleepwalker. One foot in front of the other. The pain between my shoulder blades from the drag of the sled was like a knife between them. We stopped talking, our last reserves of strength needed just to move. I dreamt of my warm bed in the blue room even as I trudged through the heavy wet snow.

Downhill should have been easier, but eventually the weight of the toboggan forced itself against us and we fought to keep it in control. As the dawn clarified our surroundings, I looked at my companion and was alarmed at the grayness of his face. The scarf had slipped away and exhaustion had deepened the cragginess of his features. He seemed hewn from the very rocks we negotiated around.

"Lee, we need to stop for a few minutes."

"Alix, are you all right? I didn't mean to make this a marathon for you."

"Lee, I'm fine. I just think a short rest would do us both good." I looked back at our cargo. "They'll sleep."

He nodded and dropped the rope. He yawned and seemed to notice for the first time that it was nearly full light. "Beautiful, isn't it?"

"You've done a wonderful thing here tonight, Lee."

"So have you." He raised his arms and stretched. "Thank God we found them."

"You found them, Lee. I just came along, Tonto to your Lone Ranger."

He turned then, and for one fleeting instant I thought he was going to put his arm around me, but he only touched my shoulder. "Alix, I couldn't have done it without you. You were my mainstay, and you probably don't even know at what point I would have given up if you weren't here."

I didn't know what to say, so joked, "Well, Kemo sabe, shall we finish this trek and go get some breakfast?"

I could see the house. With full dawn the wind had picked up a little, yet was, it seemed, a little warmer.

"Why don't you go on ahead, Alix. Call the police and let them know we have the boys."

I let go of the rope and plunged down the slope, Baddog gamboling beside me in canine enthusiasm for the latest move in this all-night game. The back door opened even before I reached it. Mrs. Greaves, bundled in her overcoat, darted out, Willie just behind her. "Where is he? Is he all right?"

"Yes, we've got them, Mrs. Greaves, we found them." I was breathless suddenly and felt the tingling of exhaustion in my eyes. "Please, call the police." She stayed where she was, staring past me and toward the path to the trails. I pushed past her and went to the phone. Almost before Lee reached the yard, I heard the wail of the ambulance and the cacophony of emergency sirens. The dawn silence carried their sound to us from miles away. I went back out to help carry in the boys.

"Alix"—Lee was still muffled behind his woolen scarf— "will you talk with the authorities? I can't." He laid Travis at the other end of the couch from where I'd put Tommy. Tucking in a new warm blanket, he turned back to me. "Alix, do this for me."

I reached up impulsively to remove his scarf, but he dodged my hand. "Alix, please."

"All right." I saw the blue flashing lights of the police car against the wall and turned to look out the window. When I turned back Lee was gone.

SOMEONE PUT A CUP OF HOT COFFEE IN MY HANDS. I clenched it, and allowed someone else to slip my coat off. A man, maybe an emergency medical technician, tugged off my boots a little too energetically, making the coffee slop a little down my sweater. He apologized and we laughed.

Others hovered around the boys, both of whom were now very talkative. Their parents had arrived hard on the heels of the authorities and the living room was filled with loud voices, weeping mingled with laughter. Bad-dog was made much of and took advantage of the commotion to jump on the couch and snuggle back down with his buddies.

To my befuddled mind it was as if being drunk at a party—I heard voices but could not distinguish words. Then I was lifted from the vortex of exhaustion by a caffeine-induced second wind so strong it was as if I had slept all night. I was embraced by a variety of people, all of whom began to clamor for Lee. I made his apologies, citing his exhaustion as cause for his sudden disappearance. My own tiredness began to creep back up on me, and it was with relief that I noticed suddenly they were gone and only the state police sergeant and Lee's doctor remained with me. I answered Sergeant Duchesne's questions for a few minutes and then was alone with Lee's friend and physician, Dr. Fielding.

"Have you seen him?" I sat in one of the Queen Anne chairs beside the fireplace. Dr. Fielding squatted next to me, my feet in his hands.

"He's pretty wiped out, but I think he'll be all right. It was a monumental feat for him to attempt, but it won't have done him any harm." Dr. Fielding had known Lee for years, and I felt enormous relief at his diagnosis.

He ran a light finger up the sole of my foot, and when I twitched he smiled and let go of my foot. "And how are you?"

"I'm okay. I think I'm warm, finally." I rubbed my face. "Just enormously tired. Any frostbite?"

"No. You're very lucky. It was damned cold last night."

"Tell me about it." I laughed. "And the boys?"

"Surprisingly healthy, but I think Tommy may lose a toe. That dog was the difference between that and a whole different ending to this story."

"Good old Bad-dog." I reached out and stroked the object of our praise, who obligingly leaned his muzzle on the chair arm. My moment of second wind evaporated and my head spun with exhaustion.

I felt Dr. Fielding pull me to my feet. "To bed, Alix Miller. You did a heroic thing tonight."

"No, I was just Tonto." I took his hand in mine and held it, forcing him to look me in the eye. "Is he really all right, Doctor?"

"If he hasn't taken a chill, and I don't think he has, he'll be fine." Dr. Fielding squeezed my hand. "You're fond of him, aren't you?"

I nodded.

"Try to talk him into accepting some credit for this, would you?"

I smiled and nodded again, too tired to answer with words.

.   .   .

I slept the sleep of the dead. Dreamless until waking, then filled with icy images and distortions of what we had gone through. I saw ledges in my dreams, and falling, I startled myself awake. The afternoon light struck the mirror over the sink in the bathroom, catching my eye as I lay under the blue coverlet and keeping me from going back to sleep. I climbed out of bed and stood for a long time in the shower, soaking up the heat from the water. I had forgotten to turn on the fan, and the small guest bathroom was filled with steam. I took my hair dryer and made a clear circle in the mirror. The face that looked back at me, framed as it was by the foggy moisture on the mirror, was untouched by the night's experience. There was nothing there that said I'd somehow joined the ranks of heroes. I didn't feel heroic, only happy. Happy. I hurried to get dressed.

.   .   .

Lee wasn't downstairs. Mrs. Greaves hadn't seen him yet. I ate the savory soup that she made for me, listening all the while for Lee's step. I wandered into the solarium where the last of the March afternoon's light had turned gray and thrown everything into dusky relief. Under the artificial light of the overhead fixture, I examined the portrait. I was pleased with it.

I was hungry again and could smell the roast Mrs. Greaves was making for dinner. "No sign of him yet?" I asked her as I helped myself to a carrot.

"Nope. Still asleep. He's worn out, Miss Miller. He shouldn't have done it. It'll kill him."

"Mrs. Greaves"—I put a hand on her shoulder—"Dr. Fielding says he'll be fine. He's not delicate, he's a healthy man."

She shook her head in disagreement, but said nothing further.

. . .

At six o'clock the phone began ringing. As if by some tacit agreement the media had let us sleep off our adventure; they were now ravenous to get the story. Every ten minutes the phone would ring and Mrs. Greaves would answer it in her deadpan way, "Crompton residence. No, he is still unavailable. Yes, I'll tell him. Good-bye." The phone would strike the cradle with a plastic clatter.

By dinnertime I was worried about Lee. I crept up the stairs to his door and listened. The old house had solid wood doors and no sound leaked through despite my straining ears. I kept thinking of Mrs. Greaves's skepticism and felt that lump of doubt grow in my chest. What if Dr. Fielding was wrong? I tapped on the door. Then opened it wide enough for the light from the hallway to lay itself over his bed, revealing the sleeping form there. I could hear his breathing, a little raspy but not labored. His foot beneath the covers twitched and suddenly I felt awkward and intrusive. Embarrassed, I backed away and shut the door.

. . .

"Alix, will you speak with this person please?"

It was thus that I began relating the tale to the media. Dissatisfied with Lee's elusiveness, they turned to the sidekick. "When he found them they were huddled together under a bower of evergreens they'd bent down to form a

132

shelter. . . . They were alert and very cold. The dog? I don't know. Big, brown, and as mixed a breed as can be. We had warm socks and hot coffee. . . . About six hours, and another four to get back down. Mr. Crompton led. He's very tired. No, he's not ill. Recluse? He's a writer." I ended the interview, unsure of how much Lee would want revealed about himself. I decided less was best. They all wanted to talk with him directly and I kept promising that he would call.

I was nearly as tired by nine o'clock as I had been at dawn and retreated to my room, leaving Mrs. Greaves to unplug all the phones. As I drifted back to sleep I thought I heard Lee stirring but was caught so firmly in the net of sleep that I could not move.

With that peculiar fickleness of weather, the next day saw the first earnest salute of spring. I could hear the trickling of the snow melting from the roof as it dripped over the slate and down through the drainpipes. Steam rose from the stones in the driveway, glistening wet in the bright sunshine. I hurried downstairs, pleased beyond reason to find Lee at the breakfast table, his reading glasses perched on his nose and his newspaper spread out before him, already marked with coffee cup rings and crumbs.

"Anything about the rescue in there?" I asked, holding myself back from leaping over and throwing my arms around him.

"This is *The New York Times*. We didn't quite make it for this edition."

"I could swear I spoke with every reporter in the country yesterday."

Lee laughed a little and folded the paper away. "Thanks for fielding all the calls, Alix. I just couldn't have done it. I'll return calls today."

I looked up at him in surprise.

"What? Why the quizzical look?" he asked.

"I don't know. I guess I assumed you didn't want to talk to them."

"Talk, no pictures. I don't have to meet anyone."

"They won't be satisfied."

"No?"

"You forget, my friend Mark is a photojournalist. He lives with the motto 'Pictures say a thousand words.' "

"Mark. Right."

I felt a little warmth in my cheeks, as if I'd brought up a bad subject. "Well, I'm sure if you just . . ."

"Alix, I've been interviewed a dozen times as Harris Bellefleur; there's never a need for photos. Not without permission."

. . .

Lee disappeared for an hour while he returned the calls and I worked on the portrait. When he finally joined me in the solarium he looked a little sheepish. "Well, your friend is right. I guess reclusive authors aren't photo-op material, reclusive heroes are. Damn reporter from the *Register* badgered me until I agreed he could come and take a picture."

"Lee, you surprise me."

"Actually, it's blatant subterfuge. When he comes, he gets to take one of you and our wonder dog there."

"Oh, I get it. You're suddenly called away."

"Precisely."

He sat down and I studied the man and the portrait, refining some of the strokes. My mind was swirling like the snow of the day before, thinking of the lengths to which Lee would go to avoid being seen. Experienced enough to know that refusal would mean open season on him, he became passive-aggressive. I smiled behind the canvas, faintly amused.

The phone rang again and he snapped it up. I was so intent on my work I didn't listen until his voice went up a decible and grew gravelly. "Mrs. Lewis, I do certainly appreciate that you're grateful, but really, no recognition is necessary. Many people were out there, anyone could have found them. I don't think the boys need to come here. No, please, they needn't meet me. That they are alive and well is reward enough." Lee glanced over at me and I could read the panic in his eyes.

"Yes, I'll think it over. But really, it's not necessary." Lee placed the handset down softly. "They want the boys to thank us in person. Both sets of parents think it's necessary."

"Lee, let them. They need to express their gratitude."

He hauled himself out of his chair. "Alix, no."

"And give me one good reason why not."

"Don't be obtuse, Alix." He pointed at his face. "You know why. I won't be a fairy tale hero. The monster may perform a good deed, but the curse is never lifted."

"Are you afraid of pity?"

He stopped pacing and looked at me, so used to my scrutiny now he no longer tried to avoid it. "Do you pity me?"

"Sometimes," I answered. "But not because of what you look like. Because of what it's done to you."

Breathless seconds passed between us. I could not take back my words, yet something in me gloried in my honesty. I had stepped over a barrier and into a new dimension in this strange relationship. He didn't answer me, but his mobile face belied his composure. Finally he simply left the room. I squeezed my eyes shut and wished I had said nothing. As I covered the portrait the content blue eyes seemed a mockery of the soul of the man.

. . .

Bad-dog and I had our fifteen minutes of fame. We dutifully greeted photographers and TV camera crews, had our pictures taken, told the story over and over again. Each time Mr. Crompton was unavoidably delayed, out of town, or ill. So sorry, please understand. Fortunately for us a successful rescue that doesn't involve heavy machinery or unhappy endings loses media attention quickly, and by the end of the following week we were left alone. I knew one of the photographers and we exchanged news about Mark. He'd met him at the airport, heading out for Somalia. I had wondered why I hadn't heard from him, although my guilty conscience had provoked me to leave three messages on his answering machine. I was afraid he'd be annoyed if I didn't tell him about my own newsworthy moment.

. . .

The town hungered for a celebration. The finding of the two lost boys had energized the community into a passion of fellow-feeling and finally it settled upon a thanksgiving service that Sunday at the Roman Catholic church where both were altar boys. First the Lewises, then the Michaliks, then the parish priest called to prevail upon the town's only legitimate hero to attend. Resolute, no, stubborn, Lee Crompton refused to be recognized. And never said why. Finally Father Vaughn, Lee's own Episcopal priest, came to call.

Unannounced, Father Vaughn showed up at the back door, bussed Mrs. Greaves on the cheek, and introduced himself to me. Tall, painfully thin, he looked almost a caricature of a rector with his white collar and tweed jacket.

"So, is our shy hero about?"

"He's in the library on the phone. Why don't we capture him in his den?" I didn't need to lead the way. Father Vaughn was well acquainted with the layout of the house, but I went with him anyway.

"You recently lost your father, didn't you?" he asked me as we went down the long hall to the library.

I was nonplussed. "Yes, last month."

My tone revealed my puzzlement and he placed a gentle hand on my shoulder. "Lee told me. I'm very sorry."

I felt a rush of delight that Lee had spoken of me to someone. "Lee was wonderful for me during the worst times." I paused before the library door. "I don't know what I would have done without him." I put a hand on his tweedy arm. "Convince him, if you can, to accept this honor. Will you?"

"That's what I'm here for." The priest patted my hand, not in a gratuitous or mechanical manner, but in an honest human gesture.

I left him at the door and went to help Mrs. Greaves.

. . .

Lee seemed to have chosen to ignore what I had said to him. He behaved as if nothing had passed between us. I itched to apologize, or to provoke some kind of dialogue to clear the air, but instead he gave me worse than no opportunity, he pretended nothing had happened. Maybe, I began to think, I took my own words too seriously. Maybe I had only thought it.

When half an hour had passed, Mrs. Greaves handed me a tea tray and I went back down the hallway to the library. I tapped on the door and went in. Lee and Father Vaughn were silent, the air thick with disagreement. I set the tray down and looked at Lee. "You won't do it, will you?"

"Do you know me so well you can read my mind now?"

"No, your face."

"You're right. Lee is being reluctant." Father Vaughn threw up his long thin hands. "I can't convince him, Alix. And we have to respect that. He doesn't want to be seen."

"Afraid he'll frighten the very children he risked his life to save." Lee shot me a look to kill but I was committed now. "Lee, what can we say to you that will convince you you're wrong?"

Stretching himself against the crookedness in his spine, Lee seemed to fill the room. His deep voice cracked from within the barrel chest. "Damn it, Alix. I have chosen a path and I am not veering from it. Drop it!"

I looked up at him, fighting the tears his anger coaxed out of me. "All right, Lee. Okay. If that is what you truly want, we can't make you."

Suddenly his shoulders drooped into their customary tilt. "Alix, I'm sorry." He looked at Father Vaughn, who had stood as well. "Hank, I'm sorry. I just can't." He looked back at me and I saw the flash of a frightened animal, then his expression resolved back into his usual face, the crags and ledges softened by a smile. "You go, Alix. You found them. You stuck it out and warmed them and hauled them down the hill. You go for both of us."

I knew then that he was truly imprisoned.

. . .

The granite church was packed. The parish priest, Father McClellan, met me in the parish hall and escorted me into the sanctuary to sit in the front pew with the boys and their families. The entire rescue effort was represented, and as I looked from side to side I recognized one of the emergency people, and there were police troopers, some in uniform, one or two in mufti I remembered vaguely. Dr. Fielding tapped my shoulder and I smiled back at him. The bulletin listed the fifty-odd searchers with Lee's and my name set off by clever printing. Special recognition was given Bad-dog as well. The day before, a huge meaty bone from the butcher's had been ceremoniously delivered by Tommy and Travis.

The processional hymn began, the organist pumping out a familiar tune, but the words seemed different. It was a beautiful service. I kept thinking it was an anti-funeral—all thanksgiving and praise. Father McClellan's homily was joyous and reflected on the acts of humans being the acts of God. What might have been a raised fist asking God why was instead raised hands praising His mercy.

Suddenly the service was over and I was embraced by strangers. I ached for Lee to be there. People surrounded me as the tangible hero, someone to see and touch. I tried to offer Lee's excuses, but they went unheeded, as those I spoke to were more set on telling me how they felt about the rescue themselves than in hearing my fabrication. And for that I was grateful. Worse than not being there, Lee wouldn't be truthful about why he wasn't. So I became the lone guest of honor, the artist heroine from out of town, while the real hero lived only three miles away and was nearly as much a stranger to them as I.

A buffet in the parish hall followed with requisite speeches from the first selectman and then shy speeches from Travis and Tommy. I was made to join them on the dais and together they presented me with a bouquet of roses.

I left as soon as I could. Sitting in my car, I undid my coat, warmed in the spring air less by the rising temperature as by the warmth of spirit shown me.

It hurt to think that Lee had, by his own massive self-consciousness, been denied this kind of love.

Mrs. Greaves laid two peek frean cookies on a plate and set the tiny silver coffee carafe on the tray with the cup and saucer. I wiped my hands on a paper towel and laid my brushes down on another. "I'll take that in to him," I offered.

"No, he doesn't like to be disturbed while he works." She tipped hot coffee into the carafe.

"I won't bother him, I promise." And I lifted the tray away from her. If she'd made a grab for it I wouldn't have been surprised. Mrs. Greaves's tolerance of me was beginning to show wear as I stayed on. Right now her stiff lower jaw spoke volumes.

I went slowly up the stairs to the bedroom Lee used as a writing room. I'd never been in it before. The door was ajar and I pushed it open with my foot. It swung open gently, the well-oiled hinges making no sound. Intending to set the tray down and slip away, keeping my promise, I came quietly into the room where the only sound was the persistent hum of the computer.

Lee hunched over the keyboard; elbows stuck out, he typed with two fingers and a thumb. Even from a distance, I could see the cursor fly across the grayish background as Harris Bellefleur gave life to Tyler Bent. Suddenly he stopped and leaned forward a little and muttered, "Tyler, you idiot, you can't do that!" With a few thumps, he'd obliterated the offending lines and forged ahead.

I began to feel like a voyeur, so I set the tray down and backed away. As I turned toward the door, I saw the painting I'd given him, framed now in an expensive rosewood frame. The late afternoon sunlight touched the greens and blues, creating a natural light for the awakening of the colors, as if a little piece of the pasture had been sliced away and framed. But above it all floated the little face, and in sudden recognition I knew it was a Death's Head. That's what that was, not Cupid or the muse it might have represented. I'd prophetically painted in Death over my landscape. I must have made a sound because he turned and saw me.

"Alix, what's the matter?"

"Nothing, I was just bringing your coffee, I didn't mean to interrupt, please"—I paused for breath—"excuse me."

"No, wait, stay. This is getting away from me, and that's when I need to stop."

"I've interrupted your dream."

"My what?"

I laughed a little. "I always call the state of concentration I try to achieve when I paint the dream state. When all else is held away and free thought guides the hand."

"Gardner."

I raised an eyebrow.

"John Gardner always said that to really write, one must allow the dream to happen."

"Well, I didn't mean to wake you, and Mrs. Greaves will have my head."

"To hell with her. Just let me get the next line on the screen and we'll talk." He turned back to the keyboard.

My eye was carried back to the painting. I was touched

142

with unreasoning happiness that he'd hung it in here, that he'd wanted something from me. The little face smiled and the sense that it was a Death's Head passed.

"I think of it as my muse."

"You read minds now?"

"Occasionally." He laughed. "Your expression is quite revealing."

"For a moment I thought it was a Death's Head."

He stopped laughing and shook his head. "No, Alix. It was never that. It shows radiant hope."

I sat in the only other chair in the sparsely furnished room. It seemed as though, even with me in the room, he was able to return to some kind of concentration as he rolled on with the work. His longish brown hair curled gently over his ears and over his collar, and every now and then he'd run a hand through it, tugging at it as if holding on to an idea, then striking the keys to catch up.

It seemed impossible that I had not always known Lee Crompton. Our ancestors had known one another—perhaps some genetic memory broke down that filmy barrier of strangerhood. Though there were many details I didn't know, I just knew the essence of him, this man who had become my friend during a crisis in my life. I was not surprised by the wash of tenderness I felt just then, staring at his broad back as he worked. In three short months, he had filled a void in my life I hadn't known existed. I drew close behind him. He wore no aftershave, but the scent of his soap was pleasant and I stood closer.

The cipher my future had seemed filled suddenly, and I knew in that moment the path I wanted.

"One more sentence," he said, feeling me behind him.

"Take your time," I said, and waited.

"Done." He sat straighter and flexed from side to side.

I put my hands on his shoulders and rubbed, pressing away the tension with my thumbs.

"Don't, Alix."

I slipped my arms around his neck and kissed his cheek. He shot up from the chair as if I had slapped him.

"Why do you flinch every time I touch you?"

"You mustn't."

"Why not? What are you saying?"

"Don't toy with me, Alix. I may be ugly, but I'm still a man. Just because I look like this doesn't mean I don't have the same desires as any other man."

"I know that." I backed up toward the door. I could feel my skin grow hot with shame. "Lee, I am not toying with you. Don't you think I care for you? Don't you care for me?" I started out of the room.

"Come back. I'm sorry. I'm being stupid." As suddenly as his flash of anger had happened, he conquered it and was apologetic. "Look, when I first showed symptoms of this disease I was going with a woman. The radiation therapy to shrink the tumor had a rather unfortunate side effect. My relationship with this woman was tenuous at best, and losing my desire was not a great advantage to it. So I discontinued the treatments, never dreaming just how, well, just how it would turn out. I eventually went back to treatment. In many ways, it was a blessing not to have any physical desire, as I was so obviously no longer desirable. But, Alix"—and here he touched my hand, clenching it in his—"ever since the day we skated together, I've realized that the impotence that shielded me is gone. When you wore your new dress for me, for my approval, I wanted you so badly I hurt. But I will not risk your friendship."

I remembered back to the first nights we spent together and my fear that he would play those will-we-won't-we games and that I would have to be unintentionally cruel, as there would be no way to reject him without offense. Now I looked full into his face and saw there, not a mis-shapen stranger, but my dearest friend.

I reached up and touched his face, and this time he didn't shrug me off. I pressed my lips against his and we kissed. I could feel him resist, and I held on. "It's all right, Lee. Let it happen."

He gathered my face between his gnarly hands and lowered his face to mine. Slowly I felt the awakening of desire, the moist flame of passion ignite as his kiss grew more ardent.

"Oh, excuse me!" Mrs. Greaves appeared suddenly at the open door, driving us apart like guilty teenagers. "I just wanted to ask what time you want dinner."

"The usual time, Mrs. Greaves," Lee got out finally.

"She knew we were up to no good," I whispered when she was gone.

"Were we?"

"Yes."

But, like the dream state, the spell was broken.

I WAITED FOR HIM IN MY ROOM, BUT HE NEVER CAME. Finally, just before eight, I gave up and went downstairs. He wasn't waiting for me in the library or anywhere else. A little throb of anxiety beat in my veins and I went to the kitchen to find Mrs. Greaves.

"He's gone out." Her face was completely bland, but her hands viciously scrubbed at a pot.

"Where?"

"I don't ask his business." She held the pot up to the light and scowled at it, picking at an invisible speck of scum on the inside.

"Mrs. Greaves . . ." I stepped a little closer.

"Alix, don't go wrecking his life with promises you won't keep."

"Mrs. Greaves, you've no business . . ."

"I have. He's been my worry for a long time. I don't want to see him hurt."

"Why do you think I would hurt him?" I felt my fists close against the accusation.

"Everyone hurts him eventually."

"I'm not everyone, Mrs. Greaves."

"I won't let you do it to him." She hosed hot water into the pot; a thin spray struck me in the face.

"Don't you interfere." Anger now flared. How dare this

woman speak to me as though I were a malicious child? "You leave us alone."

"Us? How quick you are to link yourself with him. Sure, I know your type. All you see is his money. You can look past anything for that."

So stunned was I by her accusation that I was momentarily struck speechless. I shook my head to clear it, thinking I couldn't have heard her correctly. "What? What are you saying?"

"You'll play on his loneliness for his money. I've seen it before."

The adrenaline-spiked rage twisted my hands into fists and I shook all over. "Is that what he thinks?"

"Naturally." She slammed the pot down into the dish drain. "I'll put your dinner on a tray."

"Don't bother," I said, and went to get my coat.

. . .

The open bay revealed the empty place where the MG was kept. Long night drives. Sometimes he just took long drives. I whistled for Bad-dog and struck out for the moon-lit pathway. I walked for a long time, striding along now familiar trails, ducking branches, sensing them more than seeing them as I plowed along with my head down. Eventually I came to the pond, now shimmering in the light breeze like rumpled silk. An eternity ago he and I had skated together, our hands touching, my cheek against his chest. He had rediscovered his desire then, and I had been oblivious to it. Neither of us had been oblivious four hours ago, we had both felt real passion—nothing would ever belie that.

I sat on the skater's log and held my head in my hands. How had this happened? I was a lover of beauty. My few lovers had all been handsome, especially Mark, whose smooth features were near classically beautiful. Their bodies, each of them, had been slim and strong, runners' bodies. Lee's barrel-chested torso was at complete odds with his narrow hips. Yet he skated like Boitano; hands palm downward, he sketched a circle, his skates razoring a thin single line. Gently, with courage I had not understood then, he'd taken my hand and danced me across the January ice. I sat up and looked out across the pond, and was satisfied that I knew how this remarkable love had come to be.

A duck quacked as Bad-dog flushed it. I called the dog back to heel and turned toward the house.

The entire house was dark and I thought momentarily that Mrs. Greaves had locked me out. Just in case, I fished around in my parka pocket and found my keys, a bright silver back door key recently added to the chain. I felt like a chatelaine, the keys chattering in my hand. I thought of the wind chime, its sweet melody now filling the air in the solarium when we opened a window. The morning after my return to Riseborough, I'd brought the box down to breakfast and set it before him. "A little gift for my host," I'd said. He'd held it aloft, touching the thorny brass stems individually with a delicate touch of his gnarled forefinger, then flicked them into music. "This is so beautiful," he'd said, and I was pleased when he didn't tell me, "You shouldn't have." Gracious at receiving as well as giving, Lee immediately hung the chimes exactly where I had envisioned them.

Coming around the corner, I could see that the garage bay was still empty.

.   .   .

After midnight, and I still couldn't sleep. Worry about his safety almost superseded my deeper anguish that he could possibly believe what Mrs. Greaves said. I fretted that she had his complete confidence and I imagined that her influence was stronger than I knew it to be. I shook off these thoughts repeatedly as the night wore on, yet each time they came back more powerful as I grew more tired. Where was he, why had he run away when the night had so much promise? Defeated by these mental battles, I got up and pulled a sweatshirt over my nightgown. Creeping down the stairs, I went to the solarium and uncovered the portrait.

Casually seated, ankle on knee, his notebook in his lap and his concentration on the work there, the portrait revealed to me the man I knew. I had chosen to paint him in jeans, his navy blue lamb's wool sweater and plaid flannel shirt beneath it, the collar loose, one corner sticking out from under the sweater. It was a characteristic pose, relaxed and unself-conscious. I squeezed out some paint and found my finest brush.

A sharp note of birdsong woke me to the realization that daylight now flooded into the solarium, making the artificial lights redundant. I moved to turn them off, turning the easel just enough to take on the yellow light of new day. From soft gray to pink to blue, the sky lightened, leaving the last bright star of night hanging in momentary suspension before it, too, faded. I looked out the windows and saw Willie arrive, his old father dropping him off. Bad-dog ran past the window, barking at the flock of chickadees feeding on the Yankee Droll feeder. I went back to the portrait. With a pang of sorrow, I realized it was finished.

THERE WAS NOTHING LEFT, THEN, BUT TO PACK AND GO. I took a quick shower and emptied the dresser drawers into my bag. It was only a little past eight, though it felt like midday. I was hungry and tired and deeply sad. Something had been spoiled and I had been the spoiler. I walked past the portrait gallery without stopping.

With my hand running for the last time down the smooth banister, I walked down the stairs. As the morning light streamed in from the long front windows, I could see clearly the seam I had thought not there.

The front door opened and Lee walked in, bringing with him the scent of cool spring dawn. I stood motionless on the stairs, relief banging against my chest as he closed the door behind him and looked up at me with a mixture of emotions written on his face.

"Are you all right?" I came down the stairs slowly, clinging to the banister in an effort to prevent myself from rushing toward him, yet with each step I moved faster until I was nearly there. He held up a staying hand and backed away as I reached the last step.

"I'm fine. I'm sorry if I left you to your own devices, but I needed some time."

"It's okay, Lee, I understand."

"No, I don't think you do."

"So tell me."

"Last night was a mistake."

My emotions jangling, I moved past him toward the solarium. Beneath the shadow of the shrouded painting I cleaned up my scattered brushes and tubes of paint, wiping them with a rag and setting each into the wooden box, heedless of color or size. I took down the painting and set it on the floor, leaning it against a table. I struggled to release the wing nuts of the easel, finally taking my X-Acto knife and slicing the rubber band, letting the easel crash to the floor with a satisfying sound of wood hitting slate.

"You're leaving."

"It's finished." I held back tears. This man had seen enough of my tears, but of their own volition my words came. "But I don't have to. Lee, I don't have to go at all."

"No, Alix, I think it's best."

"I see." I picked up the easel and the wooden box, then stopped. "Lee, why is it best if I go?"

"Alix, it would be wrong for you to stay. No good can come of it. Only hurt." His blue eyes glistened with anguish.

"Lee, I love you." I set the boxes down and took a step closer, but he retreated. "Don't turn away from me."

"That's not possible."

"Oh, it wasn't love at first sight, I'll admit that, but I have grown to love you as deeply as my life. Lee, don't push me away."

"How can you say such a thing?" His voice rose and the deep resonance was like a roar. "How can you think you could love something like me?"

"Never some *thing*, someone. Someone who maybe loves me."

"No, Alix! It would be so wrong, I would be ruining your

life. I can't give you what you need. A woman like you needs society and children and I won't have either."

"I only need you."

"Alix, this is no fairy tale. You will never release me from this genetic spell. I will never turn into a handsome prince, not even with the magic of your kiss."

"Beauty loved her Beast as he was. I love you as you are."

"It isn't possible. You have mistaken friendship for love; your fondness, as dear as it is to me, for passion."

"No, Lee, you're wrong. Am I wrong to think that maybe you love me?"

Barely a whisper, he answered, "No." Then swung away from me. "Go home, Alix. Go live in New York with Mark."

"Lee, it's you I love, not Mark. It was never Mark."

"You don't love me." He looked down. "You have just imagined me. You have some romantic notion that you can overlook my repulsiveness." He held up one hand. "Please, Alix, don't say anything else."

The incipient tears had dried into angry hurt. I snatched up my boxes again and headed toward the door. "Mrs. Greaves says I'm after you for your money."

It took a split second too long for him to reply and I knew then that Mrs. Greaves was telling the truth.

"My God, Lee, I never took you for a fool. How could you think that about me? I thought we were friends."

"I don't think that. Of course not. But, Alix, you have to understand, what other motive could anyone have for wanting me?"

I was thunderstruck. The man who wrote the wonderful mysteries about the masterful Tyler Bent was completely undermined emotionally by his own face.

"Who hurt you so badly you won't trust me? Who did

this to you? Who hurt you so badly you won't allow your-self to believe you are loved?"

I dropped the boxes again and grabbed up the portrait. "Look at this, Lee Crompton, look and see who it is that I have fallen in love with." I stripped the cover off the picture, but Lee wouldn't turn to look at it. "When was the last time you looked at yourself?"

"Go away, Alix. Please."

My chest felt on fire with the pain of restrained tears. I closed my eyes and sighed. "All right. I'll leave. But I'm taking the portrait. It's mine. Your mother will never miss it."

I banged out of the solarium with my boxes and the canvas, pushing past Mrs. Greaves, who appeared in the hallway. Willie had already put my bag in my car and there was nothing left to do but drive away. As I passed through the gates with the roses twisted in the iron, I chanced to see the silver back door key dangling from my key chain. I touched it, with half a mind to pull it off the chain and heave it into the dirty snow, but left it, a tiny silver memory of what real love had felt like.

ON THE DAY I LEFT RISEBOROUGH I GOT HOME AT ABOUT noon and had gone right to my own long-deserted apart-ment, desiring only the oblivion of sleep and some solitude to allow the events of the past few weeks to heal in me. The red light of my answering machine was flashing and in a passion of hope that Lee had called, I hit the Play button. A stream of calls spewed forth and I dutifully re-corded all the names and numbers of people calling to offer condolences, to check on me, to sell me cable TV. My father's attorney's secretary had called about probating Dad's will.

The next few weeks were cluttered with all the ritualistic head-bobbings of lawyers and insurance agents as we worked our way through Dad's estate. It seemed as though Dad had been well insured and, as his only beneficiary, I suddenly found that I was, if not wealthy, certainly com-fortably well-off. Handled prudently, his estate would allow me to work full-time at my art. It was as if he had always planned that I should be financially free to pursue my dream even while he badgered me about supporting myself.

I returned Lee's retainer. I wrote a short note, carefully composing each sentence to be honest without pleading. I asked him to please call me, that what I had said was from my heart and that I missed him. I lay the short piece of paper on my work table and left it for three days before I could reread it and finally put it in the mail. He will never believe me, I kept thinking. I felt more and more like some teenager, unsure about frightening off the object of my desire with uncautious words. Yet my heart persevered in wanting him.

I heard nothing from him. A card from Hospice came, a donation had been made in Dad's memory by an anonymous donor in the exact amount I had returned to Lee. The shrouded portrait sat in a corner of the studio, its back facing me. The anonymous designation on the card made Lee seem farther away than ever.

I waited until a Thursday night and paced around the telephone on the desk as if it were a time bomb. "Just do it," I said aloud and punched his number. Four rings and the answering machine kicked in. Mrs. Greaves's recorded voice enjoining me to leave a message at the tone. I hung up. Then called back, leaving a short message to have Mr. Crompton please call me. I pulled back from saying it was urgent, but in truth it was. Everything in my life hinged now on Lee Crompton.

I began to wonder if Lee had been right, that proximity had produced this unnatural passion in me. Each day I tested this sore theory; each day a rolling sense of loss answered, a loss that paralleled my grief. I mourned the loss of Lee as deeply as I mourned my father's death. It was difficult to separate the two. Both had filled my life and then vanished. But my father I had nursed to the end, had said my farewells and bidden Godspeed. Lee had been cut from me by his own hand.

. . .

Behind me the air conditioner revved. The phone rang and I let the answering machine take the call, too enervated by the July heat wave to get up and answer it. Robin's voice came on and I leapt up, banging my knee on the table and spilling a little of my coffee. "Robin! Wait!"—I punched the Off button—"Robin, hi!"

We nattered on for a few minutes, filling each other in on inconsequential details of our very different lives. Finally she got to the point. "Alix, John and I are moving the date up. We're getting married over Labor Day weekend."

She went on, "You know we're both too old and experienced to play bride and groom, so we've decided to simply do a civil ceremony and have a nice dinner somewhere. The important thing is, can you still be our witness?"

"Robin, of course I will. And I'll take the girls for you when you go on your honeymoon," I offered.

Robin demurred, her mother and John's were nearby and happy to have the two, Sarah and Caitlin. "Besides, his mother has to get used to these kids being part of her life now. What better way?"

"Well, you know I'm happy to if something doesn't work out." Actually, I was relieved that the little girls wouldn't be my responsibility.

"So how are you?"

"I'm okay," I said after a moment's hesitation. I'd gotten pretty good at dodging that question, put to me so often after Dad's death. A cheerful "I'm doing just fine, thanks for asking" wouldn't fly with Robin, who knew the other half of my sorrow.

"Still no communication?"

"No."

"But you've tried?"

"Over and over. Sometimes I think that he wasn't appalled so much by my schoolgirl declarations as he simply didn't love me."

"But?"

"But then I remember the look in his eyes and know that I wasn't mistaken. His face is incredibly expressive for all its deformity, or maybe because of it. He seems to absolutely lack the ability to mask his emotions. They are larger than life on his face. I cling to that, Robin, I cling to the memory of his eyes, and that's my lifeline and maybe the whole reason I can't seem to get on with my life."

. . .

That next Saturday Robin and I were in the mall hunting for dresses for the wedding when we passed a Barnes & Noble bookstore. There, prominently displayed in the faux bay window, was the latest Harris Bellefleur book, *Legacy for a Dancer*, A Tyler Bent Mystery. I caught Robin's elbow and pointed. "That's him."

"Tyler Bent?"

"No, Harris Bellefleur, Lee's nom de plume."

We went in and I picked up a copy from the display stack, turning immediately to the back cover to read the author blurb: "Harris Bellefleur has written several novels and short stories. He lives in New Hampshire." That was it, a terse little bit without photo. I riffled back to the front, stopping at the dedication page. "My God," I said and handed the book to Robin.

"To A. M., who for one brief moment made me feel like Tyler Bent," she read aloud.

"Keep trying to contact him, Alix. That's a message in a bottle if ever I saw one."

"One he wrote a long time ago, Robin. I wonder if he still feels that way."

. . .

Robin and John got married on the Saturday before Labor Day in a beautifully intimate ceremony with just six of us there to share it with them. We all knew one another, so the party was lively and a little undignified by the time they drove off to the Cape for a short honeymoon.

Robin touched my cheek with hers. "Go find him, Alix. Don't let him get away."

"I won't." But even to me the words rang false.

. . .

The air was silky, washing over me like gentle water as I lay on the dock. Somewhere a bullfrog bellowed. I opened my eyes and focused again on my book. The lowering sun sent streams of reddish light across the lake, tinting the trees of the little islets dotting the middle of the lake. Soon enough it would be too cold to sit out without a sweater, much less in shorts; soon enough the leaves would draw thousands of tourists and this deep breath between seasons would be exhaled.

I placed a bookmark between my pages and sifted through my bag for the mail I'd picked up on my way to the lake. I was thumbing through an art catalog when I read about a museum show to be held in January. At the bottom of the article was an invitation to submit work. I circled it with my felt-tip marker and added the name of the Percy Art Museum to the growing list of shows I was entering. So far I'd been rejected by the several I had already applied to, but, as Dad always said, keep trying. I'd been to the Percy Art Museum, a small but very well-endowed museum in northwestern Massachusetts. I had met the director and made a note of his name beside the circled address.

The bullfrog called again.

. . .

I let myself in the back door of the house. I'd long since given up my farmhouse apartment and had settled into

Dad's house. My house. Dumping my bag and mail on the kitchen table, I hunted through the cupboards for an easy meal, my flip-flops making soft thwacks against the soles of my feet as I trotted around. I was anxious to sort through my slides to find the pieces I would submit to the Percy show. Ten minutes later, I was out on the lawn with a grilled cheese sandwich and my slides.

With a little switching here and there, I pulled two from other submissions and decided that those would go to the Percy. Then I thought better of it. I got up and went into the studio, where my most recent work hung, things I'd finished while Dad was sick, a couple I'd completed since returning home. Four framed pieces hung from the center posts in the studio, a series in egg tempera. My two land-scapes soaked in the warm yellow and pink of the setting sun as they lay propped against easels. The portrait of Lee was the only thing still behind a sheet, the white rectangle orphaned against Dad's work table.

My influences and my interests were so different from the paintings captured on slides. To submit some of the older pieces was not a real indicator of my current work. Mark had always done my slides for me, and now I had work and no photographer.

Although Mark and I still spoke occasionally on the phone, we had quickly settled into an amicable distance. I couldn't ask him to shoot my slides anymore. I thought of him only infrequently and, although I tested the notion several times, I never regretted not pressing him toward a commitment. It was true what I had said to Lee, Mark wasn't the love of my life.

. . .

It wasn't until nearly Thanksgiving that I heard I'd been accepted to exhibit at the Percy Art Museum group show in January. Unbelievably, they had accepted all five pieces I submitted. The museum would host a reception on the first day of the exhibit and had sent me a box of logo'd invitations with my name listed among the other dozen exhibitors. There I was, between Darlene Lewis and Max Moeller, in lovely sans serif type, blue on blue.

I pulled out my address book and considered the roster of names there. People who'd been patrons, or classmates or fellow teachers; others who'd been briefly chums by association in some group or other; others I'd forgotten about. My more recent entries were in turquoise ink. I replaced the cover of the box and left the task to future contemplation.

. . .

Robin invited me to Thanksgiving. I knew my offering of pies and wine couldn't come close to expressing the appreciation and affection I felt for this woman who had mothered and sistered and befriended me. We made a happy party, the in-laws and various cousins, children, and one stodgy Italian grandmother in black widow's weeds and elastic stockings. Others Robin had nurtured showed up for various activities of the day, dinner or dessert or football. John's quiet demeanor was loosened vastly and he entertained us all with jokes and tall stories.

Threaded throughout this public display I saw the looks he and Robin shared with each other. Subtle touches, raised eyebrows, pleasure and annoyance, amusement and exasperation. They were already developing communication techniques that would become ingrained over the years until they were capable of speechless eloquence with each other. Such love, I thought, is a miracle. It can't happen that often.

As I went to bed that night I felt as empty as if I had fasted all day.

. . .

Two days before I had called Lee. Mrs. Greaves had answered. Although I had expected her to, I almost lost my nerve. "Is he there?" I asked with the dread certainty that he wasn't there for me.

"Leave him alone, Miss Miller. He's doing just fine without you. He doesn't need your kind of upset."

I was so startled by her candor that I couldn't speak, and before I could react the phone responded with a hum of disconnection.

It was clear to me then. He really didn't want anything to do with me. I felt suddenly as if the walls of a sand pit were crumbling around me. If I scrambled up one side, it collapsed, taking with it all the other sides.

IT SNOWED WHILE WE HUNG OUR SHOW. TWELVE OF US, disparate artists with disparate work, had the museum to ourselves except for the docent who hovered around us, guarding permanent works from contagion. Our common cause made comrades of us, six men and six women; we each took the time to look at one another's work and offer compliments, wholly truthful at the moment. We helped each other fit wires to hooks and oh so carefully set down distracted little sculptures with sharp parts. There would be a dinner for us that night; the show would open at noon the next day. Giving my five pieces a last look, loving how they looked against the soft white wall with the perfect lighting, I put on my jacket and walked out with several of the others.

The two sculptors in the group had fallen upon the snow as a new medium and were instantly creating pieces, showing off a little. Pretty soon snowballs flew through the air between the two sculptures and the younger of us took up battle lines. Half an hour later, soaked and cold, we trundled off to our respective lodgings, warmed enough to one another to look forward to the dinner that night.

Late that night, a little inebriated, I found myself necking with one of the sculptors. Long-banked sensations flared in me and it was with great reluctance I finally pulled away. "I can't, Joel," I said.

"Not here." Joel Reichert was a good-looking young man, probably younger than I. We were sitting in his car, a mistake, my father would have told me.

"No, I mean, I can't take this any further."

"I have protection." His innocent assumption was almost endearing.

"Look, Joel, I'm just getting over an emotional entanglement. I'm a little fragile right now."

To his credit, Joel sat up and simply brushed my hair away from my mouth. "Okay, so how about a nightcap?"

"Yeah, that would be great."

When he dropped me off at my bed-and-breakfast, Joel kissed me gently on the cheek. "See you tomorrow."

"Thanks." I opened the door but before I shut it, I ducked my head back in. "Hey, Joel?"

"Yeah?"

"If I was ready, I would sleep with you in a minute."

He laughed and pulled away from the curb.

. . .

The museum was filled with visitors. A soft sibilance of muted voices like lapping waves on a lakeshore beach swelled and receded room to room. I spotted Joel, the docent had him surrounded by guests and he was speaking about his two very different sculptures. Catching his eye, I winked and he smiled around his explanation of material usage and meaning. I stood and listened for a while, growing nervous, knowing that my turn to speak was coming later that afternoon. The Percy requires that the artist not only hang the work, but also explain it in detail.

I drifted back to my display, studying each one as if I hadn't painted it. What would I say? What could I say that would tell a stranger what they meant to me?

The floor beneath my feet was gritty with the sand from

the pathways. A slow-moving custodian came into the nearly deserted room, his long white dust mop floating ahead of him, side to side, gathering up all the grit and trapping it. The mop made a little snick sound at each turn. On the highly polished floor, he looked as if he were skating.

"Ms. Miller?" A second docent came up behind me. "We're running a little late, can we ask you to hold your talk until four-thirty?"

"Of course. I'll be the last then, won't I?"

"I'm afraid so. Will this be a problem for your guests?"

"I don't expect any guests. I only sent out a few invitations, I'm afraid. It's a long way to come for most of my friends."

"Oh yes, you're from out of state, I'd forgotten."

"I'm happy to go last."

He performed a little motion that might have been a bow.

I checked my watch. Only two-thirty. I could go back to the bed-and-breakfast, but I felt too fidgety to rest. A nervous energy that had grown all day infected me and I decided just to go for a walk.

The sidewalks in the small town were full of frost heaves and I walked with my head down to avoid tripping, going around gnarled tree roots thrust up between broken slabs of cement like clenched fingers.

Nature will out, I thought. I thought, too, of the invitations I'd sent, suppressing a little disappointment that no one had made it. I had sent only six, four to folks who might have made it and one to Robin and John, who would have come but Sarah had come down with the chicken pox.

The last I had sent to Lee. I scrawled a note inside it: "I

send you this not expecting you to come, but hoping you'll let me know how you are. I remain your loving friend, Alix." Before I could think better of it, I posted it, the Percy Art Museum return address at the corner of the envelope.

. . .

Chilled, I realized that I'd been walking around for over an hour and a half. Picking up my pace, I headed back to the museum. The reception was well under way as I passed through the main foyer. Tables of wine and cheese and fruit stuck out at perpendicular angles around a floor sculpture by the sculptor I hadn't necked with. I bumped into Joel and complimented him on his talk.

"I think I sold one of them," he whispered, indicating a stout older man now bending over the floor sculpture. "Talked me down on the price, but, hell, man's got to eat."

"That's great. Hope you can make it two for two."

"You too, I'll come listen and maybe I'll even buy one."

"I didn't bring any for sale, Joel. These are from my personal collection."

"Baloney, every artist will sell. Or aren't you hungry enough?"

"Nope. Not enough." I laughed.

. . .

I hate that moment when I begin talking to a group and I am aware of every word I'm saying, as if the monitor is off and I can't think before I speak. A hollow sound coming out of my mouth and a voice in my head saying, Oh my God, I can't believe I'm saying this. Then there is that sweet moment when the subject overrides the nerves and I'm launched. A fair-size group surrounded me as I stood with my back to my work. The docent introduced me, spouting my curriculum vitae from memory. Then he fired questions at me, game as any interrogator from the Spanish

Inquisition. I fielded them fairly well—medium, technique, and so on.

"The four here"—I indicated the four small rectangles with a sweeping gesture—"are of my father, Alexander Miller. He was a well-known commercial artist who died in March of pancreatic cancer." I was satisfied at the slight inhalation of breath each listener made. "I painted these from sketches I made of him during his illness. As you can see, he experienced a rapid decline, which I've chosen to emphasize by muting the colors until here"—I pointed to the last of the quartet—"where I use no color at all except this small patch of red floating above. If you take them as a series, you'll note that the patch of red has migrated from him to above him." The group did not make a sound. "I like to think of these pictures as my good-bye to him. He taught me more about art than any of my instructors here or even in Paris. He showed me how to make eyes with life in them when I was a little girl." I paused, my own recollection of distant happiness making my listeners visibly uncomfortable, like a bare patch of skin showing in the winter.

Clearing his throat, the docent squared himself and pointed to the fifth painting. "And this one?"

"This is oil on canvas."

"Please, tell us about it."

I hesitated, suddenly shy again in front of these strangers, the semicircle solidifying into a motionless frieze of faces. I felt as if I'd taken something very private and shown it to strangers. As intimate as my paintings of my father were, this one had a different pain attached to it.

"Ms. Miller"—the docent held his hands together, raising the knuckles to his mouth—"any comment?"

"No"—I turned my back to the picture—"not really." I touched the silver beads at my neck with nervous fingers.

Dropping his hands, the docent asked, "Does anyone have any questions for Ms. Miller?" and stepped back into the semicircle of people. Their faces regained individuality as they moved, restless now with the tour.

"Yes, I do." A middle-aged man with a fuzzy white beard stepped away from the group. "Why did you choose to paint your subject in this way?"

"How do you mean?"

"Using the technique you did."

I looked back at the portrait, at Lee in his jeans and sweater, his ungainly form eased by the soft brushstrokes of the Impressionist school, the whole portrait done in blues and greens and yellows.

From the center of the painting, his eyes, their blue deeper than any of the other blues, looked at me, visibly accusing, "How could you put me on display?"

The man shoved his hands into his trench coat pockets, flapping the sides of the coat as he waited for my answer.

"I wanted to show his . . ." I stopped then. "I painted this picture using the Impressionist school to"—what was I trying to say?—"my intent was to create something evocative of the quiet morning at home."

"No, no. Why did you distort the face?"

"I didn't."

.   .   .

After polite reexamination of my pieces, they all drifted away. A few stopped to offer comments, but I could hear nothing except the sound of blood rushing in my ears.

Chapter

23

THE MUSEUM CLEARED OUT RAPIDLY, THE ARTISTS GATH-
ering their friends and families, air-kissing one another in
brief hugs. "See you next week," we all said as each made
his or her way back to their lives. Joel stopped me as I
came back from the ladies' room. "Can we have dinner
next Saturday?"

I studied the parquet floor beneath my feet and
shrugged. "We'll see."

"Just dinner, Alix, no strings. We'll complain about un-
appreciative galleries." He pecked my cheek and was gone.

One by one the rooms were closed. I could hear the
loud voices of the cleaning people, startling after the
muted atmosphere of the open museum. I took the guard's
chair by the gallery archway, setting it in front of my
work. I sat down and straightened my wool skirt over my
lap. Clearing my mind, I tried to look at my paintings with
new eyes. I had been so cavalier about my memorial to my
father, though he might not have felt so. I had treated his
death as a subject, not associated with me at all. Still, the
quartet was my homage to him, as much as the portrait of
my mother had been.

The lights were turned down in the next room. I would
need to leave in a moment.

I made myself look at Lee's portrait. Not accusing me
now, his eyes had sweetened. A rush of the deepest loneli-

168

ness washed over me. Joel's kind flirting had opened up a wound I had never let heal. I looked again at the portrait and wondered for the thousandth time, when would I give up and get on with my life? What I needed was a simple human touch and I'd rejected it, clinging to a lost dream.

. . .

I heard someone behind me and I stood to leave.

"Alix?"

Lee came out of the shadows and stepped into the harsh yellow spotlight of the track lighting. Every craggy element of his face was illuminated. He came toward me, his hands raised slightly from his sides.

"Lee, you came." My hand covered my mouth. My first impulse was to run to him, but I hung back, afraid.

We stood apart, both of us terrified.

"Lee, you came." I was so afraid that any unrehearsed words would send him away that I could only repeat those words. The reality of him, after so long, struck me into numbness, yet for the first time his face did not come as a shock, no fresh surprise at the depth of his outer ugliness. Instead I saw in his eyes the unspoken, clear telegraph of human need.

"Alix, I've been a fool. . . ."

"Oh, I've missed you so." I moved toward him.

"Alix, stop—look at me." He held up one hand. "If you think you can still love me despite everything, despite my stubbornness, despite what I am, then can you give me a second chance?"

There was less than three yards of hardwood floor between us. I looked at his shadow stretching across it toward me. Months had gone by since I'd last seen him, months of regret and ache and longing for him. Months when he hadn't answered my messages. Those three yards were either chasm or bridge. I raised my eyes and looked at him. "I spent weeks studying your face, your posture, your hands. I listened to you and you listened to me. We shared the hardest days of my life and you supported me. We found those lost boys together. If I don't know how I feel about you after all that, then I know nothing. If I don't love you now, then I'm an empty soul incapable of loving anyone."

He could say nothing else as I came across the slick hardwood floor and into his arms. He folded them around me and held me so close I could hear his heartbeat beneath his soft wool overcoat. "Oh, Lee Crompton, I was so afraid I'd never see you again."

As we clung together under the yellow spotlight, I breathed in his familiar soapy scent and listened to his story. "The day you left I was crazy to go, to jump in my car and follow you. I never doubted you thought you loved me, but I was convinced that you couldn't possibly have really fallen in love with me. I told myself it wasn't fair to encourage you, and perhaps it still isn't. Love is a physical thing. To imagine your smooth face touching mine . . ."

He touched my face now as he spoke. "I've cried twice in my adult life. Once, when I was told the damage done by discontinuing the treatments was irreversible and would only get worse. The second time was the day I let you go."

"Why didn't you call me? Why didn't you answer my messages?"

"I didn't know about your calls. At least not until recently. Mrs. Greaves never relayed your messages to me."

"I wondered if she was capable of that." I remembered her bitter words to me when I'd called the last time.

"She caved in when she saw the card from the museum."

Only one question lingered in the back of my mind, and

I decided that I had to ask it or suffer the doubts. "Why didn't you ever call?"

"I was afraid to, afraid that I was right and afraid that you would tell me you realized you were wrong, that you didn't love me. I fully expected you to give me that 'let's be friends' line and I couldn't face that. I had fallen in love with you."

"But now you're here. Now you know that I have never stopped loving you."

. . .

Behind us, one by one, the room lights went off until we were standing beneath the last bank of recessed light. Lee pulled away and stroked my hair. "Let's take a look at your work."

I flushed. "Lee, I hung your portrait."

"I know. It's time I saw it." He took my hand and stepped closer to the wall. He studied the series of my father first, nodding and squeezing my hand. "It couldn't have been easy to do, but this is a wonderful monument to Alexander. I'm certain he'd like it."

All my doubts fled in the face of his understanding. He'd known my father only at the end, yet knew him enough to ameliorate the nagging little guilt I'd felt on and off—and knew me well enough to know that I had felt that way.

As he moved in front of his own image, I felt his hand tighten over mine. I was dry-mouthed, afraid then that he would disappear again, afraid he would see my work as mockery.

For a long time he studied the portrait, his usually mobile face rock still. He released my hand and his own went to his chin, touching it as if to bring what he saw into his own sense of self, a face he hadn't seen but only touched for years.

I tormented myself in fifteen seconds with a lifetime of reproach. I loved him and had painted a portrait of the man I loved, but could he see that? What had possessed me to bring this so very private portrait to such a public forum? Because it was a good painting. Everything I knew about painting from life had jelled in this portrait. Light, color, animation, depth of feeling. I had painted it in a state of growing love and the result was art.

Still looking at the portrait, he slowly lowered his hand and reached out for me. "I'm worse than a fool, Alix. I could have kept us both out of such unhappiness if I'd just looked at this portrait when you tried to show it to me."

"You just needed to trust me."

"I do, Alix. I just needed to trust myself."

I had nothing else to say, so put my arms around his middle and hugged him, shaking with the joy of his being there with me. "I love you, Lee. I have for a long time."

He rested his chin on my head, rocking me back and forth gently, then he whispered, "Alix, I won't keep you secluded with me like some fairy tale princess."

"It doesn't matter to me. I love just being with you."

"But it does matter to me. You see, I've only just made the intellectual leap that it's my problem that has kept me locked up for ten years, no one else's." He shifted away from me, holding me at arm's length and bending a little to hold my eyes. "Help me, Alix. Your love will bring me back to the land of the living."

"You've taken the first step, Lee. You're here."

"Actually, I took the first step this morning. I did something I haven't done in ten years." As he held me close again he told me of how he'd stood in front of the mirror in the guest bathroom, staring into the sink for ten minutes before he could bring himself to look up, and when he did he saw the face of a stranger. The forgotten crags and depressions were blended with new etchings around his eyes, deeper furrows as he drew his bushy eyebrows down into a frown. Testing to see if this face was his own, Lee raised his brow and smiled. The monster in the mirror smiled back. "So this is the face she loved. Amazing. Ugly, yes, but maybe not repulsive."

.   .   .

The guard came in, dimming the last light so that the room was the color of shadow. We walked out together, his huge hand easily covering mine. As we passed beneath the last undimmed light we looked at each other. If anyone as ugly as Lee Crompton could be transformed into beauty, it had happened before my eyes.

FROM THE FIRST WE KNEW THAT MARRIAGE WAS WHAT we most wanted. It seemed as though every moment in between was a lost opportunity to be joined together. I think that there was an element of the Puritan ethic in our anxiety. We wanted this so much we were both afraid it would disappear.

Not for me the outward trappings of a wedding, the gown and the veil, bridesmaids all in a row. By the very foundation on which our love was built, I knew that such a wedding would be a mockery. Lee protested that he'd do anything I wanted, invite the town if I chose, but I shook my head and said no. What I wanted was him, and if we hadn't needed witnesses by law, I would have forgone any ceremony whatever. Except that I wanted Robin to come, and Mrs. Greaves would be there, of course, and his mother.

Mrs. Greaves had been a reluctant convert to our cause. I hadn't quite forgiven her for intimating that my only interest in Lee was monetary; early on his explanation for his hesitation in answering this charge was his complete disbelief in its being launched. "I can't believe for a moment that she really meant it. I think she was grasping at straws, trying to protect her adopted chick."

"Well, I didn't believe it, either, until you didn't deny it."

"Alix, I was a man in torment. I wasn't responsible for

my actions." He drew me close and rested his head on mine, easing away the last of this painful memory. "Go yell at her," he said, and pushed me toward the swinging door between the dining room and the kitchen.

In the end we both wept, Mrs. Greaves and I, hugging each other close and swearing an end to animosities.

"I've never seen him so happy," she said, twisting her dishcloth into a band. "You've been good for him and I was a meddling fool to misjudge you."

It was almost too easy, but I think she wanted to believe the best of me now that I was a permanent resident in the house at Riseborough. I put aside my anger then, knowing that in her way she loved him as much as I, and wouldn't I have been as fiercely protective of him?

. . .

March carried too many bad memories for me, so we waited impatiently for April to be married. Father Vaughn officiated; Robin came to stand up for me. Dr. Fielding acted as best man and second witness. We had spent the last month teaching Bad-dog how to be ring bearer and were amazed at how well he carried it off, proudly sitting beside Lee's mother until called, then quietly waiting as Lee slipped the ring off his collar.

Julia Crompton looked barely older than the portrait my grandfather had painted of her so long ago. Tall and elegant, her mostly brown hair swept up in a flattering twist, she epitomized the Boston society maven. Close to seventy-five, she still moved like a young woman, a graceful roll to her walk as if the books were still balanced on her head. Except for astounding blue eyes, she and Lee did not resemble each other in any way.

She had greeted me with reserve, but then, I expected nothing less. When I touched her cheek with my lips in an overexuberant expression of greeting, I could feel her shock. Lee said afterward it had been a long time since anyone had touched Julia Crompton.

.   .   .

With my truce with Mrs. Greaves and Lee's reunion with his mother, some closure with what was past had been made. What lay ahead of us was all fresh and pure, a new canvas upon which to paint brightness and abstract representations of life; shapes and colors that stood for our incredible passion for each other. As Lee slid that thin gold band on my left hand, I felt joined to him beyond the merely symbolic, I felt as though nothing could ever come between us. Words, his métier, were unnecessary, and even if we never spoke another word to each other, we would each still understand the other's deepest needs. We needed only touch.

.   .   .

But even when there is perfect love between people it seems as though barriers eventually begin to erect themselves. It is almost as if life cannot exist without challenge. Do we really thrive on facing challenges, making decisions that affect our very souls? Lee and I knew each other well. We knew that, come what may, we intended to live forever in each other's company. We were both too old to view such love as our right; too experienced to know that love is easy. Although, sometimes, we'd relive the exact moment we each first knew that our friendship was deeper than most, we both knew that actually making this love affair happen was a near miss. Often Lee would simply touch me, a hand on my neck, a touch against my shoulder, as if to confirm that I was really there. I would lean against him, snuggle my head into his shoulder and breathe in his scent. I felt a physical attraction to him I cannot explain. "I'll never tell you you're handsome, but you have a certain *je ne sais quoi* I find powerfully attractive," I told him time and again. He'd laugh and shake his great head. "Only an artist of the modern school could say something like that."

But the inevitable barriers began to grow. Not barriers to one another, but barriers to our private selves. Lee found himself unable to write. At first he denied it. Pretended that he was between books, then he began to pretend to write. Finally, after I took a call from his publisher asking where the next overdue Tyler Bent book was, I realized that my Harris Bellefleur was blocked.

"Look, I just write for fun. If if becomes a job, then I can't do it."

"When was the last time you wrote?"

"Yesterday."

"And?"

"Unadulterated crap. Alix, I can't make two words tie together that don't sound like sophomoric slop. I'm too damned happy!"

"No excuse."

That was how our discussion of his Block, capital B, began. Then he began to get annoyed at me for reminding him. Finally, to keep peace, I stopped asking and watched as he took Bad-dog out for his millionth walk.

What made it all difficult was that I was in a major artistic wave. I couldn't stop creating. All the happiness that prevented my husband from writing incited me to paint. I had canvases scattered all over the solarium, which I had unabashedly converted to my studio.

"Temporarily, until we can get the garage space done over," I promised. But the wonderful glassed-in space was so perfect, and reminded me so much of the happy hours we had spent there during the winter I first knew Lee, that I never pestered about hiring the workmen to do the job. Winter melted away and spring was triumphant and summer began with such promise.

And then my own barrier to perfect happiness began to erect itself. I wanted to get pregnant.

I should have known that my reluctance to settle down and have children at a reasonable age was simply due to not having the right man. And now I had the right man and he was terrified of having children.

· · ·

"Alix, please, I've told you from the beginning that I would never have children, that I intend to be the end of the line for this anomaly." His voice was still gentle, but the tension of the argument showed in his cheeks.

"I know, Lee, but there is no need for any child to suffer the deformity you have. If, and you know that there is only a slim chance a child of ours would actually carry the defect, if he did, then surgery or radiation would be a cure."

"You would subject a child to that?"

"Lee, by the time a child would show symptoms, he would be in adolescence."

"Great. Do you know what being an adolescent boy with a growth problem is like? Can you put yourself in that child's place when suddenly his body begins to distort itself and makes him feel like an old man?"

"But it would never get to that point. We'd know if that child actually had the defect immediately, even before he was born, so we could prepare for that time."

"Oh, Alix. Do you think that, even if we could conceive a child, that I would allow any fetus to develop that carried this miserable gene?" Now his voice was raised, and I couldn't believe what I was hearing.

I went back to my canvas, and he went back to his study to pretend to write.

· · ·

At first it wasn't that important to me to pursue the argument. The urge to have a baby came and went, inspired by various events, getting a friend's new baby pictures in the mail or a christening at church. But as the time rolled by and I faced first my thirty-seventh birthday, and then my thirty-eighth, I became obsessed.

Obsession, for good or ill, is unreasoning. I had been obsessed by Lee, and now I was clearly obsessed by this desire to have his child. The fact that he wouldn't even discuss it gave it an almost mystical quality. There was a female mystery out there, which I was being prevented from experiencing. Forget that my husband was a genetic anomaly whose entire adulthood had been warped by his disease. I wanted a baby. It became irrelevant to me that Lee was part of this decision. I understood why a woman would choose to be a single parent. I felt great sisterhood with those women who could not conceive. I could not conceive, either. I wish that I could have answered the simple question, What chance was there that our child would carry the gene? Our public library was connected with the Boston Public Library through computer communications and I scoured the indices for the literature. I should have insisted we get genetic counseling, but I developed an unreasoning fear that the counselors would say no.

I was torn between just allowing it to happen and the fear that Lee would indeed carry out his threat that he would never let me carry a defective fetus. Of course, I knew that such a decision was mine, but how could I make him so unhappy as to knowingly bring into this world a child with his defect? I loved him too much to make this horrific possibility real. As strong as our love was, to put this between us would damage our union beyond imagining.

I SUBVERTED MY LONGING FOR A CHILD INTO A FRENZY OF work. Avoiding the urge to express my hormonal angst into soft round shapes and gravid imagery, I stroked hard angular shapes on the canvas. Dark colors crept in; blue and black and maroon dominated the field. Heaping gouache into tremulous piles, I etched triangles and lines through them, grazing to the color beneath, revealing latent impulses. Concentric circles shadowed in yellow thrust out from triangulated corners.

The work exhausted me. I was too tired to make love. I think that I could have eventually given up my obsession. Except that I became pregnant.

· · ·

Against all odds and proving to a skeptical world that it does sometimes only take once, I got pregnant when we made love one time without protection. Caught up in a moment of passion sparked by a wine-induced wrestling match on the hearth rug, things had gotten pretty far along when Lee brought himself up short.

"I think it's safe," I whispered, unwilling to let the exquisite moment dissipate with change of venue and that unromantic insertion of diaphragm. So, like those millions of parents practicing the rhythm method, we got caught.

· · ·

In the last year of my fourth decade, I was already a little sketchy with periods, so it was several weeks before I made the intellectual leap that our little match on the hearth rug was bearing fruit. Oh, but how to tell Lee what we'd done? I lay awake at night and rehearsed what I would say. Surely he wouldn't be angry. Lee was slow to anger, but neither would he laugh. As I lay with my hand against my still flat belly, imagining what it would soon be like, I knew that the most difficult discussions of our life would be taking place. In my worst imaginings, I wondered if it would drive a stake through our love. I delayed telling him, putting off the anticipated debate from weakness.

· · ·

I etched a tiny bit more of the midnight blue away from the undercoat of yellow in the curling circle flaring away from the triangle. Wiping the flakes from the X-Acto knife on my flannel shirt, I stood back to examine the work for any sign of improvement.

"Looks like something vaguely familiar." Lee came up behind me and pulled me against his chest. "I know, it looks like . . ." He started to chuckle, then stopped. "Alix, it looks like a uterus and fallopian tubes."

"Stop! It does not. That's not it at all," I countered. Lee held me closer; his arms crossed over my chest, he began to rock me slightly. I looked at the painting again and could see that he was right. What I had thought of as perhaps an homage to Picasso's bull was indeed a pretty neat rendering of a woman's reproductive organs. "Damn, it was supposed to be a bull, a masculine image."

"It's very feminine." His hands gently touched my breasts, which were already sensitive. Equally as gentle, he slid his hands to my waist, then to my abdomen. "As feminine as you are."

I turned to face him. He took my face in his gnarly hands and kissed me sweetly on the lips. "Alix, are you pregnant?"

My first reaction was a smile, then I bit it back, lowering my face as I answered, "Yes."

He let go of me then and walked toward the painting. He spent a moment looking at it, gathering his response to me very carefully. He knew that however he reacted to this unwanted news would set the stage for every other discussion of it. I could read in the set of his shoulders the difficulty of it for him. I wanted to make it easier for him, I wanted to blurt out that it wasn't my fault, that I didn't do it deliberately. But he needed to believe that of me before I said it.

BEAST

I DID BELIEVE IT OF HER. I KNEW THAT ALIX WOULD NEVER
defy me in something so important. Oh, defy is such an
authoritative word. I could never be that with her. She
meant the world to me. She was my world.

. . .

I knew that she wanted a child because she loved me and
her world was built on the normal outgrowth of that kind
of love. Her parents were in love and had her; her friends
loved their spouses and had children. Truthfully, the moment I realized that she was pregnant, that the subtle
fullness to her breasts wasn't her usual premenstrual swelling, that the infinitesimal widening of her waist was of
profound importance, I was speechless with joy. For thirty
seconds I felt the incredible rush of male pride that I had
achieved the basic human raison d'être. In the next thirty
seconds I remembered what I was, and that this being, this
collection of cells, could very likely be as frightening to
the world as I am.

I faced my wife and saw that I could utterly destroy her
joy in this achievement with a careless word. I could not
take away her happiness any more than I could have killed
her. I don't remember stepping toward her, I only remember our coming together, clinging to each other and whispering, "It will be all right. It will be all right."

. . .

Ours would be a February baby. It seemed right that our child would be born in winter. It seemed as though all significant events in our life together had been landscaped in snow.

Alix struggled to zip up her parka. There was something charming about her roly-poly struggle, and I offered to help to no avail.

"I can't believe it! I need to wear your other jacket."

I helped her into my massive down parka.

"Now I look like the Abominable Snowman," she lamented.

"Never abominable, always charming, sort of like Frosty." I patted the object of her frustration, now hidden beneath my coat.

Every day we went out and walked, ignoring the heat of summer and the cold of winter. Determined to remain fit during pregnancy, Alix was militant about this daily exercise. Even so, as she grew she began to slow down, until I was the faster walker. Now in the last of the second trimester, she was often out of breath and flushed from even a little exertion. We had worried about her blood pressure throughout the pregnancy. Clearly the doctor's warnings of complete bed rest were soon to be heeded.

So many changes come to a pair when they are expecting. None of my experience with this is new to anyone, but the exacting focus on the unborn amazed me. I would find Alix sitting rock still, listening to some internal thump or pluck, absolutely entranced, a drying paintbrush in one hand, the other seeking out the elusive movement.

In the first trimester we needed to come to terms with what might be there. As an "elderly primipara," our obstetrician's less than complimentary official description of Alix at age thirty-nine, the amniocentesis was part of the deal. Even if we had no genetic cause for concern, he would have advised it. But it wasn't mandatory to know all the results.

. . .

Riseborough is a tiny place. Boasting only the most rudimentary of institutions, elementary school, church, pizza joint, and library, it was miles from the nearest hospital and thus only attracted a pair of family practitioners to take care of most medical needs. They referred to downstate groups for specialization, and in the last two decades, had made a thriving business in knowing where to send patients with more than the treatable illnesses or well-care they kept to themselves. Dr. Trenton wouldn't begin to consider taking Alix on. Even if she had been a second- or third-time mother at her age, her skyrocketing blood pressure was enough of a deterrent to him to immediately recommend a group in Nashua.

"You're a high-risk mom," he'd said, writing the name of the group practice on a prescription pad and sliding it toward her. "You've got to keep the blood pressure under control or you'll be in for significant trouble. This group will help you."

He must have read the disappointment in her face, as I did when she reprised how she felt when he said she'd have to commute for her monthly checkups. "I'll be there to take care of the baby afterward. That's really the fun part, anyway."

. . .

"I just hate the idea of being so far from home when I have the baby." Alix dabbed a bit of paint on the latest canvas.

I knew what she meant. There had been a slim chance I would venture to the hospital while she was there if I could slip in and out at night. But to commute to Nashua, realistically it meant spending time in that town. She knew me well enough to know that I could never do that.

"Alix, Dr. Trenton is concerned about you. That's the important thing. Have you always had high blood pressure?"

"No, never. It's so strange. He told me some women just have this problem. Usually it comes with swollen ankles." She glanced down at her bare feet, ankles as slim as ever. This was still early on, and to the casual eye there was nothing different about her. "Will you still love me when I look like a cream puff?"

"Alix, please look at who you're talking to." I hugged her to me and then broached the question she had cleverly obfuscated with the talk about blood pressure. "What about the amnio? When do you have it done?"

I knew well enough that it had to be early, before sixteen weeks, so that if anomalies were detected the next awful question could be asked in time to be answered with a decision, rather than by default.

"They'll set it up for me when I have my first visit with the group in Nashua." She slipped away from me and went back to her painting.

. . .

I tried to write. Tyler Bent was clearly in trouble and Harris Bellefleur couldn't drag him back from wherever it was he'd gone. It occurred to me to try to create a new character, that just maybe Tyler was tapped out. Empty of plot or focus, maybe I needed to try my hand at another genre. I could always come up with another nom de plume and leave Harris's name sacrosanct to the detective buffs. It was no good. Detective plot or no, nothing came to mind. I stared at the few sentences I'd pounded onto the screen and gave up. My concentration was gone. Only thoughts of the unborn child filled my head. I was so afraid of the amniocentesis I shook when I thought of it. I was so afraid of finding out I was right, and then what anguish lurked around the corner for Alix and me.

.   .   .

When her medical group in Nashua declared driving alone from Riseborough out of the question, we hit upon a solution that, in its simplicity, made it seem ridiculous we hadn't thought of it earlier. We would move to her father's house until the baby was born. The old farmhouse was a forty-minute drive to the hospital where the doctors had their offices. Each month we'd head down and spend the night there, often inviting Robin and her husband to dinner. Mrs. Greaves would send us with enough provisions so that we needn't stop for anything, thus maintaining the integrity of my reclusiveness. I know that I'd promised Alix I wouldn't keep her a prisoner, but I had failed miserably to release myself. Except for friends like Robin and her husband, my circle of face-to-face acquaintances hadn't enlarged much from my pre-Alix days.

As we walked slowly out on that early December afternoon, the murky sky threatening snow for only the second time that fall, we talked about when we should make the move.

"I want to be here for Christmas." Alix shoved her hands into the pockets of my parka.

"You wouldn't want to be back in your childhood home, hanging your stocking by your own chimney?"

She slapped at me playfully. "No. We have our own nascent traditions here now and, besides, this is where our baby will have his or her first Christmas. I want my pregnant Christmas pictures taken in this house."

His or her. Alix had refused to be told what sex this child was. And had neglected to request what further tests might be done to determine if our child carried my genetic defect.

I LOOK BACK NOW AND TREMBLE AT THE MISTAKES I
made. If only I had insisted, if only I had insisted that she
take another test. No, if only I had insisted that we go to
her father's house instead of letting her talk me into staying
in Riseborough until she completed just one painting
more. Or if I had insisted that she abort this fetus right at
the start. Would I have lost her as thoroughly as I have if
I had insisted on anything?

She didn't have further tests, and I was too cowardly to
fight about it. The threat of her rising blood pressure made
me hold my tongue, and instead I fell to believing that if
there was something wrong with the child, it would be
naturally aborted. When it evidently thrived, I threw my
emotional anchor out on the belief that God would never
send us anything we couldn't handle.

We did know that the child wasn't a Down's syndrome
child; Alix had apparently allowed that possibility more
importance than the potential for giving birth to an intelligent but deformed monster.

"Lee, if this baby were a Down's, I would still have it."

"At least we know we don't have that issue to contend
with."

"No, but I would feel exactly the same if I had allowed
genetic testing. And that's why I didn't. I would still have
this child, with or without your blessing. It's my body and

my child. It would kill me not to have your full support, but I wouldn't change a thing."

"Alix, we'll never know how we would have handled it. You've taken that chance from us."

"Lee, I don't mind you being angry at me. I deserve it, but I couldn't face arguing for the life of our child against you. You aren't rational about it."

Her face had taken on the rosy color that forecast her rising blood pressure and I stopped before I said something that might have physically hurt her. Instead I caved in and embraced her and felt her warm, relieved tears against my hand. How could I insist she be any other way?

I am tempted to relate every detail of our months of waiting. The watching and waiting and the soft details of expectancy. How her friends sent along tiny things that seemed doll-like to me, lost in my massive hands, hands I could not imagine holding the being in which would be so dressed; or how we each brought a new set of names to the dinner table each night to be added to a list pinned to the refrigerator door. Molly and Todd, Oliver and Margaret, Frick and Frack. We had silly names and sweet names. We agreed on the middle names, those of either her mother or father, but were reluctant to decide too quickly on the first name of our only child. I could tell how I would wake in the middle of the night in dread, the emotions of some evaporated dream still thick around my heart.

· · ·

I have taken too long to tell the end of our story. Alix would have told it herself, far more eloquently than I, the professional writer, can, but Alix is gone.

We had delayed over and over the move to her father's house. Even when her prenatal visits became more frequent, we managed to have reasons to return to Riseborough after a day or two at the house. She never said it, but I think that she never quite reconciled herself to her father's absence from that place. The empty house was crowded with memories and she had a hard time working there. During the last of her pregnancy she had managed to work at home propped in bed. She was still working on a soft milky abstract with dashes of primary colors scattered throughout, her present to the unborn child.

"Dr. Fitch says I have to move down this week. I'm already two centimeters dilated, which means things are hopping."

I felt an internal twanging at finally hearing those highly anticipated words. "Why don't we just stay here now? I'll run down and bring back everything we need tomorrow."

When I was ready to leave, Alix climbed into the car. "No arguments. You know you'll never be able to find everything I need, and I'm mean enough to send you back. This way you'll only have to make one trip."

"But what if you go into labor?"

"It could be a week to two weeks. Being a little dilated doesn't mean delivery is imminent."

I had to believe her, because she'd been through the birthing classes. Mercifully she hadn't insisted I go.

"Besides, I have about ten minutes' worth of work left on the landscape and we can hang it before the baby arrives."

On the way back to Riseborough she'd been quiet, listening to the internal quarks that spoke to her. Suddenly she reached out and took my hand. "When you look into the face of your child you'll know pure love, love that will come to you without prejudice. We learned to love one another as all couples do, but this child will love you simply for being its father. Not because of, or in spite of, what you look like."

When we arrived home it was dark and a heavy cloud cover had descended over the tops of the mountains. Walking from the garage to the back door, I looked up and a first inkling of fear hit me. I should have insisted she stay behind.

. . .

In my mind the force of the storm that blew up that night and the sudden cruelty of Alix's labor are inextricably linked. Almost as soon as the first cries of the wind through the surrounding pine trees awakened me, Alix's first pains began.

It was the worst kind of storm—icy rain pelted by fierce winds, glazing everything it touched. The trees bent under the weight, soldiers fallen into postures of obeisance. I called for help. The dispatcher took all my information and called the emergency medical technicians while I was still on the phone. Somehow I was connected with one of them and I began to give them all Alix's history. I pressed them to hurry—already her blood pressure was rising with each contraction.

Alix was trembling with mixed excitement and fear. She tried to calm me by sending me to find all the lamps and candles against the inevitable moment of blackout. All my wires were underground, but the main lines were vulnerable half a mile away. It was midnight. Surrounded by our lamps and candles, we waited for help, our hands clasped together, our eyes on the Seth Thomas clock. Twenty minutes passed and another contraction began. Another twenty minutes, and another.

Suddenly the lights faded, surged, and then went out. It had been so expected, and yet we reacted with the laughter of surprise. Even before I could light a candle another contraction started and Alix grabbed my hand. "Just get me through this," she said, and buried her nails into the flesh of my thumb. When I got the lamp lit I looked into her face and read the pain there. The contraction had subsided, but her face was contorted with another kind of pain. In a panic I ran to the sleet-covered window and pressed my face against it to see if I could see the red flashing lights of the ambulance. The candle in my hand only gave me back my face in the window.

. . .

Eventually I heard a banging on the front door heralding the on-foot arrival of a pair of EMTs. Loaded down with tool boxes of equipment, they charged up the stairs and into the bedroom where Alix struggled. "Dad, you stand over there," one of them commanded, and I was so taken aback at the order that I went where directed. Eerie shadows played against the white wall above the headboard, elongated bobbing shapes mimicking the fierce activity on the bed.

"Oh, shit, lady, don't do this to me!"

"What's wrong?" I lunged toward the dark shapes. "Alix!"

In the movies they make the father leave the room when these things happen. But these two let me stay, kindly letting me hold the body of my wife while they freed the child from her treacherous womb. It was truly the first time I had ever forgotten myself and did not worry about what anyone thought of me.

I WANTED DESPERATELY TO KEEP IT A HAPPY ENDING. I really wanted the fairy tale to persist. But life mimics art poorly. There is never anything purely one way or another about it. The joy I felt in being loved, in being married, was tainted by my own fears; what was tragedy is ameliorated by the happiness I have found in fatherhood.

For nearly a month after her birth, I kept my daughter away from me. She had cost me my wife, the only person I ever expected to love me. I was like those old tales of aloof fathers and stranger children. She lived in the nursery, her nice little nanny there to be mother and father to her. Mrs. Greaves was barely speaking to me, torn between her genuine grief for Alix and her outright anger at me for being so cold.

Then I found the landscape that Alix had finished that evening before the storm. It had been her gift to this child, whom she had loved from her first moment of conception. The child she had loved so much she refused to know whether or not she would carry my defect; the child whose existence she defended against me; the child she had left me to care for. I picked up the canvas and went to the nursery. The nanny was in her sitting room and did not stir as I pushed open the door to the baby's room.

Alix was quite right when she told me that this child would love me for simply being her father. What I did not expect was the extreme power of my love for her. If she hadn't stirred at the very moment I crept into the darkened room, a tiny fist waving in the air like a miniature protest against injustices yet to be experienced, I might have crept right back out and not had that moment of epiphany. But that little shell-like fist waved at me and demanded that I at least see this interloper.

Helpless against the urge, I bent and lifted this bundle out of her cradle and held her away from me so that I could see for myself she was beautiful. I was not done with grieving, but the tears that ran that day were mixed bitter and sweet. My daughter looked at me with Alix's eyes and did not flinch.

Whatever may become of her, whether she grows into a lovely woman or suffers my fate, Alexandra Miller Crompton will always have one who loves her.

Epilogue

I CANNOT SAY THAT MY STORY IS AT AN END. THERE IS too much living in raising a child to ever think that. But Harris Bellefleur is part of a past that I now put to rest. Once I hid behind his name, my reclusiveness protected by Harris's fictional persona.

In telling our story I have broken the spell of my writer's block. In laboring to write as Harris Bellefleur, I stifled the exuberant happiness I had enjoyed, however briefly. Even as I began to tell her story, I knew that in some way Alix had taken Harris with her. When we first met I'd told her that Tyler Bent was a man doomed to be alone. After Alix died, I recalled that prediction and applied it to myself. But when I held my daughter in my arms I knew that I was wrong. I knew that Leland Crompton would never be alone again.

The Beast in the tale was released from the spell because he convinced Beauty he was worth loving. With that same magic Alix released me to be who I really am; she convinced me that I was worth being loved.

LELAND CROMPTON
RISEBOROUGH, N.H.
1995

HORSES
DON'T LIE

◆

WHAT HORSES TEACH US ABOUT
OUR NATURAL CAPACITY FOR
AWARENESS, CONFIDENCE,
COURAGE, AND TRUST

PQW766270

CHRIS IRWIN
with BOB WEBER

HORSES
DON'T LIE

HORSES
DON'T LIE

WHAT HORSES TEACH US
ABOUT OUR NATURAL CAPACITY
FOR AWARENESS, CONFIDENCE,
COURAGE, AND TRUST

CHRIS IRWIN
with BOB WEBER

MARLOWE & COMPANY
NEW YORK

LIBRARY OF CONGRESS CATALOGING-IN-PUBLICATION DATA

Irwin, Chris
Horses don't lie : what horses teach us about our
naural capacity for awareness, confidence, courage,
and trust / by Chris Irwin with Bob Weber
p. cm
ISBN 1-56924-581-9
1. Horses–Behavior 2. Horses–Training. 3. Human-
animal communication. I. Weber, Bob. II. Title.

SF281 .I79 2001
636.1'001'9–dc21
2001030056

9   8   7   6   5   4

Designed by Pauline Neuwirth, Neuwirth & Associates, Inc.

Printed in the United States of America
Distributed by Publishers Group West

For Anita
Thanks for the dance
of faith and fury
thanks for the silliness
thanks for pushing me
thanks

CONTENTS

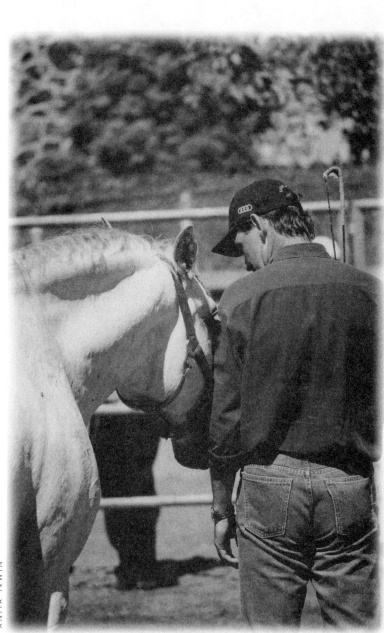

ANITA IRWIN

CHRIS BONDING WITH A STALLION

PREFACE

AGIC. THAT'S WHAT WE'VE ALWAYS THOUGHT IT would take to talk with the animals. And from ancient legends, to fairy tales, right up until Dr. Doolittle, it's one of our oldest and deepest dreams. But today, there is a new generation of men and women who have found, with horses, the reality within this time-burnished myth. They are able to get right inside the horse's head, speak to it, and command it.

Maybe you've seen one of them demonstrate it. Most commonly, these so-called horse whisperers or non-resistance trainers will walk into a round pen with any number of horses he or she has never seen before. With a few gestures and steps, the trainer has the horses pounding around the pen and within half an hour or so, the animals are following the trainer around like puppy dogs with hooves. Often, the ones that come in bucking and rearing and snorting transform the quickest. And sometimes the trainer even gets up on one of the horses and rides it around bareback. Invariably, the audience is impressed—and a little awed, too.

There's no doubt it is impressive. It's a world away from the muscles and hobbles and ropes that most of the audience is used to associating with horse training. Here, there's no force, no coercion. There's just a trainer walking around the middle of the pen, focused like a laser beam on every twitch of the horse's tail or toss of its head. Now and then he steps toward the horse or backs away from it or flicks a whip or a rope toward its butt. And then—suddenly, gently—there's that horse, enchanted, following the trainer around, muzzle just over his shoulder like his shirt pocket's full of sugar. Sure, it seems like magic.

Well, it is and it isn't. To the horse, there's no magic here. In fact, it's only because what the trainer has been able to accomplish is logical, not magical, that it works at all. But the logic we're talking about here is horse logic, not people logic. And when people start to learn from and think like horses, magic happens.

You see, horses don't lie. They don't separate how they feel and how they act. The expression "What you see is what you get" could have been coined for them. Whether they're feeling scared, confused, submissive, bold, or just relaxed and confident—and believe it, horses feel all those emotions and more—they tell you exactly where they're at and what they want from you and mean it down to the bone.

Every moment you're with them, they're taking your measure with the accuracy of a creature whose very survival depends on precise readings of its environment. You can't fake it with horses. You'll just confuse them and frustrate yourself if you try. To achieve the results I've just described, you must open your mind and allow your horse to show you how to communicate with the same depth and transparency it has. And that's when the magic starts.

It's magic because what horses need to hear from us is what many of us would like to hear from ourselves. They want us to have a calm, focused assurance. They want us to be consistent. They want us to be both

PREFACE

3

strong and compassionate. In short, horses need us to be our best selves. And by being so sensitive to our self-doubt and fear, they help us find where we keep all our inner betrayals so we can root them out.

So the hard part of horse training isn't really about the horse at all. It's all about knowing who *you* are, while learning about who the horse is, and figuring out who you need to be to bring the two together in mutual respect and trust. To teach your horse to stop resisting and be calm, responsive, trusting, and brave, you must first acquire those qualities yourself. You can't just appear to be confident and in control. You must let go of your masks and conflicts and fears and simply *be* confident and in control. Nor can you apply rules you read in a book—even this book. You have to find the parts of yourself that will tell you at a level below conscious thought what you have to do and how you have to act. Everything we can teach a horse, we can teach ourselves. And you may discover that when a horse sees you as relaxed, balanced, and centered, so does everyone else. In and out of the horse arena.

This is the first magic. But not only can working with horses restore you to your deepest self and cultivate what's best in it, these wonderful animals can change your attitude to the world around you.

Horses have a fundamentally different world view from us. In many ways, how they see the world and relate to their fellow horses is the opposite of how we see our environment. Because of that, horses have worked out different ways to get along in the world and with other horses. I believe that we have a lot to learn from their answers. I believe that becoming more horse-like in our awareness of the world and how we achieve our place in it will make us more complete human beings who work and relate well with others, yet know how to stand our ground. What's more, in today's glob-alized, interconnected world, where we're all affected by the actions of everyone else, I believe that what we can learn from horses is becoming a necessary stage of human evolution. That's the big magic.

Think this is a little airy-fairy, a little touchy-feely for someone walking into a pen to face 1,000 pounds of horseflesh? It isn't. It's as real and down-to-earth as that stuff you muck out of the stalls—just as at the same time, it's as deeply moving as galloping free across the prairie. And as I said earlier, I'm not the first to point it out. Here's what Ray Hunt wrote in 1978: "You're not working on the horse, you're working on yourself." And here's Tom Dorrance, the father of us all: "Riders may want to get an answer to their questions right early–on the surface. I want them to try to *figure out* something; I want them to work at figuring out the whole horse–his mind, body, and spirit. Maybe they will figure out what they are missing."

Dorrance called that Holy Grail of horsemanship "true unity." Today's popular culture calls it "horse whispering." Actually, "horse listening" might be closer to the mark, but whatever. It goes back a lot farther than any current fads or fashions. The point is that if you're serious–I mean *serious*–about training your horse, or about using horses to help train yourself, you'd best realize that this is not just a stunt that is used to amaze audiences at a clinic. This can be powerful, life-changing stuff. In fact, that's the only way it works, because the horse is only half the equation. The other half is you. It's hard work. It takes a lot of time and it takes the humility and courage to change the way you think. But it gets results–magical results–for both horse and rider.

BEGINNINGS

COWBOYS CALL SKILL WITH HORSES BEING "HANDY," and for such a simple word there's gotten to be a lot of mystification around it. To hear some people, if you weren't born into a third-generation horse family, you haven't got a hope. And even if you were riding before you could walk, you must still sit at the feet of some saddle-savvy old buckaroo and soak up the Zen of horses like Luke Skywalker and Obi-wan Kenobi.

Well, I didn't. I grew up in St. Catharine's, Ontario, on the little land bridge between Lake Ontario and Lake Erie. We were surrounded by orchards, water, and industrial cities.

We were almost as far from the open plains and foothills of ranch country as anyone could get. My mom tells me that as a child I was always excited when Mr. Ed came on the television, but I don't remember that and it probably doesn't mean a thing. My sport, believe it or not, was competitive rowing. Mentors? I've learned from lots of people, but mostly I've put things together by watching, doing, and thinking. The point is that handiness is learned, not bestowed. And I can prove it, because that's how I got it.

Eventually, my family did move west from Ontario to Swift Current, Saskatchewan. Swift Current, in the southwest corner of the province, is ranch country and that's where I met my first horse. He belonged to a high school girlfriend of mine, and I used to love watching the two go riding around. Or maybe it was just the girl. Either way, horses were still no big deal to me. Interesting, yes. But I was much more excited about sports, girls, hanging out with my friends, and playing my guitar. And that's mostly what I did.

As we got older and left high school, some of my buddies packed up and headed out for jobs, mostly in the Alberta oilpatch. A lot of others went to university for four more years of classrooms on the way to becoming young professionals. Somehow, neither choice felt right for me. So, in 1978, I did what seemed to be the logical thing: I built a snug little winterized camper on the back of an old pickup truck and I headed off to the mountains. I spent that winter roaming ski resorts, soaking up the challenges and beauty of the mountains, and at the end of the season found myself in Whistler, British Columbia. Wondering what to do next, I crossed the border into Seattle. Then, out of curiosity and a vague feeling that I wanted to be around horses, I went over to Longacres racetrack and asked around for work.

I didn't know anything about horses. But I got a job, the same first job almost everyone in this industry gets—mucking stalls. I lived right with the horses, in a cleaned-out stall with a bunk in it. I fell asleep listening to their nickering and woke up with their smell in my nose. And cleaning those tight little box stalls housing big, high-strung thoroughbreds, you can bet I got my first lessons on being around them.

It was clear right away that horses had personalities and moods. Some became my friends and some stayed enemies until the day I left. Most interesting of all: They seemed more afraid of me than I was of them. One day, a horse told me something I didn't understand until years later: When I pressed in on him, he turned his head away from me, then swung his head back around and took a second look when I retreated. I'll return to this later because it's important if you want to understand horses.

Anyway, I learned I didn't mind the hard, dirty work of the horse world. Maybe I got that from rowing—few sports demand more in the way of perseverance, finesse, and just working your guts out than competitive rowing. But most of all, I discovered a love for horses—the sound of them eating, how neat it is to come across a horse that's sweet and friendly and willing to spend a little time with you. I caught on to things quickly, and the trainers noticed. Before long, I was walking horses to cool them off after exercise and grooming them after that. Then I got offered a job for a little while at a breeding farm as a trainer's assistant. It was there that I learned more about the care and feeding of horses, as well as necessary ranch management skills like how to build a proper fence.

When winter came, I loaded up my camper truck and went skiing again, and that's what it was like the first while. Eventually, it got so that I was missing the horses during the ski season. I starting looking for a job that would keep me around horses during the winter, and in

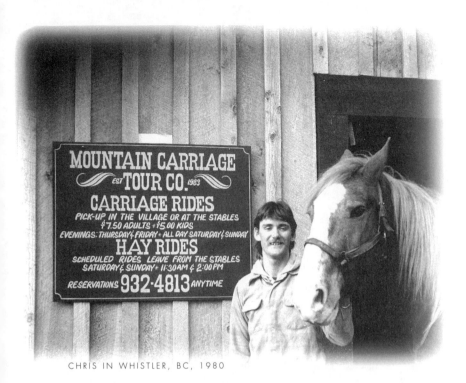

CHRIS IN WHISTLER, BC, 1980

1981, with a little luck and a lot of 20-year-old cockiness, I talked my way into a horse job. Back in Whistler, I convinced the owner of a team of draft horses who gave rides to tourists that I could handle and care for his animals. He taught me to harness them and I was off. There were some wrecks and there were some runaways, but for the most part it was a good winter. I was learning to drive and learning to ride and the bonus was that I still enjoyed plenty of memorable times on the ski slopes.

BEGINNINGS

13

The next winter, I went down to Lake Tahoe, Nevada, to visit Rick Devin, a great friend I had met while working and skiing at Sunshine Village in Banff, Alberta. Rick was a kindred spirit who was now working on the central ranch of a big outfit that ran a string of riding stables and dude ranches around Nevada and California. They had hundreds of horses, and I began helping out. Sure enough, I got offered a job. I didn't accept right away, but I did a few months later and that's when things really started to go.

Down at Lake Tahoe, it was 12 hours a day, room and board with $100 a week under the table, but I was apprenticing. I was feeding, grooming, saddling, bridling, and riding. I don't mind admitting back in those days it would get rough between me and the horses. What I knew about them amounted to how to hang on, when to stand my ground, and when to back off. One thing I did have was soft and steady hands. Maybe it came from playing the guitar, but I always had a gentle, accurate touch on the bit, just as some people can drop the needle on a record right into the groove and some people bounce it across the vinyl.

The main activity at this ranch was taking young, green horses and training them for riding. Although a lot of the guys at this ranch were pretty handy, they'd grown up under the old school and it was harsh on the horses. But there was a farrier there who taught me a lot. John Barnes couldn't read and couldn't write–he'd carve a notch into a stick each time he did a hoof so he'd know how much to charge at the end of the day– but he was really easy-going with the horses and he'd slip me a few choice words now and then.

"A horse has to go forward even to back up," was one John-ism. "When the horse does what you want it to do, then stop asking," was another. John was the first one to tell me to get out of the horse's face, to give the horse some breathing room–not just in the saddle but on the ground. He taught me that a horse shows disrespect by turning its butt toward you. I still use his lines in every clinic I give.

That fall, I had an awful accident that made a big difference in how I came to deal with horses. I was riding a lot, often at a full gallop over some pretty rough terrain. That's what I was doing one day, racing and laughing over my shoulder at Rick behind me, when my horse stumbled and we went down. I broke my leg in 13 places. I snapped three ribs and fractured my skull. The horse, a thoroughbred named Rocky, walked away with barely a scratch while I spent most of that fall in the hospital and the whole winter of 1982 recuperating. Rocky wasn't a bad horse—I just wasn't paying attention and allowed a preventable accident to happen. So when I got back to work that spring, I started watching horses a lot closer. I realized that there was real danger in this business. The result of my accident was that I was spooked enough to slow down so I could think twice about everything. I started wondering if it was possible to get a little more work done on the ground, to get the horse working with me safer and quieter before I got on. This was an important lesson.

I spent four years at that Lake Tahoe ranch, skiing in the winter and, in a basic way, training colts the rest of the time. I was literally living among the horses, out in my camper behind the corrals. I worked them all day and at night, I sat on the haystack and just watched them. The horses I'd been with at the track had all been kept in separate stalls, but here on the ranch they were all allowed to live together as a herd.

Sometimes, I'd go in to catch a horse that was in a big pen with a hundred other horses and if it didn't want to be caught, I would have to try to separate it from the others. When one horse gets going, they all get going and you end up in there in the middle of a cloud of dust and hooves playing games with the herd. I got so I could see actions and events coming before they happened. I started to notice the way the horses were interacting. I began to understand herd dynamics, and the natural pecking order of herd animals. At the end of those four years—as long as most people spend getting a university degree—I was getting pretty "handy." My approach to horses was still overly aggressive and forceful, but it was coming.

Then, skyrocketing insurance premiums during the mid-eighties eventually squeezed the profit out of trail riding and the ranch closed. I took some savings and struck out on my own, buying, training, and selling young horses. Soon I found myself falling in love with one of my first clients as a free lance trainer.

Robin was a sweetheart. She'd been around horses some, but not enough to safely handle the hot-blooded Quarter Horse-Arabian filly she had purchased. She was, however, an old hand with natural forces. Robin owned and operated a sailboat charter business on Lake Tahoe. While I was riding colts during the day, she was right across the street, taking tourists out for the sailing experience of a lifetime.

After work, we would get together. Sometimes she gave me sailing lessons but most of the time we worked with her young mare. It didn't take long before we were married and together with a mutual friend we opened a ranch retreat nestled deep in the Pinenut Mountains of Nevada. We accommodated only ten overnight guests at a time. The facilities were beautiful and the trail riding, in that setting, was awesome. My routine was to maintain the hot tub and the pool, take guests for rides, and buy, start, and sell colts.

Later, we expanded into a day program, busing up to 200 people at a time from the casinos for afternoon and evening excursions that included wagon rides, horseshoes and barbecues. Sometimes, I would even get up on stage and entertain the guests with a little guitar playing and singing.

The fun only lasted a couple of years. Neither Robin nor I really enjoyed catering to a steady stream of tourists. I was also beginning to feel homesick for Canada. I'd been gone for almost ten years. Even more depressing, I was beginning to realize that I wasn't as deep in love as I thought.

Also, our partner was far too busy and somewhat overwhelmed with other business commitments to really pull his weight at the ranch and soon nobody was happy. Fortunately for us, however, the ranch had become quite well known so it didn't take long to find a buyer. I went back to starting colts and Robin began exploring a new career in a local art gallery. Pretty soon, I was working 14-hour days, seven days a week, in an effort to avoid dealing with our fading love. It wasn't too much longer before Robin and I took advantage of Nevada's quick and relatively painless opportunity for divorce.

Needless to say, after that experience, I really began to obsess with my work. Down in that country, everybody had a round pen in their yard. They'd use it when they were taking a green horse for its first ride, so the horse couldn't run them into a corner. I had one too, and I began using it as a small space where I could work with a horse and hopefully settle down its anxieties before I got on for a first ride. At this point, I wasn't thinking about unity and communication between horse and human. All I wanted to do in those days was to keep working with the horse until he didn't want to keep running away, to try and apply what I'd learned on that first ranch.

I had started to develop a local reputation as someone

who could be trusted to start horses, to make them safe and reliable. One day, a saddle-maker from the area was watching me work a horse and asked me if I'd ever heard of a horseman named Ray Hunt. These days, Ray Hunt is one of the godfathers of our kind of work, but back then only the real cowboys knew about him. I certainly didn't. Hunt was giving a clinic in the area, and when I went to check it out, I realized that, sure enough, we were working along somewhat similar lines. At the end of the day, I was introduced to Hunt as the local boy who was handy with horses. Oh, I was so cocky. Hunt asked me if I learned anything, and I said: "Sure. I learned I should be giving clinics." To his credit, Hunt threw back his head and laughed and said, "Good for you!"

That's one of the things I like about this business—horse people are straightforward and don't mince their words, and they appreciate that quality in others. Maybe that rubs off from the horses. Just as important, I learned there were other people doing what I was doing, trying not to just beat up on horses but to bond with them. There was a fancy name for it, too: non-resistance training. I had just been calling it "horseplay."

Anyway, things were going well for me. A lot of people were bringing me horses to train. I saw old horses and young horses. I worked with horses for driving, riding, and dressage, with owners who rode Western or English style. Things were going well but they were about to get even better.

I was at a show one day when a young woman came up to me with a horse who had some behavior problems. Anita Zdancewicz was well-known locally as a competitive jumper and dressage rider and a professional instructor, but her horse wouldn't load into the trailer. I started working with her horse, and she started coming around to the stable and asking questions about what I was doing. Nobody had ever done this before. I was used to working alone and doing my work more or less on the level of instinct. Now, for the first time, I had to explain myself. Anita would ask me "What are you doing?" and "How did you know when to stop?" and "How did you see that coming?"

She knew a lot about classical riding—more than I did—but she was there every day for a week, watching me work her horse and by the end of that time I was giving an ongoing commentary: "Watch, he's getting ready to relax and stretch," or "Watch, I think he's getting ready to lick his lips now." After years of work and hundreds of horses, I knew intuitively what was going on, I knew how to talk and listen to horses, but now Anita was forcing me to reason through the actions and reactions and explain it, first to her and later to the other English-style riders she knew. For the first time, I was beginning to understand what I was doing. Smart gal, this Anita. I couldn't let her get away. We were married soon after.

That's more or less how I came to learn the basics of what people today call horse whispering. I had a lot more to learn about subtleties. I still do. But as for the horsemanship, *those* are the main sources—watching, listening to people, listening to horses, and putting things together through sometimes painful experience (I've had 33 broken bones along the way). I also took lessons from outside the horse world. My rowing days gave me the self-discipline for hard work and also developed the sense of balance, feel, and timing that any good rider needs. Playing guitar gave me soft hands. Skiing taught me to work with natural forces, not against them.

By the early 1990's, I began to understand that something was developing that was more important than simply being "handy" with horses. I'd had considerable success in the industry. I'd won 18 different American national championships with wild Mustangs, both riding and driving. A sweet little Morgan I'd trained was cleaning up in state and regional shows down in Nevada. Plus, I was getting a good reputation with everyone from draft horse people at the Calgary Stampede to the renowned dressage trainer Willy Arts. I knew I could continue as a successful trainer. But thanks to Anita, I was now interested in becoming a teacher as well.

Anyone who's ever taught knows it forces you to think harder about what you're teaching. That's what began happening to me. Standing in the middle of a round pen, horses whirling around me like a living and breathing, thundering sacred circle, I had a lot of time to reflect on what I was doing with the horses, what that meant, and what effect it was having on me.

Even back in St. Catharines, I'd always been a bit of a brooding, introspective kid. My life at home as a child hadn't been easy. My stepfather was an angry drinker who belittled and knocked me around quite a bit. Surrounded by lies and evasions and used to living with pain, I grew up full of questions about integrity, authenticity, and worth.

As a kid, in order to answer some of these questions, I first turned to the Boy Scouts. I loved the movement's

BEGINNINGS

rituals and traditions, its devotion to honor and doing your best. And on camp-outs, the Scouts introduced me to Nature. I became a leader in our local pack and I still have an old clip from the St. Catharines' newspaper of me at the head of my troop at a Remembrance Day ceremony (what Americans know as Veterans Day). All the other kids are distracted and goofing around, but I'm standing ramrod straight, seriously intent on the ceremony and its meaning.

CHRIS [left] STANDING RAMROD-STRAIGHT
IN FRONT OF HIS SCOUT TROOP

But my time with the Scouts ended badly when a local priest involved with the movement was found to be sexually abusing one of the younger boys. Finding out that the ritual I loved only hid lies and abuse, I left.

I next turned to sports. Rowing was *the* sport in St. Catharines and my longing for something meaningful drove me to do well at it. Very well, in fact—rowing for my hometown crew, we won the Royal Canadian Henley regatta, one of the sport's biggest and most prestigious events. But even this wasn't enough. Standing on the medal podium in front of thousands of cheering hometown spectators, I broke into tears. I had my gold medal and my 15 minutes of fame, but so what? An emptiness still remained.

The doubts continued when my family moved to Swift Current. Nobody was much help, either—they looked at me as if I were crazy when I asked too many questions, or told me to forget that stuff and just get a job. I read a lot. I became a Christian, even undergoing a born-again experience. However, I soon found that going to church wasn't the answer I was looking for. Although I was profoundly affected by the teachings of Christ I was still too young and idealistic to accept the painful hypocrisy that people inject into organized religion.

Those were tough days. Despite my music, despite my girlfriends, despite my buddies, despite the church, I felt beaten up and tired. As Jack Kerouac once said, I was at the bottom of my soul, looking up.

Finally, when I was about 19, I spent a couple of weeks in a monastery in Saskatchewan. Talking to those kind, wise men, I came to understand that my path would be to go off into Nature to look for a kind of healing and work my way into a better future.

That's what I was doing when I packed up my camper and headed off to the mountains. That's what I was doing when I first starting training horses. And that's what I'm still doing as I work my way along the path of life.

By the time I started to teach, I'd already noticed that my work with horses—these wonderful emissaries of the natural world—had introduced me to some qualities within myself that I was finally happy to meet. And eventually, I started thinking about how the things I was doing in the round pen related to what I was doing in life. That circle of thought started to spiral outside of myself. I started to make some comparisons, look around at what others have said and experienced, and I believe I started to get a hold on the real significance of what I was doing. Like my horses, my thoughts began to whirl.

But I'll get to that. It's time to talk about horses.

PREDATOR
AND PREY

*H*ORSES HAVE BEEN DOMESTICATED FOR THOUSANDS of years. It's thought that we first began purposefully breeding them and harnessing their strength as long as five thousand years ago on the grassy, open steppes of Central Asia. Only dogs have been with us as long, or served us as well.

We're used to seeing these animals together and when I travel around in horse country, there's rarely a ranch or horse stable that doesn't have a dog loping around somewhere. In fact, it's a question I often ask at my clinics—how many of you out there own dogs? Lots of hands go up.

But I don't see so many raised arms when I ask how many have hired a trainer for their dogs. Now, someone in the audience always says "I don't need to hire a trainer to teach my dog his job. He sleeps all day and mooches food like he was born to it." And sure, we tend to ask a lot less of our dogs than we do of our horses (I'm not even going to get into cats).

Still, few people have trouble training dogs to come when called, or stay when told, or not to chew the furniture. Even kids can train dogs to do fairly complex tasks. It just seems to be natural to a dog to focus its attention on its master, which of course is a requirement for training any animal.

So if horses have been with us as long as dogs, why are they so much harder to train? To understand this, we need to back up for a moment and look at the big picture. We have to look at some fundamental relationships in the natural world before we start discussing the specific relationship between humans and horses. And when we do look at the larger picture, a recurring pattern emerges.

Nature is full of relationships defined by two seeming opposites that are in reality constantly interacting.

ANITA, CHRIS'S WIFE, WITH HORSE SASSY AND DOGS NIKITA
AND BASHA.

The two need each other. One is defined in relation to
the other and the spark that animates them comes from
the tension and back-and-forth flow of their different
energies. Think of day and night, the positive and nega-
tive poles of a battery, think of male and female. Eastern
philosophers call this principle yin and yang, and consider it such a powerful concept—and so important to

keep in balance—that they use it to organize everything from their spiritual practices to their diet. Others call this pattern "duality," but I prefer to use the word "polarity." Horses are into polarity in a big way. They think in polarities. To a horse, you're either this or that, one or the other, in or out. "In-between" just creates stress for a horse and they don't understand "almost." So is there a polarity between horses and humans?

Yes. We are predators, they are prey. We, like our dogs, evolved to band together in packs so that it would be easier for us to kill. Horses evolved to band together in herds to protect each other from being killed. Like the ancient symbols of yin and yang, predators and prey both oppose each other and need each other to live and keep their numbers in balance.

This is why it's just wrong-headed to compare training a dog with training a horse. We think like dogs. We're both predators. What makes sense to us will naturally make sense to our dogs. But with a horse, all those bets are off. It's harder for us to understand a horse than it is for a man to understand a woman (or vice versa). To begin to open your mind to how a horse really thinks, forget about domestication and forget about all your familiar contexts of stables and barns and riding arenas.

Think of a horse as a deer. Think about putting a halter or a bridle or a saddle on a wild deer. Imagine walking into a corral and catching a deer and climbing on its back and getting it under control. That's what is really going on with a horse: a predator is not only trying to get a prey animal to trust it but is also attempting to control it. Long before we domesticated horses and tried to be their friends—or at least their benevolent jailers—we hunted them for food. The earliest representations of horses, on the walls of Iron Age caves in France and Italy, show them with our spears thrust into their rib cages. We may have forgotten this. Horses haven't.

Predators—which we humans remain despite centuries of agriculture—behave and think in certain ways. Our predatorial mind is fairly linear. We focus our attention on our prey and move directly towards it, concentrating on that goal and shutting out everything around us. We're hunters, after all. If we fail to focus on our prey, our hunt is likely to fail and our survival is put in jeopardy. So naturally, we've learned to focus well. This tendency to goal-oriented, A-to-B behavior is key to what I call predator consciousness. You can see it in everything from the way a kitten stalks a ball of string to the way a hockey player homes in on the opposing net to the way students focus in on the lecturer. It's all about narrowing attention and concentration.

But if predators think like an arrow headed toward a target, prey will tend to think like the circles spreading out around the bull's eye (the bull is also a prey animal). They're not into focus, they're into awareness. A horse is constantly aware of everything that's going on: the rustling of the trees, the movement of a nearby animal, an unfamiliar sound. They're evaluating and interpreting all 360 degrees of the environment around them all the time. They are open to everything that's going on around them because they have to be. Why? Because they know, their DNA tells them, that a predator can come hurtling toward them out of those bushes or from behind that rock at any time. To be prey is to be vulnerable, to be a victim. Think about a woman scared and alone in a dark alley in a big city late at night. That's where a horse is and how a horse feels, all the time.

Our job, essentially, is to kill. Their job, essentially, is to not be killed. That results in two widely diverging world views—quite literally. Predators tend to have eyes placed side-by-side on the front of their heads so their stereoscopic vision can judge distance ahead of them accurately. All prey animals, like horses, have eyes on the sides of their heads to give them a much broader field of view. But because horses are so familiar to us, we lose track of how very different we are. A lot of the problems between people and their horses are about the humans not being realistic about what they're up against. As naturally as a duck taking to water, or a dog chasing a cat, the horse's most basic reaction to a human being is to want to have nothing to do with us. It's in their DNA.

There are important things we can learn here. For example, think about that wonderful, 360-degree awareness that horses live in. Nothing escapes them; they are amazingly sensitive and open to everything life sends. Unlike predator thinking, which drives toward the ultimate goal and ignores all distractions, prey thinking must be aware of all the world around it and be constantly poised and ready for anything. Yet it still has to get on with the vital daily business of eating, interacting with the herd, and looking after young. It's being alert and relaxed at the same time, like being the coiled spring and the limp noodle simultaneously. I can best explain it by telling a story that I read a long time ago that has stayed with me ever since. This is how I remember it:

In Japan, a long time ago, a young man walked up to a monastery and said to the head monk: "Master, I desire wisdom. Will you teach me?" The head monk, a man named Joshu, accepted the young man as a student and put him to work in the monastery's garden. For days, the student did nothing but pull weeds and dig dirt until one afternoon, when he was bent over a row of cabbages, Joshu crept up behind him and gave him a mighty kick to his backside that sent him sprawling. The student popped up, confused and wanting an explanation, but Joshu said nothing and walked on. This happened again and again. The student would be concentrating on the job at hand and Joshu would sneak up and send him flying into the dirt. Gradually, the student changed. While still getting his work done, he learned to stay alert to quiet rustles and shifting shadows around him. He honed his senses, stood light on his feet, and remained poised for action even when doubled over pulling carrots. One day, he felt something was about to happen and whirled around. There stood Joshu, about to deliver another kick. "Master," cried the student, "I've been here weeks and all I've done is work and receive your blows! When will my lessons begin?" Joshu smiled and replied: "You have already mastered the first one."

I had to learn this lesson before I could get anywhere with horses. And make no mistake, you won't either until you understand something of this. It's the first thing we have to understand when we start working with horses. It's horse psychology 101.

But when I did learn this lesson, a funny thing began to happen. As I, a predator, started to get in touch with prey consciousness, it started to rub off. Here, slowly at first, is where my thoughts began to whirl. And after a while, not only did I understand horses better, but like Joshu's student, I began to glimpse a new kind of balance that I could bring to my life.

We need to understand prey consciousness because that's how horses think and we want to be successful with them. But understanding prey consciousness will teach us other things—things like empathy and patience.

Remember that we're taking these wild creatures that are naturally afraid of us, that have the right to be afraid of us, and we're putting them in jail. Think of that the next time you run in to one of these great, big bad horses that really get you upset and angry because they want to fight you. Think of that woman in the dark alley again and imagine that she's fighting for her life. That's what that horse thinks it's doing. So it's important not to lose track of how much transformation needs to take place for that frightened prey animal to become the confident, trustworthy being that we're looking for. It's a long path to travel and once we understand and respect this, empathy follows naturally. And once we have achieved empathy, patience too follows naturally. I hear all the time when I'm giving clinics about how patient I am with the horse, but where does patience come from? It's the result of respect and empathy for the vulnerability of a victim.

It's also learning to turn off the ego. Many people become frustrated when they fail to reach the next step with their horse and it is easy to blame the "stupid" horse. In reality, we're angry with ourselves because we believe that training the horse is simply about showing the animal who is boss. The ego says, "If I can't get my horse to do what I want, then I am a loser." But we have to stop insisting that the horse sees and understands things our way. It just can't. Like being the first to say "I'm sorry" after fighting with our spouse, we have to swallow our predator pride, learn how the horse sees things, and speak to it in a language it understands. This is a lesson a lot of men need to learn. I see it all the time—the mighty trainer entering the ring to bring the wild beast to heel. No. What's really happening is that the predator is stalking the prey and the prey is terrified.

I made this realization early on in my life with horses.

In fact, it's what bonded me to them. When I walked into that stable at Longacres back in Seattle, I realized that these magnificent thoroughbreds were scared most of the time. The very nature and presence of their captors made them want to run and run, but they couldn't. They were in jail, they knew it, and they didn't know why. Despite their power and speed, these great beasts were victims. They reminded me of myself. I very much empathized with a strong, powerful victim because—in many ways—that's what I was. Even though I was physically big and an athlete, I was running all the time from humanity.

I don't believe I'm particularly unique in this. Although most of us can be very strong in some parts of our lives, there have also been times when we've been made into a fearful, cowering victim. It's tempting to simply suppress those memories and try and forget they ever happened, but that's not the way to deal with our fears. Just as we want the horse to forget its fear and turn towards us, we must also face what scares us. Whatever we teach the horse we can also learn ourselves, and coming to terms with prey consciousness will be the first step on the road to overcoming our own victimhood.

Most of us can certainly benefit from more awareness, empathy, patience, and humility in our lives. But that's only the first step. We've barely begun to whirl. Once you start to understand how a horse thinks, you can start to influence its actions. And there is a way to do this, a way that will leave the horse doing your bidding out of respect and trust and the certain knowledge that you are acting in its best interest. If you want true control over your horse, you have to convince it that you are the better horse. And that's what we have to talk about next.

CHAPTER

3

BEING THE
BETTER HORSE

*T*HERE'S A TRICK I LIKE TO PULL WHENEVER I GIVE A lecture on how horses think. It gets everyone's attention and wakes them up right off the bat, but it also makes a point.

I borrow a watch with a second hand, start timing, and then ask the audience, "What's the point of studying horse behavior? Why are we doing this?" Now, these audiences are usually composed of riders, trainers, horse owners, vets, breeders, and other horsey folk. They're a pretty tuned-in bunch, and it doesn't take long before I'm getting answers like communication, respect, building a relationship, loyalty, all good answers and worthy, rewarding goals in themselves, but all still only means to an end.

It usually takes about a minute before I hear what I want, and I usually have to do a little coaching. The word I want to hear, the word that sums up our goal with the horse, is "control." Control has become a bit of a dirty, politically incorrect word these days but we need to come out of denial and admit the truth that control is, in fact, exactly what we need. Whether you're a rider or driver or a vet wanting to handle the horse smoothly, this is about control.

The problem with control starts in those 60 seconds the audience takes to figure out what it wants. Horses live in the moment: right here, right now. They don't rationalize and stand around waiting for us to be clear about what we want. As I've said before, they don't like ambiguity. So as we look deeper at the reasons why horses do the things they do, always remembering that control is our goal, this is going to become more and more a study in our shortcomings, not the horse's. Understanding equine behavior often amounts to understanding human behavior and why we are unable to get what we want. If you think you want to change the horse, what you really need to change is your approach to the horse.

I'll give you an example, a simple problem in cause and effect. If you've got a horse that keeps bucking you off, you're probably asking "How can I get my horse to stop bucking?" That's understandable—landing on your head in the dirt is no fun. It's always tempting to attack the symptom instead of the disease, and not just in horse training, either. What you should be asking is "Why is my horse bucking?" Maybe the horse is scared, defiant, hurting, or simply bored. To get to the root of the horse's behavior, you need to learn to look at things as the horse sees them. You need an open mind and a willingness to change. There's a good chance that the horse's problem stems from something you're doing. Fix whatever it is—and each of those problems I mentioned require radically different solutions—and you'll fix forever the undesirable behavior that stems from it. That is true control, and it starts from within you.

To learn and develop this control, we have to return to the predator-prey polarity. In the last chapter, we discussed how predator and prey behave differently in their environment. Now we'll look at how they behave differently toward each other. And the central question in any pack or herd is who is going to be the boss, and how is that going to be determined.

Every social group has some way for some individuals to dominate others. If it didn't, no one would be in charge, no decisions would get made, and there wouldn't be any social group. In predator-land, challengers work out who's going to be the leader by trying to immobilize each other. Think about those nature documentaries on wolves: There's the alpha wolf, flipping over a challenger in the pack and holding him still with his teeth around his neck. He's saying, "If you move, I'll kill you. That makes me the boss."

CHRIS AT HORSEPLAY PLAYS FOLLOW THE LEADER WITH TWO MARES

JIM KNELSON

The other wolves show their submission to the alpha wolf by rolling on their back with their feet in the air and their bellies exposed, a position in which they are essentially immobile. But you don't even have to move beyond our own species to see how predators dominate each other. Look at two kids wrestling. One will get another into a hold and keep him there. "Say uncle," he commands. If the other kid does, he's admitting he can't break the hold. He's been dominated.

With prey, it's completely different. Here, movement is the key. The most natural and necessary thing to a horse is forward movement. Horses move from place to place as they graze. Movement is a big part of their mating ritual. They need to move forward to eat, they need to move forward within the herd's pecking order to establish breeding rights. And because horses are so paranoid, the instinct to flee and run for their lives is never far from their thoughts. Everything about staying alive for a horse involves forward movement. I can hardly stress this enough: Horses feel the need to go forward all the time.

In fact, if I had to boil down a horse to its psychological essence, it would be this: a victim that needs to move. So while predators establish dominance by seeing who will back down, prey animals will do it pushing each other forward. The horse says: If you want to earn my respect, you do it by nipping my butt and making me move forward. That's why horses fight the way they do. When two stallions are rearing up against each other, what they're doing is seeing who will turn tail first and allow the other to push him forward.

This has deep implications for how we handle horses. Too often, when we want to control a horse, we attempt to stop it from moving. This violates the horse's deepest nature. And to make matters worse, we usually stop the horse by attempting to control its head and neck. That may seem natural to us, but as far as the horse is concerned, predators always go for the neck because that's where they make the quickest and most effective kill. Remember, we're predators and horses don't trust us to begin with. So when we come in and behave in a manner totally against their nature and right in line with that of their natural enemy, we're going to create fear, not trust. Our entire approach to the horse has been to stop it, confine it, put it in a box, hobble it, and tie it up. Then we take it by the head and say, "You will be mine."

Our own feelings about control make things even harder on the horse. Control is an emotional issue for people in all their relationships, whether it's between husband and wife, parent and child, or boss and employee. Often, we bring our excess stress and problems with control from these other relationships into our relationship with our horse. Imagine someone with a very stressful job, heading out to the barn after work. The horse, already nervous because it can't move freely, sees this: a big predator, full of stress, coming straight toward his head to capture him. Yikes!

So how do we establish leadership over a horse in a way that's natural to it? The same way another horse would—by pushing it forward. We do this by using one of the things predators and prey have in common. Both people and horses like their personal space. In the round pen, we can exploit this—just as another horse would—to push a horse forward and ultimately earn the right of leadership. If we step from the center of the pen into that space around the horse, aiming our drive into the flanks located between the girth and hindquarters, just in front of the hips, we create impulsive or "herding" pressure on the horse to move forward. It's just like an inflated balloon flying out from a finger pushed into it.

However, it's vital to remember that horses do not like to be pressured from the front. That's what predators do. That's how you create fear, not trust. So to give the horse a forward push it can understand, approach from the rear. As I always say in my clinics, to control a horse's mind you must first push its butt. On most horses, that spot behind the rib cage that I just described is like a button that says, "Go." To get a horse moving around the inside perimeter of the round pen, that's where I begin to walk toward, and this is how the game I used to call "horseplay" starts.

The first time I played horse for real was down in Lake Tahoe. The horse was Quincey Top Cat (I called him T.C.), a two-year-old liver chestnut quarter horse. T.C.'s curious, intelligent look caught my eye when he came in with a shipment of colts to the ranch where I was working. He was the first horse I ever bought with my own money.

I'd trained a lot of horses by the time I met T.C., but with him I wanted to try something different. This was the spring after my big accident, so first of all I wanted to take it slowly and very carefully. I worked some long, hard days on that ranch and in the evening I was often too tired for more muscle work on my own horse.

Mostly, however, I just wanted to change my ways. My horse work back then was still fairly rough and aggressive. I didn't mind getting violent with a horse and, in fact, I must admit, a part of me liked the adrenaline rush. But I knew in the back of my mind what I was doing when I was strong-arming some poor colt was unloading a lot of rage and hurt from my past. I didn't want to, I didn't mean to, but that's what I was doing and the catharsis made me feel a little better for a while.

What I chose to do with T.C. was a little different. With him, my own personal horse, I wanted to bond with one of nature's greatest creatures and do it without a fight. So I decided to just take it slow and make some time to play with him. I was in no hurry to get on him— I'd been riding colts all day—and I'd just get in the round pen with him and I'd walk around, watching, listening, and reacting. Hour after hour, day after day.

Without really knowing what I was doing, T.C. and I eventually joined into a partnership. We never had a bad moment together. With T.C. I got a taste of what it felt like when a horse gave its heart to you. It felt really good and it felt really healing, and it made me want more. By that fall, I knew that it was time for me to leave the ranch and strike out on my own to explore what T.C. and I found together.

One of the first things I learned was that once this

game is under way, it's crucial to stay on top of it all the time. You always have to move with the horse. If I push a horse forward and it trots away and increases the gap between us, I'm not really pushing that horse any more. That horse is running away from me and leaving me behind. It knows it's winning and it's not going to learn the respect for me that I want it to have. If, however, I push too hard on the horse and constantly close in on it, it's going to create fear when what I want is trust. The balance has to be just right, based on what the horse is telling me.

Remember, a horse is a profoundly physiological being, by which I mean that its mind and its body are deeply linked to the point of being one thing. Unlike humans, it's just not in a horse to pretend. When you are able to read a horse's body language, you are quite literally reading its mind. A horse is constantly giving off signals about what it feels, whether it's anger, defiance, fear, boredom, fatigue, relaxation, or submission. To know how much forward pressure to apply, you must learn how to read these signals instantly and learn to respond appropriately—that is, as a better horse would. It's like a dance, even though one partner has two feet and the other has four.

To gauge the right amount of pressure and read the horse's response simply takes experience and dedicated observation. I can give you some hints and start you off, but I can't show you how to do it in a book and that's not really my goal here, anyway. Still, it's worth going through the body of a horse, reading it like a book's table of contents, if only to demonstrate the rich emotional vocabulary in the lift of a tail or the line of a back.

Since I've already said the way to a horse's mind is through its hindquarters, let's start there. A tail tells all kinds of tales (sorry). A tail that is puckered right down tight against the hindquarters and the back of the legs indicates that the horse is frightened. A swishing tail signals agitation. Stiff and pointed up, that horse is excited. If it's just hanging light and loose, the horse is calm. A tail that goes beyond swishing into circular wringing lets you know that the horse is angry. What's under the tail can convey a message, too: a little manure dropping out can signify a tense, suspicious horse is starting to relax. Or in another context, it can mean you're literally scaring the crap out of it.

A horse can send you even more important messages with its butt. When one horse turns its hind end to another, that's a big insult. It signals a complete lack of respect, as well as defiance and aggression. It's like flipping you the finger and the horse is literally saying "I dare you to bite me."

Same kind of message from the hind legs. If they're kicking out, the horse is saying: Screw you. The tail, the butt, and the hind legs can all work together, too. They can signal everything from mild disdain to outright contempt.

If you want a horse to respect you, don't ignore any of these gestures. Ever. Ask yourself this: If you let a horse give you its ultimate sign of disrespect, does it make sense to the horse to think of you as dominant? No. In fact, the horse thinks the opposite. So when you try to ride that horse, the horse won't buy it. It won't necessarily buck you off, but it's always going to be testing you, questioning your authority and never automatically doing what you want. All kinds of behavior problems start here, with a rider that hasn't properly earned respect from the very beginning.

Moving forward along the body, the horse's barrel can also tell you what the horse thinks of you. If the horse is bending on an arc through the length of its spine, leaning against you on the ground, or against your inside leg while you're riding, the horse is pushing into you and invading your space and challenging your control. The horse will use its shoulder to do the same thing.

As well, somewhere in the front of the barrel right around the girth is a line I call the equator. Behind that line, you're in control. You can push the horse forward with assertiveness to earn respect. But the horse knows where that line is too, and an aggressive horse will try to keep you from getting behind it. A horse that keeps turning into you or pushing against you or being aggressive with its head is saying "If you don't go back there, you don't win." It's like a bouncer at a nightclub, saying "Sorry pal, you don't even get in the door."

The level of a horse's head says other things, too. If the head is up, the horse is saying something's wrong and it is resisting the impulsive drive to go forward. Even though the horse may be moving, if the head is up then the brakes are somewhat on. It's worried or concerned about something, or it's challenging another horse. Or you. Head up with a tight tail is fear. Head up with a swishing tail is annoyance. Head up with a wringing tail is anger. Head up with a calm, curled tail is stubborn defiance. If the head is lowered and staying that way, that's likely saying it's submissive—but submissive and sullen. If the horse bows but then brings its head back up high then it is respect through fear. If the horse holds its head level with its back, then bows it down and then comes back up to level, that's the best signal of all. The horse is bowing to you with respect that is balanced with trust. It's saying, "You're the boss and I'm okay with that."

Again, the horse will use its head to challenge you. People always think it's cute when a horse nuzzles its head right up to you, but unless you've invited that attention in towards you that horse is deliberately invading your space. It needs to be pushed away to learn more respect for your personal space.

There's more, much more. If the horse's front legs are even, that's a calm, stable position. One leg forward means it's restless and ready to move. The ears will tell us all sorts of things: back means something (hopefully you) has got its attention; pinned down flat is angry; pricked forward is distracted, intent on something in the far distance. Ears that are constantly moving around, like an equine radar dish, are the sign of a relaxed horse tuning into the environment around it. We need to watch the face, too. Does the horse have a frozen, stiff look? Again, it's stressed due to fear, anger, defiance, or confusion. A relaxing horse will blink, roll its lips around, flex its nostrils, sigh, maybe blow out a little snot. A horse will yawn not because it's tired or bored but as a means of releasing mental stress.

With all these little messages—and myriad others as well—a horse is telling us what our attitude toward it should be. If the horse is defiant, maybe it needs a little more forward pressure to be shown who's boss. If it's relaxing, it could be time to reward and encourage it by backing off. One thing you'll learn for sure the more time you spend around horses is that they have almost as many ways of challenging unwelcome authority as people do. Like a teenager rebelling against its parents, they can fight you aggressively, by running away, rearing up, or pressing in against you. Or they can fight you passively, by being evasive, stubborn, or just plain lazy.

To understand what the horse is telling you and how strong the message is, all the signals have to be considered together and your response to it has to be appropriate. If your horse is calm and its body language is speaking gently, you don't want to rile it up with sudden violent or abrupt gestures. That's like shouting in the middle of a quiet chat.

Equine body language has a subtle vocabulary of great range. I'm still learning it and I doubt that any human learns to read a horse's body language as well as another horse does. But you can learn it well enough to first dominate the horse, then teach it to respect and trust you on its terms, not just on terms of fear and intimidation.

Let's imagine we're back in the round pen. We're pushing a horse by moving into his space and pressuring his Go button at the flanks. At first, it's a contest. The horse doesn't welcome your push, or doesn't think you can do it. So it resists, maybe by moving in towards your space. Meanwhile, it's tossing its head at you, tail held out rigid. You keep the pressure on, consistently herding it forward, assertive but not threatening, always aware and absorbing everything its body is telling you. When the head comes down and when you start to see other signs of relaxation, you back off and give it a little more space. You keep the horse moving forward, but not so aggressively.

Finally, when you see the horse accepting your herding ability, when its head is level and body is relaxed and loose, you begin to step back toward the opposite wall of the round pen and let the horse come up to you. At this point, it'll turn. If it points its butt toward you as it turns, you haven't won the game yet. Tap its hindquarters and get that horse moving again. Tap into the herd impulse and push forward for more respect. But if it doesn't, it's acknowledging that you're the better horse. It'll lower its head and bow to you. If you know how to walk like a leader it'll follow you all over the pen and watch you like you're the most important thing in its life. You've given all of yourself to the horse, and it's giving its own trust and spirit back. I've done this thousands of times, just with me and the horse or in front of a crowd, and I never get tired of it. It's a beautiful experience.

This kind of work between a horse and trainer pays immediate benefits. A lot of a horse's behavior depends on its confidence in the handler. Quite often, you'll see a horse sail over a jump with its trainer that it wouldn't dare go near with its owner. Same jump, same horse. But if the rider doesn't have the respect, trust, and confidence of the horse, that horse won't face its fears willingly. Confidence in a handler begins with establishing that herding reflex. The horse must feel it's being herded by a better horse.

Now, authority and control are not foreign or cruel to a horse. Horses dominate and control each other in the wild. It's natural and even necessary to them. To some

ANITA IRWIN

CHRIS AND BAHAMA AT A DEMONSTRATION AT SPRUCE
MEADOWS, CALGARY

extent, it is also natural to a lot of human males. That's why the dominance part of horse training can come easy to us (and the gentling part is something we men have to work at a little harder).

Many women, on the other hand, are socialized to think dominance is always bad. They think of horses and they see loving and nurturing and grooming and caring for their horse. Those are wonderful things. But you don't want to ever lose track of the essential fact that *one* of you is going to be the boss, and that it's going to take some show of assertiveness to boss around 1,000 pounds of frightened animal.

In the horse whispering world of Hollywood and of fiction, a lot of sincere people think that if they just understand how the horse thinks, and talk quietly enough, all you have to do is go work the round pen for 20 minutes and you've got a best friend for life. It's a nice concept, it's romantic and sometimes it does actually work like that. But most of the time, you've got to establish emotional authority. Passive, non-assertive people don't usually do well with horses. Assertiveness—measured appropriately, in a language they understand—is as much a part of handling horses as is empathy.

Get this part right, and the horse will thank you for it.

CHRIS AND BAHAMA AT SPRUCE MEADOWS

After all, the higher a horse is in the herd pecking order, the more responsibility for the other horses it has, the more challengers it has to fight off, and the more stress it carries. It's a great relief to find someone stronger and more dominant who can take care of him for a change.

In fact, learning how to compete using prey consciousness has a few useful lessons for we predators. When humans compete with each other, it's very adversarial. One wins, the other loses. One gets a massive ego boost; the other is crushed, pinned beneath the alpha wolf or bankrupted by the sharper businessman. Horses compete, too—that's what's happening in the corral or the round pen—but they don't seek to vanquish their opponent. They compete to find their proper niche, to find out how they're all going to live together in the herd. Horses have worked out how to compete without causing the fear, pain, and distrust that we go through because in a herd, the horse that loses the battle is not regarded as a victim. In fact, in prey consciousness the loser is actually empowered because it now acknowledges a stronger horse that will look after it. Horses know that after any contest of wills, they must still all live together in the herd. They compete in a way that makes that possible for them—a way that offers us a model of how we can earn our own rightful places in society while strengthening its fabric instead of tearing at it.

The lessons don't end there. You may be strong enough to establish leadership, but you also have to be consistent enough to keep it. Horses, like kids, need consistency. They don't think in terms of 70 percent or 80 percent. Either you are the boss or you're not. You need zero tolerance for disrespect, and that's just the way horses think. That's not to justify going in there and being abusive. What you do is respond appropriately, according to the level of their disdain. If I walk by a horse and it stomps its foot and throws a kick out at me, I'm going to give it a good nip on the butt. But if I'm grooming a horse and I get a little swish of the tail, I'll simply give it a little tap, just to let it know I'm aware of what's going on. You have to measure your response. But don't ever ignore disrespect or misbehavior. That sends an ambiguous message, and horses don't understand ambiguity. This ambiguity is why most people have trouble with their horses. One day we're really sharp as a hawk and not missing anything, the next day we're letting things slide. Horses would rather we not let them get away with anything, because then they know the rules. Otherwise, behavior erodes very quickly.

It's a refrain I hear all the time: "My horse was great when I bought it." Let me say it again. You have to learn to monitor the body language 100 percent of the time. Every single moment. There is no cruise control. You must retain awareness, for the horse has got nothing better to do than to remain aware and wait for your mind to wander. People want their horses to be like their cars and computers and all their other toys, complete with on/off buttons, but it just doesn't work that way.

We began this chapter talking about control, and how human ambiguity and indecision gets in the way of that. Now that we've got that horse circling the round pen, being herded and dominated in the way it's familiar with, we need to let our thoughts circle back to where we came in. It's time to consider how our own minds enter the equation.

Horses don't lie—they always tell the truth with their bodies. There is no separation between what a horse thinks and what its body says. People, on the other hand, bluff and pretend and hide. We learn to pretend interest in small talk, to play social games, and tell white lies. We're taught to do it from our earliest age, the first moment mom or dad tells us to stop fidgeting in church and act like we're interested or insist we respond politely to people we feel like yelling at. We've even made an art form out of faking what's in our heads and pretending to be someone else—it's called acting.

Altogether, you might say the ability to be less than forthcoming with our thoughts and feelings is almost a requirement of civilized life. We've gotten pretty good at it, and so, of course, we try it on our horses. People go in to work their horses to show them who's boss when in reality, there's a big question mark in their own minds as to whether they really are. Sorry. You won't fool the horse. Remember, horses are prey animals, they are finely and intensely attuned to their environment. They can spot a faker before he or she even opens the gate. The human has to learn to speak honestly and confidently with his or her own body language. And ultimately, this means that confidence can't be an act. It has to be real. This kind of quiet, unshakable faith in oneself isn't easy to learn, but it can be done. We'll talk about what that learning takes a little later. For now, it's enough to know we need it—and that once we have it, it stays with us no matter what we're doing.

So now the circle is complete. To train and work with calm, focused, confident horses, we must acquire these qualities as well. Everything we do with the horses we must also do with ourselves. And as we've seen before, what we learn with our horses will ripple out into the rest of our lives. Now, we have to take those circles, stand them on end, and learn how to ride 'em.

CHAPTER

4

RIDING
THE WAVE

*E*VERYTHING IN THIS BOOK KEEPS COMING BACK TO circles: the swirling thunder of horses circling around me, the 360-degree circle of the horse's awareness, the herding of a horse in the round pen, the ripples that spread out within us from what all this has to teach. This shouldn't come as a surprise; nature abhors a right angle and is full of cycles and circles. Horses come to us from the world of nature—I sometimes think they were put here to teach us about it—and thinking in terms of circles and arcs and curls is often the best way to understand them. Take the way they move.

Forward motion in a horse starts in the hindquarters and it rolls forward like a wave on the ocean. The hindquarters in a healthy horse are smooth and round and powerful, and the energy they create surges and cycles forward through the barrel, through the shoulders—more roundness—along the neck and breaks like a wave at the head. I can't emphasize that back-to-front, circling flow of energy enough. When you say "Go" to a horse, that word becomes like a stone thrown into a pond, sparking a wave of energy that just keeps moving forward.

Once this is understood, it has profound implications for how we ride a horse. We don't want to get in the way of that forward energy. We want to ride that wave, like a surfer rides a wave in the ocean without disturbing it. And more than that, we want to control and direct the energy of the horse like a dam controls and directs the flowing energy of a river. I know the metaphor is mixed, but I like to think what I'm trying to do on horseback is riding the wave into the dam.

Before we get there, though, we have to backtrack a little. In the last chapter, I described how horses win respect in the herd by driving each other forward from the rear. Humans have to do the same thing if they want the respect and attention of their horses. Direct their butts, and their hearts and minds will follow. This does-n't stop once you get into the saddle. In fact, it's even more crucial. Riding is like squeezing a tube of tooth-paste: to get the most out of it, you can't start near the top. In practical terms, what this means is that we have to learn to guide and communicate with our horses pres-suring our seat, hips, and legs into the barrel of horse. We can't, as too many riders try to do, simply use the reins in our hands.

Perhaps the problem starts with the fact we're so used to our cars and trucks. Turn the steering wheel, the front tires twist at the desired angle, the chassis follows smoothly along. It's a natural reflex to think a horse turns the same way—pull one rein, turn the head and the body comes right along with it. This—as anyone who's experienced a horse that refuses to turn no mat-ter how hard the reins are yanked—is not the way it works. Think, instead, of a fish. They turn by bending their whole body through their midsection, all the time powering themselves along with their tail. This is also how a horse turns naturally, by bending through the barrel, and it's how a horse should turn with a rider in the saddle. It seems like a basic concept, but I'm con-vinced that the significance of bending is one of the least understood aspects of riding. And it's one of the most important: if A in horsemanship is "go forward," B is for "bend."

How does the rider initiate that bend? The same way he or she communicates with the horse in the round pen, with subtle weight shifts and body language. In the last chapter, we talked about how we can push a horse forward to earn its respect by applying impulsive pressure, that is, moving into the space around the horse's hindquarters. Now we have to return to this idea and get a little bit more specific and a little more physical.

Obviously, once we're in the saddle we can't really get to the hindquarters. We could persuade them with a gentle nip from a whip, but that only says "forward" and we need to do more than that. Fortunately, there is a way. There is a network of pressure points I call "buttons." They're in a slightly different place on every horse, so you have to go looking for them, but once you find them they are the secret to creating that natural bend, and all kinds of other gymnastic and lateral movements, that will allow you and your horse to develop the agility of a fish in the water.

One button, found back in the flanks, will initiate forward motion. Come reasonably close to that button with your heels or legs and that tells a horse "Go." There's another button just behind the girth and down low that says "bend." A little pressure here will cause the horse to bend out, making the pressing leg the inside leg or pivoting point of a turn. Back on the hips, right where most horses get branded, is a button that will create movement like a pendulum swinging from side to side, exactly how a rudder turns a boat from the back. Go in front of the girth and there is another button that asks for a similar pendulum-like response from the shoulders that will also cause the horse to move away from the pressure. You can use the outside shoulder button to finish off the turn you started with the inside girth bending button: press the button just behind the inside girth to create bend through the barrel and initiate the turn; then move to the outside leg and press just in front of the girth near the shoulder button to push the horse's shoulders into the turn and finish it off with help from the hands on the reins. That outside leg is like following through with a golf swing or a tennis racquet.

When I say finish it off with help from the reins I'm trying to make the point that the reins do nothing to create a turn—they are only to support a turn. The reins are like the training wheels on a child's bike. The purpose of the reins is never to tell the head of the horse where to go but only to tell the head of the horse where not to go. Earlier I used the metaphor of a river moving forward into a dam. Let's now talk about the banks of the river. The banks of the river do indeed control the direction of the forward flowing water. However, the banks of the river control the water by establishing consistent blocking boundaries that tell the water where not to go instead of direct pressure pushing the water, telling it where to go. This is what the reins are for. To build the solid banks of the horse river that tell the head of the water where not to go. Unfortunately, the main cause of resistance during riding is caused by that predator instinct of ours that wants to use the reins on the horse like a big dog on a leash telling the head where to go.

Note the sequence here: go forward from the flanks, the turn starts from inside the barrel, moves into the outside shoulder, and finally through the neck and head. The purpose of the reins is not to initiate a turn but to assist in supporting or maintaining and balancing a turn. We wouldn't be balanced in a left turn if we allowed our horse to look right. So we can use the left rein, not to pull left, but simply to block or not allow the horse to look right.

Power and control in a horse always move from back to front. So many people try to turn a horse from its head. That's just riding backwards. Of course, for this to work the rider must have done his or her homework in the round pen. The rider has to have established respect and trust. As we've already discussed, horses won't allow themselves to be bossed around by a horse or human it doesn't respect. So if the horse doesn't respect the rider's legs, it won't bend in response to the buttons being pushed. It'll just push right back. The horse's barrel then stays straight or even flexed in the opposite direction going into the turn, and that creates all sorts of problems.

ANITA JUMPING SASSY THROUGH A FIELD OF OATS

JIM KNELSON

The first thing that happens is that the rider usually pulls harder on the reins, which usually causes the horse's head to come up. Remember, horses raise their heads when they're fearful or being challenged, and by raising the head you've just created the stressful state of mind that goes along with it. And that's not all. Raise the head and you consequently lower the back, which is a stiff and awkward way for a horse to move. That means the ride for you is more awkward because you are in the trough of the wave instead of on the crest, which will probably make it harder for you to keep your balance, which makes the horse even more stiff and nervous, which will probably make you hold even tighter on the reins, which is where this whole vicious cycle begins again until the rider gets off and says "This horse just won't turn." But it's not the horse's fault. The rider had no emotional authority from bonding with the horse to begin with and also doesn't know how and when to use the buttons for centered and balanced riding. This series of problems is, definitely, the underlying cause of dysfunctional relationships between horse and rider. I see it all the time.

Turned properly, however, the horse stays balanced and supple. The head stays down and the back-to-front transfer of power is smooth and strong, like a stretch of a calm river flowing forward with no obstacles or resistance causing rapids. Anything the rider does wrong is like a rock in that river, churning up what naturally should be gliding smoothly forward.

Now, think back to that surfer, poised on the edge of a wave. The surfboard has to be positioned just right: too low on the wave and the surfer gets swamped, too high and the wave will roll right past. The perfect position for the surfer is to find the spot on the wave where the water is changing from a lifting-upward rise to a falling-downward drop. There is a sweet spot on the wave where the water is suspended, where rising energy will transfer to falling energy, and this is where the surfer must ride. There is a similar sweet spot on every horse—not so much an up-and-down spot, but a spot where the horse's fore-and-aft, left-and-right motion balances out. With a rider solid, sure, and balanced in the sweet spot, communicating clearly in a language the horse understands, the horse's power swells up in the hindquarters, curls up over the barrel and shoulders, and breaks over the neck and head. This is riding the wave.

So far, I've primarily talked about our legs on the body of the horse. Is there more that can be done with the hands? Well, I've already mentioned the role they have in maintaining–not creating–a turn. But they also have a much more important function. Think back to the second half of that mixed metaphor I drew at the start of this chapter. Now that we're riding the wave, it's time to build the dam. And that's where the hands come in.

As any river flows forward into a dam, a reservoir of water grows behind it. That reservoir has many uses, but the one we're interested in involves power. The dam, holding back a lake of water from its natural flow, is collecting a reservoir of power. The hands on the reins and the bridle of a moving horse do a similar thing. At the same moment, we tell the horse "Go" with our legs, we also create a little blocking pressure on the bridle. We're asking the horse to create more forward motion, but we're not allowing it to go any faster. This creates pressure, as if we're taking the horse's energy and compressing it. We create a little resistant pressure and like the dam and its reservoir, we let out only as much of the horse's energy as we desire. Using the reins to build this dam and gather a reservoir of horse power is called "collection." It's a subtle thing. I'm not suggesting you pull back on the reins. Just as the dam never pushes back against the river, the hands should never impede the forward flow of the horse.

Collecting the horse requires no backward pressure from the hands, just a solid, steady feel that closes and anchors itself all the way back through the rider's body, deep into his or her spine. Hands that are collecting horse power are like the floodgates on a dam that open one way only. They can be wide open, partially closed or barely ajar, but they will never swing past the center of the door frame and slam the horse in the mouth.

Done correctly, collecting a horse gives you much greater control over it. It's a little bit like gearing down a sports car. The car stays at the same speed, but in the lower gear the engine revs much faster and creates a lot more torque the driver can use to power through a corner or quickly accelerate.

Riding as I've just described—controlling direction from the barrel with your legs and using the hands to finish turns and collect power—allows you to shift from being a reactive to a pro-active rider. A reactive rider is "behind" the horse, constantly reacting to fix problems, trying to fix mistakes and regain balance. This rider tries to control the horse from the head and is likely to be scrambling from one problem to the next, just recovering from the last awkward maneuver when it's time to enter the next one. It doesn't sound like much fun, and it isn't. Pro-active riding begins with being "on top" of the horse, maintaining balance with no need to recover from mistakes that aren't made in the first place. But best of all is riding perfectly positioned on the sweet spot of the wave, fully focused and aware at every moment, aggressively projecting your desire to go forward, riding strongly from one moment comfortably into the next.

As we have seen, mastering riding requires the ability to synchronize several tasks. The rider's body must be balanced and flexible, each leg and hand performing independently and simultaneously to apply the subtlest of pressure to guide the horse. There are any number of sports that can test an athlete's skill and courage, but the mind, body and spirit of the horse makes horse-manship uniquely demanding.

In other sports, if you're not having your best day, it doesn't bother your equipment. Your golf clubs don't care if you slice and your surfboard doesn't care if you fall off. Horses, however, care intensely. Remember, they're counting on us to provide clearly consistent leadership—we are the ones who are supposed to know what we're doing. So when they sense a wobbly, unbalanced, on-the-edge-of-control rider, it troubles them. It shakes their trust and leads them to rebel against what they are being asked to do. And as typically seen, here's where all sorts of horse behavior problems begin.

So an equestrian must possess more than physical skill. The rider's mind must remain constantly focused on the moment-to-moment application of pressure and weight. The rider must be constantly aware of the surrounding environment, looking for distractions that will shift the horse's focus from the work at hand. The rider's spirit must calmly and confidently project straightforwardness into the horse. We ourselves must possess these skills of the body, mind and spirit so that we can impart to our horses the attributes of impulsion, balance, flexion, focus, awareness, trust, calm, confidence, and willingness.

I know. This is a tall order, and that in itself creates another challenge. It's hard to find courage and persistence when being overwhelmed with new information, and it's hard to aim higher when what you're already attempting is dragging you down. "Hard" creates frustration, frustration creates stress, and stress creates resentment, anger, and fear. And you know by now that all that will go directly into your horse, making things harder yet. But here's a couple of tips to help you get started.

First, breathe. I know it sounds too simple to be true,

RIDING THE WAVE

81

but deep, controlled breathing will go a long way toward building the relaxed, focused attitude we need with horses (and in other areas of our lives, too). And breathing's not as simple as you think. Actors and musicians spend hours talking about and working on correct breathing. Meditation starts with deep breaths. Often, our first reaction to stress is to stop breathing or take short, shallow breaths. We can short-circuit this whole feeling if we just stop and focus on a nice, relaxed, in-goes-the-good-air, out-goes-the-bad-air. That will help calm ourselves both on the ground and in the saddle, and our horses will notice. The cornerstone of self-control is breathing.

The second thing to remember is to give yourself a break. You're learning, too. We need to let go of our ego and allow ourselves to make a few mistakes. Impatience is an ego-driven problem.

We all want to improve, the sooner the better. Remember: patience. Even a batter in baseball is allowed to make at least two strikes before he has to connect. Mistakes are, after all, an essential aspect of any learning process. People who don't make any mistakes aren't trying anything new.

The riding arena can often feel uncomfortably like a

stage, and nobody wants to look bad in public. The trick is to get around that by respecting who we are and where we are at this stage of our development. Think, "I'll get better, but right now this is where I'm at and my intentions are honorable." Competitive athletes cannot reach their peak until they make peace with their desire for recognition. They must stop playing to the crowd and learn to play for the sake of themselves and the sake of the game. If we want to learn patience and respect with our horses, we must first learn it with ourselves.

Let's not, after all, underestimate what we're doing here. We're dealing with powerful forces, and I mean that in the most concrete and physical sense. Controlling the power and strength of a horse and asking more and more difficult and dangerous tasks of it should generate a little stress in the rider. I can tell from personal experience that the stakes in terms of pain and injury are significant. But personal growth doesn't come from avoiding risk, challenge, and stress. The key to success is in learning to embrace the stress. If you love your life and where you are and what you're doing, stress is exhilarating and inspiring. Facing stress and welcoming it under these conditions is the source of optimism, faith, trust, and perseverance. If we wait for the stress to come to an ending then we've completely missed the point. Stress won't go away; we must make peace with it. We must learn to face these fears just as we ask horses to stop running and face their fear of us.

I think my first inkling of this came back when I was growing up in Swift Current, watching my old girlfriend ride her horse. Like me, she was a bit of a brooding soul with a lot of conflict and doubt in her life. But she was a pretty good rider, and when she was on her horse I could see all that darkness fall away. When I watched her ride, I could see that she was happy.

The ultimate ride on a horse is to take an energy that is calm and ride it as it builds like a gathering storm, swelling with power until the forward wave crescendos to a peak. We surf that peak, riding the balanced, harnessed power. Our lives can be like that too: moving from our stasis forward into new challenges and responsibilities, then enjoying the rewards of discovering a new source of mastery. But of course, it never ends: We get a glimpse of the next level and back we go into the ocean of life, looking for new surf. Or up we get into the saddle, riding the exhilarating equine wave of mind, body, and spirit.

TRAINING
THE RIDER

A T THIS POINT, I'M STARTING TO FEEL LIKE A writer in one of those home decorating magazines. I've described this wonderful room full of grace and beauty that we'd all love to live in. I've told you about how it was designed, all the meaningful objects it contains, and how magical the hours spent in there can be. What I haven't told you about is how you can enter this room and experience it for yourself. It must be starting to feel as remote a possibility as a perfectly ordered and designed parlor in a household with two kids and a dog.

Well, it needn't be. This room is open to anyone. And while you will still have to walk through them yourself, this chapter will tell you where the doors are. In short, this chapter is about how to effect change—change that will allow you to develop the qualities and skills you need in the horse arena. And maybe in other areas of your life as well.

Change is a journey. Like a journey, it requires preparation. A traveler isn't likely to end up happily arriving at her desired destination just by setting out and trusting to luck. Before we talk about the path that will lead us to that room we want to be in, we have to pack a little mental luggage.

The first thing in our saddlebag should be a clear, unequivocal decision that change is needed. If there's one thing that's common to all the self-help books I've read, this is it. Remember our horses' distaste for ambiguity, for weasel words and justifications and rationalizations and excuses? Well, that's the horse showing us how to get started. We have to turn that clear kind of thinking on ourselves. The first question to ask is "Am I satisfied? Am I happy and content?" There's no room for "maybe" or "sometimes" or "half-and-half" in our response. Either you want more or you don't. In the

CHRIS AND THE WARMBLOOD STALLION KAISER IN MEXICO

same way, you can't answer, "I would be happy, if only this or that in my life would change." If you want change, nobody else can do it for you.

This isn't news for most of us and in fact, it's something of a self-help cliché. But that basic insight is just the first step. A clear desire for change is no good without the will power to drive that change. There's a lot of unused fitness equipment in a lot of basement rec rooms bearing dusty testimony to that. To turn desire into action, we need to believe two things: First, we need to believe that we are worth changing and second, we need to believe that we are capable of change. In short, it's a question of believing in ourselves.

I know, this may not be as easy as I'm making it sound. We all grow up learning attitudes that cling to us like burrs on a saddle blanket. Many people don't even realize that they are living with deep-seated beliefs that hold them back until something shakes them up. My friend Rob, for example, somehow grew up with the idea that he wasn't very athletic. Sure enough, he wasn't. Then he was unemployed for a while. With a lot of time on his hands and not much money to spend, Rob hauled out a pair of old cross-country skis he'd had as a kid, just to fill in his days and work off some frustration. Today, Rob skis marathons and makes tracks all over the mountains. He's got a few bicycle racing trophies, too. Far from thinking himself awkward, and somewhat to his surprise, he's now comfortable and confident in his body.

We can't change our height or the color of our eyes, but we can change how we think about ourselves. It takes lots of soul-searching, if for no other reason than to assess what our self-image actually is. It may also take some healing and some letting go of past wrongs. I know from personal experience that most of us have some emotional luggage from our childhood that we're still hauling around. Learn to leave it at the station. You can blame whoever you like for your problems, but that blame is a like a big roadblock keeping you from the confidence you need to move forward. It keeps us from believing in ourselves because it hands over power to someone or something outside ourselves.

Tell yourself to be on guard against blame. Every time you hear yourself blaming your parents or your spouse or your kids or your boss or your employees or your horse, you are in denial. You are denying that you are free to control your own response to the situations life sends you. If you are in the habit of blaming other people and external circumstances for your discontent, then the only way you will be able to go forward effectively is by going back and dealing with your past.

Guilt is another mental habit that sucks the faith and optimism right out of us. It strikes right at the heart of the belief in our own worth that we need to help us change. Lord knows, we all live with some guilt; the trick is to learn to probe into its origin. Are others making us feel guilty because we don't live by their standards? If so, what are our thoughts about those standards? Maybe we need to learn more respect for our own standards. But maybe we're guilty because we're not measuring up to our own standards. Take a minute to ask yourself why not, and write down a few of the answers. If any of them involve blame, see above. Once you know the real roots of that behavior you feel guilty about, ask yourself how you can change that behavior. Here's where your going forward begins.

Now you've packed your bags with the right attitudes. It's time to think about the journey, time to draw a few maps. You can't ride a horse without telling it where to go (by telling it where not to go), and you can't engineer change in yourself without setting both goals and boundaries. There's a common theme in the self-help movement that dates all the way back to Dale

Carnegie winning friends and influencing people, and that's the power of positive thinking. We have to be cautious with this attitude. We're told over and over that we can do anything if we psyche ourselves up enough, even walk on fire, as if the human mind were as simple as the Little Engine That Could saying "I think I can, I think I can."

Positive thinking is fine, but unless you've already given a lot of serious thought about what you want to achieve, and also what you no longer want in your life, you're just huffing and puffing. You can't brainwash yourself into success without first knowing exactly what it is you're aiming for. All that energy spent striving for improvement with your horse or happiness in your life is going to be wasted if you don't know where you're focused on going and where you're definitely not going.

This is a tricky one. Everyone's going to find their own goals differently. And what's more, it's not something you do once and then never have to do again. Goals change over the course of our lives, sometimes radically. For that reason, it's often just as important to know how to find what's important to us as it is to have the answer. The process can be just as important as the result.

For me, it began with learning to listen to my subconscious rather than trying to program it. Dreams at night told me much about who I was and what I did and did not want. I found it useful to write them down in a little notepad I kept by my bed. I learned it was important to write down whatever was in my head, whether or not it was pleasant for me or someone I cared about. And then I gave myself time to think about what I had written.

Lists can be another useful tool for goal-setting. Just like when you're shopping for groceries, lists can help us organize our thinking and make sure we cover all the bases. Make lists of everything you want to change about yourself, physically, mentally, and spiritually. Lay them out in front of you and compare them. Do they reinforce or contradict each other? For example, are you asking your spirit to be more spontaneous and your mind to think things through more carefully? Then, make another list of what is keeping you from making these changes. Think about the roots of these roadblocks. Do they originate from within yourself, in feelings of blame or guilt? Ask yourself what you need to do to overcome them.

Once you've got a reasonably clear idea of your goals, decide which ones are truly the most important to you. Write them down. I find writing them down makes them seem more attainable. Remember to break big, long-term goals down into manageable steps. For example, if you make $30,000 a year and your goal is to make $100,000 annually, you are setting yourself up for failure unless you understand that before 30 becomes 100 it must first become 31, then 32, and then 33. If your horse improves one percent a week, within two years he'll be 100 percent better.

All packed with a reasonably reliable map of your destination, carrying a load of the right mental baggage, you should be ready for your journey of change. But before you actually set sail on your adventure, here's a few travel tips that I've found useful—some mental and physical exercises that will help you keep moving forward.

Learn to breathe. Nothing is more important to your body than breathing, yet it is the first thing to be thrown out of whack when we are stressed. Many unproductive mental states are linked to similar physical states—tension, for example. And you can't approach a horse, or anything else, with a calm, confident, loose manner if your head is all ajangle with fear and confusion. Controlled, regular breathing can help a lot. Think of a woman giving birth: To keep herself as calm and strong as she can, she focuses on breathing. Faced with a tough situation, learn to take a second to remind yourself to inhale and exhale deeply, completely, and regularly. Practice this so you can do it easily when you need to.

Feel your body. We communicate with our horses mostly through our body, so we need to be as fluent with it as we can. Get in shape. Use your body. Develop a physical program that focuses on flexibility, not just strength. Disciplines such as yoga or Tai Chi or other martial arts courses are very suitable for this. A simple routine of quality stretching before your regular riding session, or whatever sport you do, can go a long way towards enhancing performance.

Nurture your spirit. I believe meditation is the basis of all spiritual discipline. Meditation is not the absence of thought; it's allowing the mind to let its thoughts flow unrestricted and unjudged. Give your mind the unedited freedom to allow your spirit to come to the surface of your thoughts. Soon, with practice, your spirit will come to life and give you inspiration and guidance. And this will be a powerful source of optimism and fortitude to face the challenges of change.

Repeat affirmations. In practice, our mind is rarely still and quiet. It always seems to need a bone to chew on. However, we can decide what that bone will be. When doing a job that doesn't require your full attention—doing the dishes, weeding the garden—try using the opportunity to program your mind. Find yourself a mantra that furthers your goals: "I am relaxed and centered," or "I am free of guilt," or "I ride tall in the saddle." Soon enough, these little affirmations will take on a life of their own and you'll hear yourself saying them when you need them the most.

Visualize success. This is a very common and empowering advantage used by athletes in training. When you're having trouble accomplishing a particular maneuver or feat, sit quietly and run a movie in your mind of successfully completing the task. Imagine exactly what you want to do, then close your eyes and run the film over and over. Run it in slow motion and carefully savor the details of your performance. You will find this much easier and more effective if you've already learned to clear and calm your mind through breathing and meditation.

Reject judgment. When you get something wrong, resist the temptation to see it as a reflection of your own worth. Don't think "I can't get my horse to turn left around that obstacle. I'm such a loser." That's an example of where not to go. Instead, use your visualization skills to examine what you're doing objectively. Don't assign labels of wrong or right; just try and analyze what you're doing and where your body is at each step. Instead of looking for things you're doing wrong, look for ways to make what you're doing work better. Nobody gets everything right the first time. The sooner you realize that, the sooner you'll be able to learn from your mistakes instead of letting them defeat you.

Recognize success. When something works for you, take a moment to savor it. Use your visualization skills to replay it in your mind. Try to remember how it felt in your body. Draw on those memories when you have to repeat the act, remembering that no two situations are ever exactly the same.

Don't forget to laugh. Keep things in perspective. Remember to have fun. Obviously, none of these suggestions are going to teach how to saddle your horse, jump a fence, or perform a flying lead change. Those are technical skills and teaching them is not my intent in this chapter. The point I do want to make is that following these simple guidelines is going to make the path of learning those specific technical skills a lot easier. Furthermore, horses will respond much better to a

CHRIS IN MEXICO COACHING JUAN JOSE DEL VALLE ALVARADO, PRESIDENT OF THE WORLD LUSITANO ASSOCIATION, RIDING HIS PRIZE STALLION

rider who learns to cultivate a calm, collected mind and spirit, untroubled by self-defeating emotions. And in my experience, so will people.

All through this book, I've stressed the importance of a clear, confident stance toward your horse, an attitude that doesn't have to be put on like a pair of riding boots— because it comes naturally from within. I know, developing this attitude is a lot harder than I make it sound in a series of neat paragraphs. It will take time. It will take work. Just remember that change is inevitable, so we might as well work toward change for the better. Ask yourself every day, "Did I move a little forward toward my goal today?" If the answer is yes, then there's a law of physics that's working in our favor: An object in motion tends to remain in motion. If we are patient and focused, improvement, like bank interest, will compound.

CHARACTER AND CONSCIOUSNESS

*W*E'VE BEEN PRETTY PHYSICAL SO FAR IN THIS book. We've watched horses in the field, we've worked with them on the ground and finally, we've mounted them and begun riding. We've talked a bit about the attitudes necessary to approach this work, but now it's time to let our thoughts whirl a bit further out and think about some of the wider consequences of this kind of horsemanship. At the end of the first chapter, I was standing in the middle of a round pen, horses swirling around me. At that point, I was slowly becoming a teacher and starting to think more deeply about what I was doing. I was cataloguing all the things I'd learned–or tried to learn–since I started working with horses and was looking ahead to the new directions my ideas were taking. I'd like now to return to that figure surrounded by pounding hooves and roiling dust. The previous chapters have detailed what he's learned about the demands horses place on his body and his mind. What about his spirit?

Most of what I had learned to that point was the result of instinct, repetition, painful experience, and bonehead luck. Not a course of study I would recommend–it takes a long time and leaves a lot of bruises. But it was the only one I knew and it worked for me, even if it did leave me operating on the level of intuition and what felt right. It was my wife Anita's perceptive and persistent questioning that forced me to think out loud and articulate what I was doing and why it worked. The last several chapters are the result of what she started. But once this process of self-examination began, it picked up a momentum of its own. And as I probed into what I was doing with the horse, I also started to think about what the horse was doing with me. Two things were changing: my character and my consciousness.

I've already hinted at some of the qualities that working with horses will call up in you, if you let it happen. Mostly, those discussions have come as an afterthought, as we were chiefly concerned with the horse. Now it's time to turn our gaze inward and examine those qualities a little more closely. We've talked a lot about confidence, and with good reason. If respect is the most important feeling a horse can have toward us, confidence is the most important feeling we must develop toward the horse. As we've seen, respect and confidence are the proper roots of the horse/trainer relationship. Nothing gets accomplished without them and unless they're firmly established, all kinds of behavior problems creep in.

We know that respect means focus, trust, and control. So what do we mean by confidence? Well, confidence is not is a cocksure swagger, a booming voice and a heavy hand. That's not confidence, it's bluster, and it's worse than useless in the horse arena—and anywhere else, for that matter. For us, confidence has more to do with always knowing exactly what we want, exactly what we don't want, being resolute about achieving it, and expressing that knowledge and resolution in everything we say and do.

Think of a major league batter stepping up to the plate. He doesn't come in talking trash to the pitcher or pointing to where in the stands he's going to smash the ball (unless he's Babe Ruth). He steps up firmly, grips the bat, settles into his stance, and coolly looks out toward the mound. At that moment everything in his mind and his body is saying: "I will hit this ball." Of course, chances are he'll go down on strikes, pop out, or get tagged at first base. Even a good hitter only gets on base once in every three at-bats. The batter knows that too, but he doesn't ever allow that to dent his inner surety. And every now and then, he'll knock one out of the park.

This is the kind of confidence I came to understand that horses needed from me. Because it has purged itself of conflicting desires and knows clearly what it wants, this confidence is calm and still. Because it is reflected in every word and gesture, it's consistent. Because it understands that there will be setbacks, it doesn't get easily rattled. Because it reflects the mind's desires clearly through the body, it's transparent.

Horses respond to this kind of confidence, and it comes into play both in the round pen and in the saddle. It doesn't take much to make a horse nervous, maybe only an unfamiliar object like a garbage can suddenly placed alongside a familiar path. When a horse does come up to something that upsets it, the first thing it does is ask its rider, "How do we feel about this?" The worst thing that rider can do is feed the horse's apprehension. A tuned-in rider will know to look for the question and then be able to clearly respond, "I don't have a problem with it. It's OK." Relieved, the horse will carry on.

Confidence is closely related to the next quality that horsemanship will draw out in a person. Once you're clear about what you want and are confidently expressing it, you are able to focus. We've already talked about the need for focus. Focus doesn't mean narrowing down your attention to a few details of horse behavior. It means paying attention to and balancing a wide variety of inputs. While our body is engaged in the moment-to-moment task of pushing the horse forward, our mind must also be totally aware of the constant messages being sent back from the horse. Our mind must also remain focused on responding immediately to those messages or even anticipating them with the appropriate measure of forward pressure.

Meanwhile, our spirit must project a continuous aura of calm determination to be the leader of this dance between human and horse. We have to be able to do all this at the same time. Compare two camera lenses: While the telephoto lens isolates small details of a scene, we need to be the wide-angle lens that sees the big picture and brings everything into equally sharp relief.

We also need to be able to keep this lens in focus over the long haul. Like our horses, we are easily distracted and too often, we come to the ring with a head full of unrelated thoughts and issues and general mental noise. But if we want our horses to learn to focus their attention on us, we must learn to focus ours on them. That's easy enough to do in spurts. The real trick is to learn to maintain it for as long as we need to. There's no automatic pilot on horses. They're constantly sending you messages and they constantly need some response. Horses, by being so sensitive to our self-doubts and fears, allow us to spot them within ourselves and root them out.

As our confidence grows, and our ability to focus increases, we need to learn how to use assertiveness to put our desires into play. Assertiveness can be a tricky one. Make no mistake, we need it. We're trying to earn the respect of an animal much bigger than ourselves that has definite ideas of its own. It's going to get physical out there. The only question is how much strength, and when.

Men tend to rely too much on strength—and not just in the horse ring. Plenty of home handymen, confronted with a part that doesn't quite slide into place, growl, "I'll make it fit." Then they reach for the hammer, or as it's called in these situations, The Persuader. Often as not, they break the part and have to start over. Horses don't respond well to that type of persuasion any better than hardware does. Nor do many other situations, really.

Women, on the other hand, are sometimes afraid to use a little muscle. They're brought up to believe that just a little more love and nurturing will solve any problem. This, unfortunately, isn't always the case—especially with a herd animal like a horse which needs to know where it fits in the hierarchy of the herd.

The challenge is to assertively establish dominance and lead without abusing. Too little force and you won't realize your goals in anything. Your horse won't do what you ask, your children will walk all over you, and your employees won't follow your agenda. Too much force, and all of the above will respond with fear, not respect, and will eventually rebel against you. Judgment is the key. Clear, confident goals and accurate, focused understanding, give us the tools we need to develop and use our strength with good judgment. A real Mr. Fixit soon learns that considering the problem, then sliding the stubborn part home with just the right twist works a lot better than bashing it with a mallet.

But judgment must also be tempered by two other qualities: empathy and patience. We can't only take our own goals and understanding into account when we're trying to respond to behavior. It's vital to understand where the other side is coming from on both rational and emotional levels. This empathy will give us much greater insight into what we're really asking and how far we expect the horse to come. Once we understand and act on that insight, patience comes naturally.

Often, we're not aware of how hard what we're asking really is. A friend of mine once explained how that lesson was brought home to him. Gerry was training to be a lifeguard and swimming instructor. He was, of course, an excellent swimmer and completely at home in the pool. Diving off the board was no big deal. So to make him understand how scary the diving board was for a kid in his first or second year of lessons, Gerry's instructors took him up the high board, blindfolded him, and told him to jump. "That's what your kids feel like when you ask them to jump off the regular board," they said. With that lesson firmly in mind, Gerry went on to become a fine swim teacher.

The next quality that grows from true horsemanship flows from these lessons of patience and turning toward the other's point of view. Horse people—all people, I believe—should learn humility. Our egos would have us think that we are always right the first time and that to admit error is to be diminished. When we're wrong in public—and nothing can feel more public than a riding arena—we lose face. No one wants to lose any of those things, and this is how our egos hold us back and keep us from venturing outside what we already know. Humility can set us free from those ego-imposed restraints by allowing us to acknowledge our ignorance. Humility gives us permission to be wrong; it shows us the length of our own journey and allows us to grasp that it's going to take a bit of traveling. Humility allows us to stop worrying about how others see us and lets us focus on where we actually are. It makes patience with ourselves possible. There's an old saying that an expert is simply somebody who has made thousands of mistakes and learned something from them all.

There's something I call the law of 1-2-3-4; it's my way of describing the learning curve of both humans and horses. Say you're trying to get a horse to do something, maybe to go all the way into a corner instead of shying away. You work at it and work at it, and eventually the horse does what you want. But that's just once.

Once is luck. You keep at it, and the horse does it right the next time, too. But that's just twice. Twice is coincidence. The next time around, the horse gets it right again. That's three—the horse has spotted a pattern. If the horse does it right the fourth time in a row, then he's learned something.

People often learn in the same way, not only in simple physical skills but in complex matters that are central to our lives. Few of us find real love without going through three or four serious relationships first. It's almost as common to find someone who's experienced several different fields before settling into their true career. We have to accept these false starts and not think less of ourselves because of them. Humility lets us do that. It allows us to reclaim our past by showing that it wasn't just a series of mistakes, it was the path we took to get where we are. In the same way, acknowledging we'll probably mess up again makes it easier for us to try something new. Humility frees us to explore our future path.

And once humility has removed the roadblock of ego, horsemanship will now call up one final quality—courage. Not just physical courage—although you'll need that, too—but the courage to change. Just as our horses need to go forward, we also need to find the courage to take risks and go forward as well. We need courage to accept the danger we face with our horses and also the courage to accept the mantle of leadership we ask them to grant us. These kinds of courage are often the hardest to find. But with our calm, focused confidence, patient strength, and humble awareness of our ignorance, we're already well on the way.

But horsemanship can change more than just character. The more time I spent with horses and the more I thought about things, the more I came to realize that my new, emerging understanding of myself was only half the story. For me, the final step in my journey came when I realized the impact horses were having on the way I understood the world.

For example, I've already talked a little bit about what I've called prey consciousness: an orientation toward overall awareness instead of narrow, focused concentration on a goal. To recap briefly, humans are hunters, and hunters learn to concentrate their attention on their prey. A moment's distraction can cost the kill and endanger the survival of the pack. It's effective—humans, after all, are a pretty successful species—but it tends to reduce the world to two categories: food or not-food, and everything not-food can be safely ignored. Horses, however, are prey. Their food—grass—is all around them, so there's no need to focus on the particular patch they're grazing on. Their survival depends on detecting and warding off attacks from hunters, and for that they have learned to be highly attuned to everything in their environment. A predator is interested in the grazing deer; prey are interested in the entire meadow.

And that is one of the most valuable things horses have to teach us. Sure, like Joshu, we can learn poise and balance, to walk on the balls of our feet and stay alert to our surroundings. That's worth knowing, but there's more here than that. What we really need to learn is that the world is more than a gallery of prey— and I use that word in the broadest sense. Sometimes our prey is money, sometimes it's power, sometimes it's sex or success. Whatever we're stalking, we have to realize that there's more to the world than a place for us to conduct our hunts, thinking only of our own ends with no concern for the context of our actions.

Like a herd of horses, we must become sensitive to the interactions and interrelationships between ourselves and the people and our world around us. Also like a herd of horses, we must come to realize that our survival depends on those linkages and cross-fertilizations. To behave otherwise is destructive both socially and environmentally, and there's just too little of the natural world left for us to keep hunting down and killing whatever of it we desire.

We'll always remain predators and we'll always need something to hunt. But if we learn to think more like prey, we'll get better at putting the results of that hunt in context. Maybe we'd find new goals to chase down and conquer, goals that strengthen rather than weaken the social and natural fabric of our world. Horses don't only show us what we must learn; they show us how to use that knowledge.

Think back to our discussion on how horses compete. They compete with each other while keeping the welfare of the herd in mind. Horses know they have to stick together to survive, so the loser of a battle for dominance is not vanquished. In a way, the loser is strengthened because he now has an ally more powerful than himself to rely on. The herd is also strengthened, as the chain of authority is clarified and those most fit to lead will naturally rise to the top without the loss of any members. It's competition, serious competition, but it's non-destructive.

Pondering all this set me up for the last and deepest lesson I believe horses have to teach us. Remember our

CHRIS AND BAHAMA DEMONSTRATING HOW TO
CROSS OVER WATER

discussion about dualism or, more accurately, polarity? Earlier, I described the type of qualities that being a predator summon up in us: boldness, confidence, courage, and strength. Humans love a challenge, to undertake quests and focus on goals. We see the world as a stage for individual action.

But then I went on to say that we have much to learn from prey consciousness. And prey consciousness is all about observing, not acting; receiving and understanding the world as it is, not going out and changing it. Prey consciousness sees unities instead of parts and makes connections instead of breaks. Individuals take their meaning and worth from their role in the group.

We see this polarity again and again. Some call it the struggle between passion and reason; others, instinct versus intellect. It opens up every time we have to decide whether to follow our head or our heart. It colors our idea of the human journey: We associate youth with passion and inspiration, while maturity is thought of as cooler and more calculating. It also shapes how we look at the world, for the natural world is considered free and spontaneous while civilization is called artificial and rule-bound. And although both sexes share qualities on either side of this divide, this polarity continues to be the greatest influence on how we think about gender.

The greatest lesson horses have to teach us is how to resolve this polarity and bring together these two sides of our nature. If we can think like predators and feel like prey, as I believe horses want us to, I am convinced that would go a long way toward healing our wounds within. We would live easier with each other, and yet we could retain and nurture the spark and crackle that makes the human adventure worth experiencing.

Ultimately, I don't think we can confront our deepest attitudes toward ourselves and our world without looking toward the Power that lies behind them. I believe that just as we must teach our horses to conquer their fear, stop running and focus their attention on us, we must also learn to face our fears and stop running from God.

Humans will fear spirit just as horses fear us because we believe that nurturing our spirit will force us to sacrifice. We won't be able to do as we please any longer, we will lose our freedom, we may even die. But just as a horse can find freedom and trust in its relationship with its rider, we can find the same things in our relationship with, well, call it The Creator, call it Jehovah, call it the Great Spirit, or even call it Fred if you like.

We are here to allow our spirit to drive our body and our mind forward in the experience of life. We are to learn to be responsive to the constant flow of experience that life has to offer us and to direct and control the flow to find our goals. As we focus on the spirit, we discover a realm of balance and harmony. Just as our work in the round pen is a dance, life is a dance too, sometimes frantic, sometimes a slow waltz. But we are always meant to face the spirit and ask it where we should go. And the answer will come back: "Forward."

CHAPTER

7

ETIQUETTE

*T*HIS STORY HAS COME A LONG WAY, FROM SWIFT Current to Seattle to Nevada, and the inner journey has been even longer. But there's still a little way left to go, and one more lesson for you and I to learn. To complete the circle, I need to pick up the threads I put down a few chapters ago. I need to talk about the horse that taught me you *can* go home again.

I left off telling my story when I was still in Nevada. It was 1993 and I was doing pretty well training, buying, and selling horses. Some of my horses, especially the Mustangs I worked with, were winning state and national championships. I was the young up-and-comer, a growing fish in a good-sized regional pond.

Through my wife Anita, who was a riding instructor at a large local equestrian center, I had been introduced to the world of English riding and was beginning to make inroads into that community. In fact, the owner of the place where Anita worked—the Carson Valley Equestrian Center—invited me to move in and become the resident trainer.

It was while training horses at that facility that I first heard of Willy Arts, a Dutch dressage trainer and well-known breeder who lives in Fresno, California. That's where he raised and trained Olympic-class dressage horses. Willy used to come through our place once a month for a clinic and he was coaching at one of these events when he noticed somebody driving horses in the next arena. Impressed at the driver's skill, he grew more and more distracted until he finally asked the crowd if anyone knew who that guy over there was. Luckily, Anita was in the audience and she spoke up: "That's my husband." So Willy and I got together and we hit it off. Willy liked how I handled a team and he liked how I handled unruly horses. And, as it happened at the time, Willy had an unruly horse that needed a lot of handling.

This horse was something to see. First off, he was huge—a big old warmblood 16.2 hands high, tall enough to stand shoulder to shoulder with me with his head towering over me. And I'm not short. He was also handsome, strong and big-boned, and had an amazing amount of what horse folk call presence—a tough thing to define, but it's the same quality that in people marks a born leader or draws your eye inevitably towards a movie star.

But this was one troubled animal. He was mean, angry, and very nasty. He attacked both people and other horses with equal fury. He'd chase grooms out of his stable and they couldn't even walk other horses by him. He was no bluff, just really bad. His name, ironically enough, was Etiquette.

Etiquette had been brought to California by a woman who dreamed of starting her own high-end breeding farm. He was of the finest, purest pedigree, and a couple of his brothers were on European Olympic equestrian teams. Etiquette was intended to be the foundation sire of an entire breeding program. But, of course, those dreams don't come cheap and the woman who was chasing them ran into money problems.

Etiquette's training was delayed again and again.

ETIQUETTE

PAT MITCHELL

ETIQUETTE AT A SHOW IN CALIFORNIA

Despite his value, this magnificent animal's development was neglected. Eventually, Etiquette's owner went out of business and ultimately, his training never even started. The woman owed Willy money and in lieu of some of that cash, he took over Etiquette.

By this time, Etiquette was five or six years old. Believe it or not, he'd never been ridden. He'd never even been started. He'd been left a stallion—although Willy was soon to change that—but he'd never covered a mare. You couldn't even put a halter on him and grooms had to feed him by throwing hay over the fence at him. Then they put water in his trough while Etiquette was distracted by the food. He was that mean. "He'll never make a woman's horse," Willy said. And because the great majority of dressage riders are women, he decided to turn Etiquette into a driving horse.

That's when he asked me to see what I could do with him. Train this beast to the point where he's saleable and we can split the money 50-50, Willy said. Again, I agreed. But I almost wished I hadn't when Willy drove out to our place to deliver Etiquette. There he was, rearing up in the air, screaming and hollering, the snarliest and angriest horse I'd ever seen. I swallowed hard when I realized this was my project.

ETIQUETTE

We let him sit in the round pen at the Carson Valley Equestrian Center for a day. The next day, with 30 or 40 people watching, I stepped into the pen with him for his first session. Sure enough, Etiquette came at me. I was more like a rodeo clown than a trainer for a while as I dodged his attacks. But I didn't let that huge horse chase me out of the pen and I didn't give up. I kept right on playing horse with him, challenging and trying to earn his respect the same way I'd done hundreds of times before and the same way I've described earlier in this book.

And Etiquette tried to do the same with me. We were running circles around the pen, sometimes Etiquette chasing me and sometimes me chasing Etiquette. It was loud, aggressive body language all right. For 45 minutes, we shouted at each other with our gestures and pushed into each other's space as we fought over who was going to be the better horse. Eventually, it was me. After a long hour had passed, Etiquette finally accepted. And when he did, he came all the way. Focused and centered, he walked right up in front of me. It was beautiful.

I could see his anger beginning to give way to a serious work ethic, so I kept at him. I haltered him and gave him his first lesson on a lunge line. I didn't stop there, either. I kept working my way in closer and closer from the lunging position of about 20–25 feet out. Closer and closer I got, until I was driving him from close at his side. I improvised a set of reins out of the halter rope. And then I just swung up on the back of this big, scary horse and he let me do it. He was a little annoyed at my presumption, but he let me do it.

Right away, I felt a powerful connection with this horse. I felt as if we were somehow each other's destiny. I turned him left and I turned him right, and when I squeezed him up into a trot it was the biggest wave I'd ever felt in my life. It was like going from bobbing around on a lake to surfing Hawaii.

By the end of the first week, we were cantering cross-country, jumping bushes, and crossing creeks. And he still had that presence, that powerful male energy. When Etiquette and I came trotting along, other horses and riders just parted before us. I knew I couldn't sell him at this point and I bought him outright from Willy. With Etiquette underneath me, Willy was able to teach me all kinds of things about dressage I wouldn't have been able to learn on any lesser horse.

Anita rode him too, introducing him to show jumping. She sometimes allowed the best of her students to

ETIQUETTE

ride him, just to feel what that kind of energy was like. After our work with Etiquette, Willy once announced to a group of his peers, "When you've got a good horse, call me. When you've got a bad horse, call Chris." That felt pretty good. And sure, I'm proud of what we were able to accomplish with Etiquette. But that's not why he's such an important part of this story.

With all the other horses I've trained, their spirit became a tiny bit smaller after I was finished with them, their energy slightly dimmed. The change grew less noticeable as I got better at my work, but something was always lost in the domination. And I never felt I was achieving complete unity with a horse if I was asking it to give something up that I didn't have to. Etiquette, however, lost nothing. He accepted me with complete trust, but it didn't cost him one iota of his presence, his energy, his equine machismo. Riding Etiquette convinced me that the balance I've been talking about isn't just an ideal or a pretty piece of New Age theory. It's as real as flexing muscle and flying mane. Etiquette was living, galloping proof it is possible to balance both the cooperative and competitive sides of our nature and compromise neither of them.

And one more thing. Kept isolated from both horses

and humans, nobody had ever played horse with Etiquette. That's a terribly unnatural situation for a horse. But it turned out that what this "bad" horse wanted most of all was to join up with someone. He just needed to be challenged on his terms, in a language he could understand. Once he had been, and was convinced to face and put aside his fear and anger, he was the greatest horse I've ever ridden. Etiquette's willingness to go beyond his painful history and move on to accept the work he had been born to do made a deep impression on me. I guess I was susceptible about then, because things were coming together for our little family. Anita and I had a daughter by now, our beautiful little Raven, and we wanted to raise her in our native country. We also felt there would be a lot of opportunity for our kind of work in Canada. And truth to tell, we were starting to feel a little homesick. So as I watched Etiquette transcend the trauma of his past, I came to realize that I too had made a lot of progress dealing with my own childhood and that maybe it was time for me to stop running away from things. It was time to come home. That's what we decided to do.

There was, however, a catch. We knew we would need some start-up money. We looked around for options,

ETIQUETTE

but we both understood that Etiquette was our greatest asset. To return to Canada, we would have to sell the horse who helped us realize it was time to go. We started looking for a buyer who would give him the home he deserved and eventually, we sold him to a woman who belonged to a hunt club in Nevada and needed a big, strong, spirited horse to chase coyotes over hills and through creeks and over bushes. That's where Etiquette went, to ride boldly through the desert countryside. I thought he'd like that, but it didn't make the transaction any easier for me. I'd bought and sold hundreds of horses by that time, some pretty good ones too, but that was the only time I really felt a twang in my heart when one of my best friends walked into somebody else's trailer. I've always been able to let them go, but losing Etiquette was hard.

It was, however, the money from Etiquette's sale that gave us enough capital to make our new start. So in 1995, we moved to Stewart Valley, Saskatchewan, not 30 miles from my old Swift Current stomping grounds. How's that for coming full circle? Now I'm back in my prairie roots, raising our family amid the wooded coulees and shortgrass prairie along the South Saskatchewan River. From our ranch, I travel out to share what I've learned and at home, I work with horses to give them a new start.

Raven and my little boy Adler often watch me when I'm working horses around the ranch, and that's one of my greatest pleasures. But as they watch me in our round pen, the center of a pounding ring of horses, they have no idea how those circling animals have inspired my thoughts to spiral out over the years. Lord knows, I had no idea where they were going to take me, either.

And sometimes, when I consider that I'll have enough to do for the rest of my life just working through what my horses have already shown me, it feels like that journey is over. The challenge now is to stay on the path I've started and to practice the life that I'm preaching. I don't feel so much these days like I'm reacting to my past. Thank God, I think I'm finally through with the bad old days and, like my horses, I'm moving forward.

But I know my journey isn't really over. There's always more to learn and what feels like a destination is probably just a new beginning, the next rotation of the circle. And always, horses stomp and whirl around me, my thoughts astride them, riding forward into new and deeper understanding.

ETIQUETTE

131

THE MAGIC
OF HORSES

I BEGAN THIS BOOK WITH A PROMISE OF MAGIC. As we've gone along, I've done my best to describe the magic of horses and how to find it, for magic is exactly what horses have been in my life. I believe that magic is available to us all, and most of us, in our desire for transformation and growth, can use all the magic we can get. But still, it seems like a lot to ask of an animal, no matter how strong and beautiful. Haven't horses got enough to carry without filling their saddlebags full of our dreams and needs?

The answer is that horses have been carrying that

load for us for as long as we've been together. The spiritual relationship that exists between horses and humans is ancient and well-documented and is no New Age fad. Neither are stories of those who have understood that relationship.

Belief in the magical power of horses was widespread in the ancient world. Horses were used as clan totems as far back as the early Stone Age, when they also came to symbolize the cosmic order of the universe. By the time of the ancient Greeks, horses were keeping company with the Gods, especially those Gods associated with the sun and with water. But at around the same time, the tribes of northern Europe were going one better.

To these people, the horses themselves were godlike. The ancient Celts were a nomadic people to whom the horse was essential equipment. They needed horses to move, to help them fight their enemies, and to establish social prestige. Perhaps that's why they had such a well-developed idea of the divine horse. Epona was her name—she was generally represented as a mare or a woman on horseback—and she was associated with freedom and creativity, as well as with fertility and battle.

The name Epona seems to have appeared first among Celtic tribes in Gaul during the Roman Empire and her worship soon spread throughout northern Europe. In fact, the Roman cavalry legions occupying these areas adopted Epona for themselves, honoring her under the name Epona Augustus or Epona Regina. Under the names Rhiannon and Macha, she also had devotees in what is now Wales and Ireland. Her shrines were common in stables and barns, and some people think that the pre-Christian horse effigies in England are ancient sites dedicated to Epona. Carved into a chalky hillside in Berkshire, England, is the graceful, stylized image known as the White Horse of Uffington. It is believed to be a representation of Epona from the first century A.D.

Just as these ancient cultures recognized the spiritual power of horses, they also recognized the spiritual bond between horse and rider. Leaders in the old Teutonic clans swore oaths by the heads of their riding horses. If those promises were broken, the heads of both were severed. The link was even more explicit in the tale of the Irish mythical hero Cuchulain, who could live no longer than his horses.

Tales of people who understood these bonds and used them to communicate with horses are just as old. The Roman historian Tacitus wrote of a group of Germanic priests who cared for some sacred horses and used their snorts to tell the future. Stories of men who used charms, herbs, or magic words to tame unwilling horses are common throughout Britain and date back to at least the sixth century A.D. There was probably more to their technique than that, but it is true that these old-time horse whisperers existed. They even had a union. The Horseman's Word was a secretive, hard-to-crack guild that preserved their secrets of horse management as well as a good working knowledge of horse medicine.

Some of these traditional horsemen are known to us by name. In the late 1700s, an Irishman named Sullivan became famous for quieting unruly horses, which he claimed to do by whispering an Indian word in their ear. As one account said, "He would lead the animals away into a darkened barn and no one knew for sure what happened when he closed the door . . . All the witnesses knew, was that when Sullivan led the horses out again, all fury had vanished."

In those days, such an ability created a certain amount of public awe and fear. In 1760, a mysterious man named Benjamin Gold became friendly with King Louis XV of France because of his skill quieting horses. Eventually, however, he was accused of dabbling in the occult. A successful demonstration of his skill before all the court didn't help—Gold was forced to flee to England, and eventually, they say, to the court of Catherine the Great in Russia.

I'm not suggesting that we should all become neo-pagans and build shrines to Epona. Nor do I think we should accept those old horse whispering stories as gospel, either. I'm just pointing out that I'm not the first person to come to these conclusions about the spiritual power of the horse and its relationship to us. People have been bringing this power into their lives for thousands of years. There are many historical precedents for what I'm saying. There's a thread here, a thread of magic, and I believe it's no coincidence that people are starting to pick it up again.

As Western civilization progressed, we became so preoccupied with the practical uses of our horses that the spiritual side of our relationship has been overshadowed. It's not hard to see why, given the importance of the horse to our development. Their strength tilled our farmland and carried our goods. Their courage took us to war. Right up until the Industrial Revolution, the fastest way to get anywhere on land was on horseback. They have been so important to the daily business of human life that horse ownership was the best measure of someone's wealth and power. Any job that required power or speed required horses, and Western civilization would be hard to imagine without them.

Now, of course, those days are gone. Our farms are mechanized and our cavalry divisions drive tanks. We fly quickly and easily from place to place through skies that once belonged to Pegasus. Except in a few specialized cases, horses no longer serve any practical purpose. For the first time in human history, we have no need of the horse's physical strength. What we do need, perhaps more than ever, is the horse's spiritual power. We need that power to resolve conflicts within ourselves and between ourselves. We need that power to bring us back together with our damaged planet. Great as the horse's gifts to us have already been, this one may be the greatest.

Today, the human spirit is poised for transformation. That old predatorial warrior spirit has brought us a long way, but it is now struggling to achieve a balance with the peaceful co-existence of prey consciousness. Many women are well on the way to that balance. Men, always waiting to the last minute, are beginning to consciously search for their own path to a greater sense of spiritual identity. It is imperative that people stop attacking themselves, each other, and the earth and learn relationships that are mutually advantageous. Win-lose is predator thinking. We see now a new age of horse people that are committed to making peace with nature—the hardest lesson that western culture has to learn. But we'll learn it. We have to.

As for me, I still think a lot about Etiquette. I mentioned the powerful, almost predestined connection I felt with that horse—believe me, I've been on a lot of horses and I've never felt anything like that before. It was as if he was the horse that would allow me to realize my ideals and, in fact, that's what he turned out to be.

A horse like that you want to ride for the rest of your life. I've had close relationships with a great number of horses, but with Etiquette I wanted to develop that bond for years and years and see how deep we could get. It didn't work out that way. But I haven't given up hope. If there is a next cycle for me, it will begin when I find another horse to ride along that path that Etiquette and I began. This horse I'll buy and play with as carefully as I can. And I'll never sell him.

I can see him in my dreams—or rather, I can see both of us. We're doing the kind of riding I've always loved best, roaming free over the prairie, down into willowed coulees and up over the silver-sage benchlands.

Sometimes we're at a full gallop, sometimes an ambling walk, sometimes I'm just dozing on the grass in the sun while my horse grazes idly nearby. And in that dream, I can feel us talk. Just whispers really—a few words, a snort, a gesture, a flicked tail is all we'll need to know exactly what the other is thinking and feeling. To others, it'll look like magic. And you know what? They'll be right.

CHAPTER

9

CONNECTING
TO OUR
CONSCIOUSNESS

*T*HREE YEARS HAVE PASSED SINCE I WROTE THOSE dreaming words about how I hoped I would soon be able to laze around in the shortgrass while my new horse grazed nearby. And in those three years, many of the dreams I had expressed have indeed come true—although not exactly in the way I expected. Just when you think you've got things all mapped out, life has a way of surprising you. As I'd sensed, I was about to enter a new cycle of exploring the horse-human polarity. But I thought I was about to mount the back of a second horse like Etiquette and see how complete a unity we could achieve. I thought I was about to get closer to the horse side of the equation. Instead, I was about to get closer to the people side. Just as I'd hoped when our little family moved back home to Saskatchewan, it turned out there was indeed an audience for what I had to show and say. I was mostly training horses at home and also going out on the road about fifty days a year to give clinics.

After this book was first published, I began to tour more seriously, conducting clinics at first across Canada and then into the U.S. I soon found myself on the road 200 days a year and as you might imagine, that was a real emotional challenge for my family. I'll never repay the debt of gratitude I owe Anita for keeping our home more than just together, but genuinely happy. I spoke at quite a few horse conventions and met many other renowned trainers. I learned from almost all of them, for most of us thought quite a bit alike. I watched lots of round pen work and I met a lot of trainers with a pretty good understanding of how the mind of a horse thinks. But as I conducted workshops in little towns and big arenas all across the continent, I was starting to notice something that no one else, I thought, had picked up.

At clinic after clinic, something was beginning to happen that I had only sensed before. This didn't happen all the time, but people kept coming up to me after a demonstration and would say something like, "This is amazing. You walked out there and talked about horses for two hours and all I could think about was how it applied to everything else in my life." When I began giving clinics, I had been afraid that my thoughts and ideas were just too far out there—that I had ventured far beyond what most people were even prepared to think about, let alone accept. I felt I was taking a big risk. The last thing I needed was to end up labeled as some kind of New Age flake by the conservative and often close-minded horse industry. But in fact, I needn't have worried. As it turned out, I wasn't that far ahead at all and many people were ready to listen. They were making similar connections all on their own. It got so I could predict when the penny would drop. I knew, for example, when I was talking about giving respect to get it and controlling behavior through indirect pressure, some woman in the audience would ask jokingly but hopefully, "Does it work on husbands?"

Someone asked that question at every clinic I gave. Every single one.

Sensing the interest, I responded. I still did plenty of lectures and demonstrations of round pen work, but I began to broaden the metaphors I used. I talked about how, when we're riding, our mind should be like the captain of a sailboat because the mind of the horse is very much like the wind. Everybody inherently knows that a sailor does not fight with or make vain attempts to control the wind by force but instead learns to become accountable for how well he or she can work with their sails. I began to talk about the relationship between the dance in the round pen and the rest of our lives. And as I did more of this, my audience began to change. Mixed in with the horse owners and trainers and riders I saw more and more people whose lives had nothing directly to do with horses. I saw a lot of teachers—in fact, teachers were often the first people to understand what I was driving at. I was even invited to speak at a few teachers' conventions. I told them the same things I'd been saying all along. I told them that their attitude towards themselves was reflected in their attitude toward the horse. I told them that if it was their goal to teach the horse to trust and respect them, then they too would have to learn how to demonstrate trust and respect. I told them that if they wanted to control the horse, they had to be prepared to take the responsibility as well as the power. I showed them that the horse could help them learn these things. Although it was the same talk I gave to the horse people, the message crossed over to the teachers right away. What they always told me in return was, "It's just like teaching kids!"

Social workers and therapists were starting to come to the demonstrations, too. One day a man walked up to me after a clinic, introduced himself as Bob Friedrich, and then told me he'd read my book and went on to lay out an interesting proposition. Bob worked for the social services department of the Canadian government and he asked me if I'd be willing to put on a workshop for a group of social workers. I said I would, and soon after I found myself working a horse in a round pen before a group of social workers and their clients, young people who were having problems. Some of them were street kids. I worked with the horse for a while and then asked if any of the kids wanted to get in with me and see if they could establish a bond with the horse. One boy who looked about fifteen was just shining with desire, so I opened the gate and ushered the little tough guy in. I coached him, and before long he figured it out. He found the right balance of assertiveness and restraint and he was able to control the horse without scaring it. After the session, a TV reporter asked the boy how he'd felt when he'd gotten the balance right. The kid beamed up at him and said, "It's the first time in my life I've been able to get what I wanted without having to start a fight for it." (Incidentally, I checked in with Bob about a year later and he told me that same young man was now off of the streets, that he'd made great strides, was doing really well, and he actually had a job working in a horse barn.)

At a clinic in Orlando, Florida, I met and worked with a man named Michael McClain. Michael works for a large NASA contractor responsible for launching and processing the space shuttle. Michael's job is to coordinate and communicate between different departments and he's used to translating ideas from one context to another. He thought that what he'd learned while working with his horse that weekend was also valuable to his colleagues. Respect, trust, and clear communication are always big issues in any workplace, too. The ideas we talked about soon began appearing in the company newsletter he wrote and he tells me that his coworkers really responded wonderfully to the predator-prey message.

Then there's my friend Ronnie from Sacramento,

California. Ronnie's a firefighter, and he was a good one, too, until he was leading a group of men through the zero visibility of a burning house filled with thick smoke, searching for the owners they believed were trapped somewhere inside, when the roof suddenly caved in on them. Fortunately, Ronnie was not too badly burned, but he suffered a terrible psychological trauma. Aside from believing he was about to die a horrible death, the worst of it was that at first, Ronnie had heard the other firemen screaming, and then they suddenly stopped, and he was overwhelmed with the thought that these brave men, his friends, had just died in the cave-in. Even though he was rescued and soon learned that everyone had actually gotten out safely, Ronnie never got over the overwhelming guilt and fear he'd felt when he thought his two comrades had died on his watch. After all, it had been his call to go in. After that, Ronnie couldn't work anywhere near a fire and ended up on disability leave to heal, both physically and mentally. He needed help but was resistant to a heavy course of mainstream therapy. Ronnie loves horses, too, and he trains colts as a hobby. I joined him in his round pen for a couple of sessions and I could see he was struggling with something inside. We went out for a beer after the second session. He looked at me, shook his head, and sighed. "Working in the round pen with that horse of mine pushes more buttons in me than when I go into my therapist's office," he said. One day, a friend shot some video of Ronnie and a horse. Watching himself, Ronnie realized how clearly his body spoke of stress seething under the surface. That realization was Ronnie's first step forward toward real health and now he's doing great. Ronnie is a hero to me because he is walking, talking proof that what doesn't kill us can only make us stronger if we have the humility, courage, and determination to go forward.

Clearly, some link between horses and the human psyche was surfacing. And in the fall of 1998, I got my first e-mail from Dr. Jane. Jane MacNaughton is a medical doctor, who works hard as a family psychotherapist at her practice in Kingston, Ontario. Like most of us, she knows all too well how challenging it is to balance her career with her family and still find some quiet time for herself. She is married with three children and she's also a horse owner and rider. Sensing that something was missing from her relationship with her horse, she'd gone into a bookstore looking for something that would help her understand horse psychology. Struck by the title, she walked out with *Horses Don't Lie*. And before long, she was on the phone with me, asking if I had any interest in discussing the ties that might lie between horse work and therapy. I was very interested indeed. As it turned out, we had a lot to talk about.

In her practice, Dr. Jane often uses principles of Jungian therapy, a branch of psychoanalysis that tries to weave a balance between the outer world of action and events and the inner world of dream, fantasy, and symbolism. A distinguishing feature of Jungian analysis is the concept of archetypes, symbols rising from the deep, dark psychic pool of the collective unconscious where humanity's common experience is stored. Archetypes express a complexity of images and emotions that accompany the defining experiences of human life. Examples include the Hero, the Divine Child, the Great Mother, Transformation, Death, and Rebirth. They are the same for us all, no matter who we are or where we come from. It's as if they are built into the wiring of our brains. And one of the most commonly recurring archetypes is—you guessed it—the Horse.

We spent hours on the phone, Dr. Jane and I, comparing ideas and notes. We talked about what the Horse archetype has meant throughout the ages. It has been closely linked with our instinctive, primal drives. Jung thought the Horse's appearance could signify instincts out of control. The horse evokes intense feelings and unbridled passion instead of cool, collected thought. We also talked about some of the things I'd seen happen with horses and humans, things like the young boy's encounter with the horse when I'd done that clinic for the social workers. Dr. Jane could see benefits right away.

Issues around uncontrolled passions were constant in Dr. Jane's therapeutic practice and she asked me if I'd ever considered whether horses might play a practical role in therapy. We knew we were on to something and even tossed around the idea of doing a series of joint lectures, but we lived so far apart it was tough to make anything happen. Then, in early 1999, I got an e-mail from a woman named Linda Myers.

Linda's son had picked up a copy of *Horses Don't Lie* at a horse show and given it to her for Christmas. After reading it, she wanted to tell me about the Equine-Assisted Growth and Learning Association. EAGALA dates back to the early '90s and begins with a man named Greg Kersten. Greg grew up on a ranch and when he was a young boy, his father died. That led to some difficult years during which Greg skipped school more than a few times. He used to hide out in the barn, tucking himself into the horse stalls. That's where he learned to read horse body language, the same place I did. Eventually, Greg became a counselor, although his love of horses remained and he never lost his horsey ways. He used to come to work in a cowboy hat and boots, and some of the kids he worked with would ask him about where he'd been. He'd promise to take them out to the ranch as a way to reward them for making progress. When he did, he noticed that bringing the kids together with the horses always seemed to lead to more progress. Then he got a call from Lynn Thomas, the director of the Aspen Ranch, a working cattle ranch that is also a youth treatment facility. She hired Greg to work at the ranch, and together the two of them started developing a series of techniques to bring horses together with the people who need their help. EAGALA was born soon after. Today, there are hundreds of certified therapists in Canada and the U.S.– social workers, psychologists, psychiatrists and other professionals who have all taken the training pioneered by Greg and Lynn. One American college, Virginia Intermont College, offers a minor in equine-assisted therapy and several other colleges are considering it.

I was floored! Here I thought I was on my own and it turns out there's a whole school of thought moving in the same direction. It was just like when I started lecturing and was worried about being too far in front of my audience—when an idea's time is right, it suddenly and simultaneously appears all over the place like magic. And so many members in EAGALA had stories that echoed my experiences. Linda's is just one of them.

Linda had been working for years as a counselor with troubled adolescents, but was growing increasingly discouraged. Nothing she was doing seemed to make any difference to the kids she had devoted her career to helping. They were impossible to reach, sealed off behind a curtain of evasion and mesmerized by drugs, booze, and a shallow, distraction-addicted culture. And their families didn't seem to care, at least not enough to commit to progressive change. The kids would leave her office just as sick as when they came in. Beaten down and disillusioned, Linda was ready to quit. She was going to chuck it in and become a realtor. Before she did, cancer intervened. Linda fought it successfully, but was forced to take a year off to recover. Linda had ridden horses as a little girl, and she returned to riding during her convalescence. She was amazed at the mental and physical healing effect it had on her, and when she returned to work she resolved to try and harness this tool for her clients. She became one of EAGALA's very first certified therapists and opened her new practice, complete with indoor riding arena, in October 1998.

Sherri was one of the first kids she worked with, one of a group of kids recovering from a chemical dependency. Sherri had also been sexually abused, and being victimized was commonplace to her. One day, Linda was a bit late getting to the group session. When she walked in, several of the boys were holding Sherri upside down, teasing her and making sexual jokes at her expense. Linda stopped them, but the damage had been done. Sherri had been victimized again. She was at the bottom of the totem pole, the butt of everyone's jokes.

Linda decided to try her newfound equine therapy skills and took the group to the round pen. Her goals were modest. She just wanted to get the group to work as a team to draw in and move the horse from one end of the arena to another. That's all she wanted, but she got quite a bit more.

Linda showed the kids how they could make a horse go forward by approaching its back end and make it stop by standing in front of it. When the boys tried it, they could all make the horse go but none of them could make it stop. They couldn't stand in front of the horse with enough confidence. The horse would keep moving forward and the bluffing boys eventually started backing up. None could stand their ground. But when Sherri tried it, she planted her little feet in the sand, held out her arms and chest, and that was it. The horse couldn't move her. Instead, she moved the horse. She got so good that she could push it all over the ring, all by herself. Nothing could have been more empowering, and that session was a turning point for her. Linda never took those kids back to her basement office again and they had many, many sessions together in the round pen. Sherri became a group leader. She learned to say "no" to the horse and "no" to her peers. She learned how to be assertive without being confrontational. She learned what a mutually consensual relationship felt like, and she transferred that to her everyday life. She learned she didn't have to be a victim.

I heard many such stories from EAGALA therapists. I was starting to have a few of my own, too. In many different situations and in many different ways, horses were enabling people to make contact with feelings they'd buried deep inside themselves. There didn't seem to be any doubt that equine-assisted therapy worked. The question was, why? Linda believes that it works because horses are big and powerful and because they are so attuned to body language. Their size and sheer presence makes them impossible to ignore. A client may be able to tune out a counselor droning on about taking charge of their life, but they can't tune out a 1,200-pound horse in the arena with them. Horses also give us a comforting sense of familiarity, a safe reminder of all things basic, a primal memory and perhaps an ancestral connection to our grounding roots to Mother Nature. As well, working with the body helps you work with the spirit. At the very least, working with a horse will force you to look up. And as Dr. Joanne Moses, a remarkable therapist in Tucson, Arizona, who has pioneered equine-assisted psychotherapy says, "When you're dealing with a deeply depressed person, just getting them to look up is a major step forward." Finally, a horse gives you instant and honest feedback on what you're communicating. "It's almost like the horse is a huge biofeedback mechanism," Linda says.

I think she's right about all those things, but I also think there's more. The reason horses can help us make such deep and profound changes in our lives is that they evoke something deep and profound in us. That something goes back to the conversations Dr. Jane

MacNaughton and I were having. In our talks, we came to the conclusion that the horse offers us a powerful opportunity to reach inward and touch our deepest selves. When we get into the round pen, suddenly there's 1,200 pounds of prancing, snorting archetype right there in our face. Linda's right. We can't ignore a horse, any more than we can help what we feel when we stand in front of one. Horses, by embodying one of the deepest archetypes in our consciousness, most definitely stir us up. All those things that are buried away or girdled safely up start swirling around in our psyches.

After my talks with Dr. Jane, I came to believe that horses can be a direct connection to the unconscious. When we look at a horse, and especially when there's a horse strutting across the pen in front of us, we see the flesh-and-blood incarnation of powerful forces bottled up within us that we wish we had the guts to saddle and ride. These are the forces that Jung called the "shadow self." We know those forces could take us to our dreams and turn us into our best selves. We also know those forces could destroy us. That's why we bottle them up in the first place. And when such hidden feelings are stirred up and agitated, that's when we have the chance to work with them and learn to control them. Horses give us this opportunity. They do this to us whether we're aware of it or not. But what a powerful tool to be able to use consciously!

Carl Jung also talked a lot about life's paradox, and how important it is to embrace the seeming contradictions as we travel the never-ending journey towards becoming fully human. Horses, which can both free us or hurt us, embody this paradox. How we handle this paradox in the arena becomes a metaphor for how we handle it everywhere. Only in this case, it's such a potent and direct metaphor, that we can use it to change our reality. Horses force us to face our "shadow selves." Once we do that, we discover much greater freedom as we go forward in life. This, I believe, is where my next cycle will take me. I've spent years studying the how of horse-human communication and now it's clearly time to turn to the why. Fortunately, I've got lots of help. Friends and associates such as Dr. Jane and Linda continue to contribute much to my education. In return, I think I've been able to offer them the kind of thorough grounding in horse professionalism that the growing field of equine-assisted therapy needs. These therapists, after all, are coming from the clinical side. I've spent two decades getting to know horses inside out. We have much to teach each other. But I have other guides, too. Writers, thinkers, and dreamers throughout history have returned frequently to the archetype of the horse and I look often to them. You don't have to go far to find examples. You can start with the Greek and Roman myths, as so much of our culture does. Those ancient and thought-provoking stories aren't just simple fantasies. They're shaped how they are for a reason, and they often give us powerful insights into our inner lives. Take Neptune, the old Roman god of the sea who rides a chariot throughout his watery domain. Right there, you have two strong symbols of the unconscious, water and horses. Water is deep, formless, and unchanging, like our subconscious, and the horse gives us, like Neptune, the power to move through it. It's up to us to harness our inner horse and direct the journey. I'm convinced that these ideas I've come across are not new concepts. They are, in fact, some of the oldest ideas we have, and I believe that the time is right to rediscover them. And as I travel and talk to people and show them what I've learned, I'm convinced that's what's happening. When I first started out on this path, I was afraid I wouldn't be taken seriously. Then, I was afraid I was the only person spreading this message. Both times I was wrong. People

all over North America had come to the same conclusions I had and many others needed only a slight nudge
to connect the dots. And all over North America, the
evidence is pouring in that these ideas do indeed work.

Before I began my current life of lecturing and
demonstrating, I thought things would evolve differently for me than they have. I pictured myself on horseback, perfectly attuned to my mount and my inner self.
We would ride over the prairie, free to explore the limits
of the horse-human relationship. I now realize that
vision, while beautiful, was incomplete. There weren't
any other people in it and that wasn't the direction
my life was heading at all. My life these days is full
of people—Anita, Raven, and Adler, of course, but also
the dozens and hundreds of people who come to hear
me talk and watch me work. Often, I walk away from the
round pen after a public session with tears of joy stream-
ing down my face after watching people discover something about themselves through the kind, patient help of
a horse. And the best part about it is that those discov-
eries have nothing directly to do with me. With the help
of a horse, people make these breakthroughs all on their
own. I am just a messenger who shows them the door
and every time, they walk through it to find the message

on their own. So I'd like to change the picture I painted for you at the end of the last chapter.

The next cycle of my life isn't going to be about galloping over the hills in solitude or dozing on the grassland while my horse grazes gently nearby. I'll still be on horseback, but now I imagine myself riding over to a neighbor's house. We chat, and then they saddle up with me and we ride off to the next home on the prairie. They join us too, and it goes on like that until we've got a whole string of horses and riders confidently riding off to explore uncharted territory. There's lots of talk and laughter. The horses hold themselves relaxed and easy. We stop together and start together. We all know what our goal is and we all helped to set it. Nobody gets bossed around, but when decisions need to be made we know how to make them. We're all happy as we amble together through the short-grass. And this, too, will be magic.

ACKNOWLEDGMENTS

$\mathcal{I}$T IS WITH A GREAT GRATITUDE AND APPRECIATION that I'd like to acknowledge the following people for all they have done for me and my family. Thanks to Sally Snow, Rick Devin, and Mike Warren for encouraging and inspiring me to never give up on my dreams. To Richard Bach and Dan Millman for helping me to look beyond the illusions. To Robin Chapin for her unconditional love and acceptance. To Gary Poley and Bill Henderson for showing me "the ropes." To Theda Roper, Karen Malloy, Anna Richter, Elaine Partington, Sue Sliger, Kathy at *Canadian Horse Journal*, Susan Stewart,

Dr. Jane MacNaughton, Linda Meyers, and Jorge Garay for believing in me and for having the courage to take chances with me. To Bob Weber and Sylvia Strojek for their friendship, literary expertise, wisdom, and wonderful sense of humor. And, last but certainly not least, to my business partner Margot Trembath who is a great friend, a tremendously supportive partner, and the catalyst to the success of Horsepower Productions.

ABOUT THE AUTHOR

CHRIS IRWIN, INTERNATIONALLY RENOWNED horseman and equestrian coach, is a leading pioneer in equine-assisted therapy and its beneficial influence on human potential. He conducts clinics and demonstrations throughout North America, and is a widely read equestrian columnist, a regular guest lecturer at numerous colleges and universities, and a motivational speaker at teacher, therapist, and business conferences. Irwin and his family live in Western Canada, where he is currently developing a "ranch-retreat" in British Columbia for guests who want to "Discover Their Horsepower."

Chris Irwin can be reached at:
Horsepower Productions
www.chrisirwin.com
1-877-394-6773